CHERYL ST.JOHN

The Rancher Inherits a Family

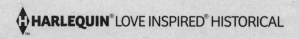

HARLEQUIN® LOVE INSPIRED® HISTORICAL

Special thanks and acknowledgment are given to Cheryl St.John for her contribution to the Return to Cowboy Creek miniseries.

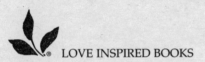

Recycling programs
for this product may
not exist in your area.

LOVE INSPIRED BOOKS

ISBN-13: 978-1-335-36962-8

The Rancher Inherits a Family

www.Harlequin.com

Printed in U.S.A.

"I'm glad you and your boys are all right."

"Well, that's the thing…"

"What's the thing?"

"They're not my boys."

"They're not?"

"I never saw them before I boarded the train headed for Kansas."

"Well, then—"

"They're yours."

Had he taken a blow to the head, as well? "I assure you I'd know if I had children."

"Well, as soon as you read this letter, along with a copy of a will, you'll know."

At the sound of paper unfolding, he opened his eyes. "What are you talking about?"

"It seems a friend of yours by the name of Tessa Radner wanted you to take her children upon her death."

* * *

Return to Cowboy Creek:
A bride train delivers the promise of new love and family to a Kansas boomtown

The Rancher Inherits a Family—
Cheryl St.John, April 2018
His Substitute Mail-Order Bride—
Sherri Shackelford, May 2018
Romancing the Runaway Bride—
Karen Kirst, June 2018

Cheryl St.John's love for reading started as a child. She wrote her own stories, designed covers and stapled them into books. She credits many hours of creating scenarios for her paper dolls and Barbies as the start of her fascination with fictional characters. Cheryl loves hearing from readers. Visit her website at cherylstjohn.net or email her at SaintJohn@aol.com.

Visit the Author Profile page at Harlequin.com for more titles.

Trust in the Lord with all thine heart; and lean not unto thine own understanding. In all thy ways acknowledge him, and he shall direct thy paths.
—*Proverbs* 3:5–6

This book is dedicated to my aunt Marilyn, a kind and gentle spirit. Surely now there are chocolate chip cookies in heaven.

Chapter One

Cowboy Creek
April 1869

Seth Halloway heaved a burlap sack of dry beans over his shoulder and carried it to the back of the wagon, where he vaulted into the bed and stacked the bag beside kegs and crates. He yanked a faded bandana from his back pocket and wiped his face and neck. The sun was warm for April. Good for the early hay.

"Hadn't you better clean yerseff up and git over to the station?" Old Horace, shuffling from the interior of Booker & Son general store, slowly drew a cheroot beneath his nostrils and inhaled. He paused at the nearest porch beam and struck a match. The loamy dark scent of tobacco drifted upward. "Bride train's arrivin' any time now."

Seth tucked away the bandana. "Too much work waiting to go gawk at women keen on a husband," Seth answered. "There'll be plenty of eager grooms crowding the rails."

"Might be you'd take a shine to one of those young fillies," Gus Russell said from the bench where the two old men sat a healthy portion of the day when they weren't playing horseshoes behind the church.

"A wife is pretty far down my list," Seth told the two men, who knew all the comings and goings in town. Last fall, he'd sold his land in Missouri to start a ranch here in Kansas, and getting the White Rock stocked and operational took all his time and energy.

"You need sons to help you run that ranch," Old Horace advised, peering up through a trail of smoke. He punctuated his statement by pointing his pipe stem at Seth.

Seth thought the same thing. He'd learned ranching from his father, and he wanted to pass down land and know-how to his own children, but the war and some unfortunate turns had put a kink in any plans he may have had. "Plenty of time for that."

Shouts reached them, and the clanging bell across the intersection at the corner of The Cattleman hotel echoed along Eden Street. Seth's immediate thought was a fire, and a jolt of unease rippled through his chest. He jumped to the ground.

Hoofbeats alerted him to a fast-approaching rider.

"Train derailed to the south!" the cowboy hollered from atop his prancing piebald. "Need ev'rybody's help!"

Abram Booker appeared in the doorway in his clean white apron. "I'll get another wagon from the livery. We'll need to bring in the injured."

"Help me unload these onto the boardwalk," Seth called to the cowboy. They made quick work of stacking his purchases, and Abram tossed in an armful of blankets. "I'll be right behind you."

"I'm comin', too!" Old Horace climbed up to the seat. Seth helped Gus into the back, and by the time they'd gotten to First Street, half a dozen more men and a few women had joined the old men in the back of the wagon. Seth urged the team past the now-deserted railroad station and south alongside the creek after which the town had been named.

He spotted a thin line of black smoke before he came within sight of the train. The engine and tender were overturned, and men worked at putting out fires along the tracks. The hazard of a prairie fire seemed to be under control. The foremost passenger cars had been overturned, and beyond those the stock cars were detached and had skidded together in a zigzag pattern.

The wailing of crying infants and children could be heard, along with shouts of men and whinnying horses. Other townspeople had arrived, as well. A few women offered water and assistance to passengers seated or lying on the sloping ground.

Seth set the brake handle and helped Old Horace down, then joined one of the small groups of men gathering to search cars.

"You're strong and agile, Halloway." Chesley Lawton, the portly gray-haired barber, gestured to him. "Come with our group." He glanced over Seth's shoulder. "You, too, young fella."

The five men passed the closest cars and made their way farther along the tracks. A snake slithered from behind a rock and disappeared into the grass ahead. Seth chose a car no one had reached and surveyed the exposed underside facing them. He found hand- and footholds and climbed upward, another young man joining him. Finding the doorway, Seth sidled inside.

Two dozen passengers, having found no way to reach the doors or windows above them, appeared visibly shaken with various cuts and bruises. Together the men helped move debris and assisted women and children out and down to safety. The men made their way out last.

"Anyone still in here?" Satisfied everyone had escaped, Seth climbed out.

The young fellow beside him stuck out a hand as they headed for the next car. "Freddie Simms."

"Seth Halloway."

Entering the next car didn't go as smoothly. The door was jammed and blocked. Freddie ran ahead of him to the front and yanked open the metal door. The cowboy led a group of frightened passengers out of the railcar.

"No wonder the rear door didn't open." Once inside, Seth surveyed the destruction. An entire row of seats had come loose and, along with a piece of interior ceiling, were piled at that end. He located an unconscious man with a head wound and kneeled to press his ear to the fellow's chest. Freddie returned to stand behind him. "Heart's beating."

Together, they got the man as far as the doorway, and then shouted for help to get him down the twisted platform to the ground. The three on the ground took the unconscious person's weight and Freddie helped ease him onto the grass.

Seth turned back inside. "Anyone here?" he called. Crunching broken window glass beneath his boots, he maneuvered toward the rear one more time. A muffled sound caught his attention. The size of the pile blocking the door prevented him from spotting anyone trapped beneath.

He kept searching, moving aside mangled metal and splintered wood. The car lurched, settling beneath him, and his heart jumped. He'd surveyed the ground by the railcar before entering, and there was nowhere for it to slide, so the movement was unsettling, but didn't pose a threat. The battered seats and metal overhead were a true concern however.

He shoved aside a valise to discover a pair of women's feet encased in high-top black boots. He wrapped his hand around her ankle and felt for a pulse. The leg moved, along with the dust-covered fabric of her skirt. He let go and wrenched away the cushions and frames, exposing a space where the fallen seats had formed a protective barrier. After dislodging the seats, he discovered a huddled woman and three children. He stifled his amazement and asked, "Are you all right?"

"I—I think so."

The reverend, Virgil Taggart, joined Freddie behind him. He breathed a prayer of thanks and reached to take the children's hands one at time. All three boys' faces were tear-streaked and the youngest's jagged breathing demonstrated his fear and recent crying. Freddie picked up the smallest one and herded the others toward the door.

"Come on, ma'am." Seth helped the woman to her feet. She was taller than he'd expected—younger as well. Her red-gold hair had fallen from its mooring and hung over her shoulder in a shiny wave, with hairpins protruding. "You and your boys are safe. We'll get you all to a doctor."

"Peony is still under that pile somewhere." The young woman backed away from the reverend's outstretched hand and stepped closer to Seth. Her wide hazel eyes, with flecks of gold and green, had the uncanny ability to plead with his sensibilities. "I can't leave her."

Startled at that disturbing information, Seth turned

back to the corner where he'd found them. Another child buried, injured or worse? "Where was she?"

"Right beside me when the train crashed, but I'm afraid all the shifting debris has covered her."

"Get back." He grasped her by the upper arms and moved her. Clearing away twisted metal, he got on his belly and pressed farther into the space from where he'd only just uncovered the passenger and her other children.

A mewling similar to a baby's drove a shiver up his spine. An infant? *Lord, help me find her and get her out of this.*

The sound came again, much louder this time.

"That's her! That's Peony!"

He spotted a small cage at the same time the woman's voice and the feline squalling registered. "A cat? Peony is a *cat*?"

"Do you see her?"

The railcar shifted again.

"Come on, lady!" Freddie bellowed. "I've got her. Get out of there, Halloway!"

Seth inched closer, reached for the cage and inched backward. Backing out of the narrow space wasn't as easy as going forward. He had to push with his elbows and wrists and then scoot the cage along, a fraction at a time. Finally, he had his body out of the tunnel, but a loud creak from above alerted him to imminent danger. He threw his arm over his head a split second before an unhinged seat broke loose.

Seth's shoulder and wrist throbbed under what he guessed, due to the numbing cold, was an ice pack. He opened his gritty eyes and squinted against the light that was making his head hurt. He didn't recognize the room or the pungent earthy smells. The pain in the other hand was appallingly familiar. He'd taken more than one shot during the war, as well as a couple after. A groan escaped his lips.

"Mr. Halloway." The soft voice near his side added to his disorientation. "Are you in pain?"

Ivory-skinned and hazel-eyed, with a halo of red-gold hair, the woman from the train came into view. She'd rearranged the shiny mass back on her head and had only a scrape on her chin as a result of the ordeal. "You fared well," he said, barely managing to get the words out.

"I'm perfectly fine, thank you."

"And the children?"

"They have a few bumps and bruises from the crash, but they're safe."

He closed his eyes with grim satisfaction.

"I'm Marigold Brewster."

If she was one of the brides, she was certainly a young widow. And more power to the man willing to take on all those kids. "Seth Halloway."

"I know. The other men told me your name. Thank you for rescuing me."

"I'm glad you and your boys are all right. Reverend Taggart must've been praying the whole while."

"Well, that's the thing…"

His head throbbed and the light hurt. He closed his eyes. "What's the thing?"

"They're not my boys."

"They're not?"

"I never saw them before I boarded the train headed for Kansas."

"Well, then—"

"They're yours."

With his uninjured hand, he touched his forehead gingerly. Had that blow to his head rattled his senses? No, he hadn't lost his memory. He remembered what he'd been doing before heading off to the wreckage, and he recalled what had happened inside the railcar. "I assure you I'd know if I had children."

"Well, as soon as you read this letter, along with a copy of the will, you'll know."

At the sound of paper unfolding, he opened his eyes. "What are you talking about?"

"It seems a friend of yours by the name of Tessa Radner wanted you to take her children upon her death."

"Tessa… She's dead?"

"This letter says she is. I'm sorry."

He remembered his friend well. They'd been neighbors and classmates in Big Bend, Missouri, a hundred years ago. He'd joined the infantry alongside her husband, Jessie. Jessie had made it nearly all the way through the war and had been killed at the end of the Appomattox Campaign in Northern Virginia's final battle. Seth winced at the magnitude of senseless loss.

Miss Brewster held up the letter, so he could read it. Tessa had gotten sick and her main concern was for her children. She'd believed she was getting better, but had taken a turn for the worse. Arranging to send her children to Cowboy Creek had been her frantic effort to see they were cared for. She'd been a young widow, frightened to die, frightened to leave behind her children. Seth's chest ached with sorrow and sympathy for his childhood friend. But sending her beloved babies to *him*? She must have been desperate to believe he was her best choice. What was he going to do with them?

He realized she was still holding the letter and his

vision had blurred on the words. He glanced up. "So… you're their chaperone?"

"No, I'm the new schoolteacher. I've been hired to replace Miss Aldridge. The town council paid my fare. I met the boys—Tate, Harper and Little John—soon after the trip started, and asked why they were traveling without supervision. I shudder to think what might have happened to them. Tate showed me this letter, which explained why they were alone. Harper and Little John looked so frightened, and Tate was trying to be brave and act as though he had everything under control. He's only seven himself. All I did was help them out as best I could."

The news was a lot to take in. He would show the letter and the will to his brother, Russ, who was an attorney. Russ would know if everything was on the up-and-up, but Seth didn't know what choice he had. If these were Jessie and Tessa's sons, and they had no other family, he had no choice. He always did the right thing, the responsible thing.

He swallowed, finding his throat dry. "Well, I reckon we're even then."

"Pardon?"

"We're even. You took care of the boys, and I rescued you."

"I suppose so," she agreed.

The door opened and Dr. Marlys Mason entered, wearing a crisp blue dress and a white apron. "How are you feeling, Mr. Halloway?"

"Call me Seth. I've been worse."

"Yes, I noticed that when I removed your shirt. Besides several other interesting scars, one from a .58 Minié ball, I'd say."

He quirked an eyebrow at her. "You can tell the caliber by the scar?"

"Indeed, and you were fortunate it was the Minié ball because the greater weight and velocity allowed it to penetrate and come out the other side. Another inch and it would have shattered your shoulder or become lodged in the bone and necessitated amputation."

Beside him Marigold sucked in a breath of surprise.

"There are a couple of wounds I don't recognize, though," the doctor added, clearly fascinated and peering again to have another look. "These inch-long scars on your upper arm and your shoulder."

He raised his arm only to regret it when pain shot through his ribs. "Arrows."

The doctor's eyebrows rose. "Arrows?"

"Comanche."

"They didn't pierce bone, however."

"I was a moving target."

"Fascinating. How were they removed?"

"Grin and yank. The ones that had gone clean through were easiest because I could break off the tips."

Dr. Mason's fascination was evident in her raised eyebrows. He had spoken to the doctor other times, and was accustomed to her logical thinking and straightforward speech. Her intelligence and intuition impressed him. He glanced over, and Miss Brewster, on the other hand, appeared a shade paler and unimpressed. "I'm glad they brought me to you, Dr. Mason. I respect your natural remedies. What's ailing me at the moment?"

Marlys peered into his eyes one at a time. "You took a blow to the head, but seem to be clearheaded now. I want to observe you overnight however. Besides the head injury, you have several contusions and your ulna is broken."

"My arm?"

"Yes, this bone," she said, raising her arm to show him the underside. "It's a clean break, and will heal properly in a few weeks. I'll put a cast on it as soon as the swelling is down. I'll make a poultice for those ribs and we'll wrap them. I would say a large object struck you there, rather than something with an edge, which would have broken or cracked ribs. Bruising will heal far more quickly, but is still quite painful. I will supply you with herbs. Those ribs will hurt every time you move until they've had a couple of weeks to heal."

He closed his eyes against the worrisome news of recovery time.

"You have ranch hands," she said, as though she'd read his thoughts.

Yes, if he counted a full-grown boy who came after doing his own chores and an old man.

He attempted to sit up and swing his legs over the side of the bed. "What I have is a ranch to run."

Marigold recognized the overwhelming apprehension on her rescuer's face. She'd taken care of her sister and her niece for a long time, and she understood the weight of responsibility. Poor Mr. Halloway had just learned he had three more mouths to feed and was now unable to handle his chores for the unforeseen future.

"You're not going to be doing any ranching for a while," Dr. Mason told him, her voice and expression stern. "Do not use that arm for any reason."

"I can't lie around doing nothing."

The doctor placed a gentle but firm hand on her agitated patient's shoulder and eased him back to a prone position. "Rest now will spare you a future impediment. A brief respite only makes sense."

He swiped a hand over his face in obvious frustration, causing Marigold to speak up.

"I will help Mr. Halloway get home when he's ready," she told the pretty lady doctor. "It's the very least I can do after he's saved our lives. He's only just learned he has three boys to take home as well." Belatedly, she thought about his situation. "Do you have a wife to help out, Mr. Halloway?"

"No," he replied. "Just me and my mother."

She truly hoped his mother was an understanding and capable woman. As a teacher, she knew full well how active these boys would be.

"I'll need to find someone who knows what's been done with the luggage. I was told I'd be living with the students' families, so I'm not sure what to do with my clothing and personal belongings just yet. But books and supplies can be delivered to the school. It's a fairly new building, I understand."

Marlys nodded. "You can see it from the front windows of this office if you look northeast. It faces Lincoln Boulevard, so from here two sides of the yard and the south side of the school are visible. I hear the children when they're at play."

Marigold smiled. "I'm relieved to know you're so close. I feared I'd be in a rural area with no neighbors or help if I needed it."

"Not at all. The schoolhouse faces a growing neighborhood to the east, and it's only a block from the main thoroughfare."

Marigold stood. "I'll take the children with me now, so they can see a bit of the town. Once we've located our belongings and I've arranged to have them moved, I'll be back."

"I had my wagon and team with me at the site of

the wreck," Seth told her. "My supplies should still be stacked in front of Booker & Son. Hopefully someone took care of my horses. Can you drive a team?"

"I'm sorry to say I cannot."

"We'll find someone to transport your supplies," Marlys assured him. "Why don't you plan on staying here tonight, Miss Brewster? There's a room in the rear where I lived before I was married. I'll be staying here to keep an eye on Seth and the other patients, so my husband will take the boys home for the night. We have a son, and he'll be glad for the company. It won't be a problem. Tomorrow, after everyone is rested, will be soon enough to take Seth and the children to the ranch and learn where you're staying."

"Will you send a rider to let my mother know what's happened and that I'm all right?" Seth asked.

Marigold gave her rescuer what she hoped was an encouraging smile. "Yes, of course."

"And one other thing, if you don't mind. My brother was likely among the men helping at the wreck. If you could ask around to see if anyone knows his where-abouts and let him know I'm here? His name is Russ."

"I'll take care of it."

She sensed his gaze on her back as she slipped from the room. She paused in the outer office area, collecting her senses. She'd made the decision to come to Cowboy Creek, hoping for a new start, but so far nothing had gone according to plan. She captured her thoughts. Just the fact that she was alive and her young travel-ing companions were unharmed was cause enough for thanksgiving.

"Thank You, Lord," she breathed. "Give me strength and fortitude for the days ahead."

Her gaze lit on the three towheaded boys in the waiting area, their wide, uncertain eyes focused on her. She hadn't the vaguest idea what she was doing.

Chapter Two

After asking Dr. Mason if it was all right to leave Peony in her cage in the waiting room, Marigold led Tate, Harper and Little John out of the doctor's office and glanced west.

"I think your kitty is hungry," Harper, the five-year-old, said with concern in his dark eyes.

"Dr. Mason fed her," Marigold assured him. "She's still frightened from the train ride and the accident. All this is strange for her." She glanced up and down the street, her attention lighting on the closest building, which bore a sign that read Bath House. "Once we find our luggage and have clean clothing, I think a trip to the bathing establishment is in order."

Harper shook his sandy-colored hair and ran his fingers through it so dirt and bits of unidentifiable rubble fell out. "I don't need no bath."

"Harper don't like baths," Tate told her. At only seven, he took responsibility for seeing to his younger siblings' needs and wishes. He was slender, with shaggy blond hair and a serious expression.

"I'm afraid baths are in order for everyone today," she told the three of them. "After our journey and then lying under all that wreckage, none of us are present-able. And we probably don't smell very good."

Harper sniffed his arm and shrugged.

The three-year-old, Little John, stuck his thumb into his mouth and gazed up at her with wide brown eyes. The contrast of his large dark eyes and pale hair gave him a waiflike appearance. She took in his soft-looking round cheeks, his spiky dark lashes, and an ache knotted in her chest. He was so young—all of them were too young to be without their parents. Too young to be traveling across the country without supervision. Who put children on a train all alone? What if Seth Hallo-way hadn't been in Cowboy Creek? What if he'd denied knowing their mother and turned them away?

She collected her thoughts and concerns. Mr. Hallo-way had been here. He had come to their rescue, and he was taking responsibility for the three of them.

"You all must be hungry. I know I am. Are you hungry, Little John?"

He nodded.

She drew herself up straight. "Let's go find the mer-cantile and arrange for Mr. Halloway's wagon to be found and his supplies delivered. We'll figure out a meal."

A touch at her wrist drew her attention down. Little John found her hand and grasped it securely. His fin-gers were small and damp. She clasped them back. An arrow of distress pierced her conscience at his trust. What was she doing? How had she found herself exactly where she'd planned never to be? She was not going to develop an attachment to someone else's children, no matter how deserving. She'd come to Cowboy Creek to start over, to distance herself from her past, from the losses and the hurt. She was determined to choose her own path for the future. She refused to have circumstances thrust upon her.

Her uneasy conscience warred with self-preservation. It was her Christian duty to help these children. She owed Seth Halloway for rescuing them. Who knows how long they might have been trapped in that railcar if he hadn't been persistent or intuitive, or led by the hand of God? A fire could have broken out. Anything might have happened. And he'd been injured in the process. The least she could do was help until they all got home. She took a deep breath and pushed back the sharp twinges of panic.

She spotted Booker & Son and led the boys across the street, where several people conversed. "I wonder if I might trouble one of you for some help?"

A short, stout woman separated herself from the group and hurried forward. "Land sakes, look at these little ones. And you. Are you one of the brides?"

"I'm Marigold Brewster, ma'am. I'm the new schoolteacher."

The woman introduced herself as Aunt Mae and presented the others on the boardwalk. "We weren't aware you were bringing children."

"No, no, I didn't bring them. I met them on the train." Briefly, Marigold explained the situation with Seth and what was needed.

"I saw Russ leaving town on a train a day or two ago," one of the younger men said. "I'll watch for him to return and let him know Seth's at Doc Mason's."

"Seth's wagon is at the livery, and his horses are cared for," another explained. "I'll go for the rig and we'll get these supplies loaded."

The men had Seth's supplies loaded quickly. A young cowboy with long jet-black hair and beadwork in the shape of Texas on the back of his vest tied his horse behind, tipped his hat to Marigold and headed out to let Seth's mother know her son was all right.

"Let's not stand around here gabbing any longer. Come with me. That's my place right there." Aunt Mae pointed to a boardinghouse across the street. "I'll get all of you something to eat. Afterward, these gentlemen will help you find your belongings."

Marigold had never met such helpful and warm people. As she led the Radner boys across the street, Little John took her hand once again, and she glanced down. His brown eyes were nothing like the hazel ones in her memory, but they lodged protective feelings in her heart all the same.

Lord, help me guard my heart.

Living up to her name, Aunt Mae treated them like family. The motherly woman prepared them a satisfying meal. "Do you have any idea how many patients Doc Mason is seeing to?"

"I'd say at least half a dozen are there right now," Marigold replied. "But she spoke as though only Seth and one other were spending the night."

"They missed their noon meal. I'll send trays for six." Aunt Mae lowered her voice. "She's a fine healer and a kinder person never lived, but she's not much of a cook."

The boys had washed up at the dry sink on the back porch, and she suspected she looked as silly as they did with only a clean face and hands, and her hair dirty and disheveled. They boys ate ravenously, and Marigold exchanged a glance with the older woman. She carried a second pitcher of milk to the table and they held out their glasses for refills. She agreed the bath house would be their most efficient option, since her boardinghouse had only one tub.

Thankfully, there was a knock on the front door and Aunt Mae returned minutes later to say her trunks and the boys' bags had been left on her front porch.

"I suppose they can sit there until we figure out where we're going," Marigold said. It was unsettling to be uncertain of where she'd be staying. "I'll gather clean clothing for today."

At the bath house, they were assigned curtained-off chambers and provided with soap and towels. Tate insisted on bathing himself, but Aunt Mae and Marigold put Harper and Little John in one tub and shared the chore of scrubbing two little boys who didn't want to be washed. They both had a few scrapes and bruises from the accident, so the women gently cleaned their injuries. Harper endured the washing, but Little John cried, and Marigold felt dreadful for his discomfort. These children had lost their mother and been shuffled across the country, ending up in a heap of train wreckage.

"It's going to be all right," she said to him and used the corner of a towel to dry his reddened face and his watery dark eyes. "After we're clean and dressed I'll read you a story. Would you like that?"

The toddler's lower lip continued to tremble, but he lifted his wide trusting gaze to hers and nodded.

"All right," she said with an encouraging smile.

"Do all of us get to hear the story?" Harper asked.

"Yes, of course."

"Poor little lambs," Aunt Mae said after they'd dried the boys and supervised their clean clothing and hair combing. She waited with them while Marigold took her own bath and washed her hair. Her chin hurt to the touch, and she had a bruise on her shoulder that ached, and another on her wrist she hadn't noticed.

Marigold thanked the woman for all of her help, but

Aunt Mae just gave a shrug and hurried home to tend to her boarders.

A deep orange sun hung low in the sky and cast long shadows in front of the four of them as they walked back to Dr. Mason's office.

Dr. Mason was ushering a cowboy with a bandage wrapped around his wrist from one of the examination rooms. He greeted Marigold with a crooked smile. Taking a hat from the rack near the door, he glanced back at her two more times, his gaze skittering away each time, before he finally exited the office.

"Get used to it," the doctor said with an amused grin. "There's a shortage of young women in this town, and especially pretty ones like you. You'll receive a lot of attention." She reached for Marigold's chin and tipped up her face to get a better look. "You have a bruise here I didn't notice before."

"It was probably covered with dirt. I have some aches I didn't notice at first."

"I'll make you a poultice for it. It will take down the swelling."

Marigold admired the other woman's efficiency, the way she moved about her offices with confidence. She liked the idea of working to support herself and of being indebted to no one. If she decided to marry one day, she would do the choosing.

"Did you enjoy one of the meals Aunt Mae sent?" she asked the doctor.

"Yes, she is thoughtful. Let's see if Seth is ready to eat something. He was sleeping last time I looked in on him so I didn't disturb him." She gestured for them to enter his room. "I figured he and the children would want to get acquainted before they leave for the night, so I carried in a few chairs."

Dressed in wrinkled but clean clothing, their damp hair parted and slicked back, the boys entered the small room ahead of Marigold. Tate took Little John's hand and guided him forward.

"Mr. Halloway?" Marigold said softly.

He was already awake, a purplish bruise having formed on his cheekbone. With an assessing coffee-brown gaze, he took in the trio of youngsters without revealing his thoughts. He was a large man, seeming to take up the entire narrow bed where he was resting, a sheet covering him to his waist. It had taken several men to lower his unconscious form from the railcar, and three strong ones to carry him into the doctor's office. Above the bandages that wrapped his torso, his shoulders and upper arms were powerfully mus-cled, attesting to arduous work. His russet-brown hair was chin-length and wavy, and he wore a thick, neatly trimmed mustache.

Little John turned and clung to Tate's waist, obvi-ously frightened by the bear of a man sizing him up.

"Mr. Halloway?" Marigold said again. "This is Tate Radner."

Tall for his seven years, with dark blond hair, Tate took a jerky step forward and bravely extended a hand. Little John immediately released his older brother and attached himself to Marigold's leg. "How do, sir."

"Pleased to meet you, Tate. You look like your fa-ther."

Obviously pleased, Tate puffed up his chest. "You knew our pa?"

"I did. We enlisted together. Served in different reg-iments, but ran across each other from time to time."

"This here's Harper," Tate said, turning back to the

five-year-old, whose fair hair had dried with a cowlick at the crown. Tate gave his brother a little tug.

Harper shuffled a few steps toward the bed, stared at Seth's enormous outstretched hand for a moment, quickly placed his narrow fingers into the palm, then released it and scuttled back beside Marigold.

"You look like your mama," Seth told him.

Harper glanced from Seth to Tate and back.

"And this here is Little John," Tate said, pointing to the three-year-old with wispy platinum hair.

Little John's wide eyes opened even wider. He stuck his thumb into his mouth and Marigold was relieved that he didn't immediately burst into tears.

"We call him that 'cause he's little. Pa named him Jonathan, but Mama said that name was too big for a little sprout."

Seth's mustache twitched and his mouth settled into an amused smile. "Little John sounds about right."

"Why don't you boys take seats?" Marigold suggested. "I'll read the story I promised while Mr. Halloway eats his dinner."

"Seth," he said, turning his dark gaze on her and catching her by surprise with his intensity. No wonder the boys had flinched under his scrutiny. "They should call me Seth."

She gave a nod. "Very well."

Marlys, who'd been standing behind them during their introductions, moved near the bed. "I'll slide some more pillows behind you so you can sit up."

He cast her a doubtful glance.

"The herbs will help with the pain so you can move enough to incline a bit. Don't try to do it alone today. Let us help." She glanced at Marigold.

Marigold jerked into action and stood beside the bed.

"Each of us will take an upper arm like this." She demonstrated, placing her forearm along Seth's forearm and clasping his bicep securely. "Then we'll let our arms do the work, and not your back or ribs. Got it?"

Seth glanced at Marigold, likely sizing her up for the job. She rested her right forearm along his and placed her hand around the muscled circumference above his elbow. His arm was warm and work-hardened, and decidedly masculine. An unfamiliar and uncomfortable sensation fluttered in her chest. Her gaze moved to the scars on his muscled arm, where he'd been shot with Comanche arrows. This man was as different as night and day from anyone she'd ever met before. Her gaze slid hesitantly to his. Seth assessed her hair, her eyes, her chin and lips, and her skin flushed under his perusal.

"On three," Marlys said.

He had another scar above his right eyebrow, where the skin wasn't tanned like the rest of his face, and a fresh cut under the same eye she hadn't noticed before. Two neat sutures held the cut closed.

"One. Two. Three."

He grasped her arm gingerly, undoubtedly holding back so as to hurt neither her nor the lady doctor, but she gripped his and pulled firmly. His lips formed a white line, but he sat up and leaned forward. Marlys quickly slid pillows behind his back and the women allowed him to inch back onto the added support.

A fine glow of perspiration glistened on his forehead, and Marlys used a damp cloth to blot it away.

"Are you doing all right?" Marlys asked.

Seth released a breath. "Yes. I'm fine."

Marlys hurried from the room, returned with a tray

and settled it on his lap. "I'm going to see to one of my other patients now."

"Thank you." After the doctor had gone, he glanced at Marigold. "And thank you, Miss Brewster."

Marigold uncovered the plate and handed it to Seth, along with a fork. His attention moved to the boys, who were taking up only two chairs, because Little John huddled on Tate's lap.

She got the book she'd brought along and seated herself beside Harper. "My books are still packed in trunks, but I had this one with me. It's about a little girl, but we'll have plenty of time to read stories about boys later."

"What is the book called?" Harper asked.

"*Jessica's First Prayer.*"

"What's it about?"

"It's about a little girl abandoned in London, but she makes an unlikely friend."

"Who is the friend?"

Marigold grinned. "You will have to be patient, listen and find out." She opened to the first page. "'In a screened and secluded corner of one of the many railway-bridges which span the streets of London there could be seen a few years ago, from five o'clock every morning until half past eight, a tidily set-out coffee-stall, consisting of a trestle and board, upon which stood two large tin cans, with a small fire of charcoal burning under each so as to keep the coffee boiling during the early hours of the morning when the work-people were thronging into the city on their way to their daily toil.'"

"What's a coffee-stall?" Tate asked.

"An open booth where a vendor…where a *person* sells coffee."

"What's a trestle?" Harper asked.

"A bridge," Tate replied.

"Well, there are trestle bridges," she answered, "but this is a makeshift table."

"Trestle is the wood frame that's holding the board on top to make a table or a bridge," Seth explained.

Marigold gave him a relieved glance. "Yes, exactly. The table is set up so the coffee can sit upon it."

"And then the little girl sells it," Harper suggested.

She gave Seth an apologetic glance. "This might take a while."

The fork hovered above his plate. He studied the faces of the curious boys, his overwhelmed expression revealing doubts about his ability to raise three young boys while he ran a ranch. He met her gaze. "I'm not going anywhere."

In that instant and with those words, much as he'd ignored pain for the sake of remaining calm in front of the children—as well as for the sake of his pride, no doubt—she watched him deny his sizable struggle and accept the responsibility that had been delivered to his door. These children frightened her. But he frightened her more. She needed control of her future. She sensed the threat each of them presented to that control.

She wanted people of her own choosing in her life, but so far, since arriving, circumstances were determining her actions. Marigold turned back to the book. She could handle anything for a short time.

The doctor's husband, Samuel Woods Mason, was the local newspaperman. Marigold recognized his name right away, had followed his articles covering the war and read the book he'd written afterward about his army experiences. He was a talkative, friendly man and arrived with a handsome young son some time later.

"You're the new schoolteacher?"

She extended a hand. "Yes. I'm Marigold Brewster."

They stood in the exterior portion of the doctor's office.

"When things settle down, I'd like to do an interview and write a piece for the *Webster County Daily News*. Your arrival will be of interest to the citizens."

"Well, I don't know how interesting I am, but I'd be happy to let people know my plans for the students."

"Everyone is interesting if I ask the right questions," he said with a smile. "And in this town women are of utmost interest. This is August," he said, indicating his son. The slender boy had jet-black hair and lashes like his father's, and appeared a couple of years older than Tate.

Marigold extended a hand. "I expect we'll be seeing a lot of each other at school."

"Yes, ma'am."

"August loves to read," Marlys told her. "He's learned to speak Chinese and now together, we're learning to write the characters. He can also understand German and is picking up some Shawnee."

Marigold looked at the boy in surprise. "My goodness. That's impressive, August."

He gave her a bashful smile. "Marlys teaches me languages. We visit the people who speak it so we can learn."

He'd called the doctor *Marlys*, but looked to her with affection.

"Come meet the children who will soon be in your class." Marlys rested her hand on his shoulder and introduced the boys, who'd been sitting on chairs in the waiting room. The four of them looked each other over.

"You're going to stay with us tonight while Dr.

Mason looks after your—after Mr. Halloway," Sam explained. "We can get up early and have breakfast at The Cattleman."

"They have flapjacks and sausage," August told them.

The boys looked at Marigold for confirmation. She felt so out of her league with these children. She'd taught in stressful circumstances, with inadequate supplies, and in cold classrooms during the war, but she'd always been confident she had something to offer her students. These children needed so much more than she could give them.

But right now, they simply needed assurance that they were going to be safe and together, and she could offer them that. She kneeled in front of the trio and took Little John's damp hand. "August and Mr. Mason are going to take good care of you tonight." She looked from one little face to the next. "You're all safe and you're together. Tomorrow we'll get you settled at Mr. Hallo— At Seth's ranch. Your travels are over, and you're going to be just fine."

As she stood, Little John dug his fist into her skirt and clung to the fabric.

"Let go, Little John," Tate told his smallest brother.

Little John's lower lip trembled.

She thought quickly. "I'll tell you what." She moved to a nearby table, under which her open bag sat. Attached to her skirt, the toddler followed. She reached into the satchel and withdrew the book they'd started earlier. "You take care of the book for me, Little John. And tomorrow we'll read more."

After a moment's thought, he released her skirt to grasp the book and clutched it to his chest. "Aw-wight."

"That's a good boy. Thank you." She handed Sam

the small valise that held their belongings and he led them out the door.

An ache opened in her chest as she watched them leave with a stranger. She'd been a stranger to them until a few days ago, and now she was their lifeline. They were vulnerable and helpless in a world of unfamiliar people.

Except for Seth Halloway, of course, she reminded herself. He was a strong capable man, willing and able to take over their care. Just as soon as he was on his feet again.

"I'll show you where you'll be sleeping tonight," Marlys told her. "It's perfectly comfortable. I lived here before Sam and I married last year. I carried your pet's cage into the room earlier."

"Thank you, doctor."

"Marlys, please." She led the way into a long narrow room that ran the width of the building. It held a bed and bureau, a woodstove and a table with two chairs. "Feel free to make yourself a pot of tea. There's wood in the bin. The necessary is at the end of the path out back. It's visible in the moonlight."

It had been six days since Marigold had dressed in her nightgown and been afforded a comfortable place to rest. Her entire body ached, and exhaustion was catching up with her. From her cage, Peony, too, was making her displeasure clear. Marigold unfastened the latch and the long-haired ginger cat stepped out, immediately inspecting the area.

Marigold had dreamed of a cup of tea, but tonight she settled for a glass of water and poured a bowlful for the cat. Marigold slipped the thick braided ribbon leash she'd made for the train ride around Peony's neck and let her out for a few minutes, talking softly to her the whole time. Bringing Peony on the train had been challenging, but Marigold had lost so much already, she couldn't bear to leave her pet behind. Peony symbolized home and stability—a small comfort, but a much-needed one. It would be good to get settled, so the poor dear could get used to a home again.

She changed into a delightfully unrestrictive soft cotton gown and climbed under the covers on the narrow bed. Peony leaped up and stretched along her side, her purring loud in the small room. Sweet comfort engulfed Marigold, and she stroked the animal's soft fur. She prayed whoever took her in first was amenable to having the cat as well. "Thank You, Lord, for hearing my prayer in that railcar and sending Mr. Halloway."

She thought of Little John's frightened eyes, of Harper's inquisitiveness and Tate's brave front. Seth Halloway was going to take good care of them. He was a responsible, hardworking person. Even lying down, he probably looked like a giant to them. Fingers curled in the cat's long silky fur, she imagined the giant tied down by the six-inch inhabitants of Lilliput in *Gulliver's Travels* and smiled.

It was the last thought she had until sleep claimed her.

When she opened her eyes again, sunlight was streaming through the small window at the end of the room. She couldn't recall falling asleep, but she remembered the strange dream. The grainy mirror over the bureau reflected a rested yet disheveled young woman with a garish purple bruise on her chin. She set her valise on the bed and found her hairbrush. Several minutes later, after dressing, gathering her clean hair into a tidy knot and feeding the cat, she put Peony back into her cage and stepped into the office.

She discovered Marlys working in an enormous cabinet filled with hanging stems and dozens of bottles and jars. The earthy aroma was strong, but not unpleasant, and unlike anything she'd ever smelled.

"I didn't intend to sleep so long," she said, apologizing after she greeted the doctor.

"You needed your rest. I remember what that journey was like."

"How is Mr. Halloway this morning?"

"It's going to be difficult keeping him still," Marlys told her. "He's dressed and eaten already. Aunt Mae sent food for all of us." She pointed toward a tray on the nearby table. "There's yours. While you eat, I'll make you a small poultice for your chin."

Marigold looked over the labeled jars and crocks, the bunches of hanging dried plants. "What is all this?"

Marlys explained about her practice, how she gathered most of her herbs and roots, how she'd learned healing techniques from the Cheyenne and Chinese. She was a fascinating woman, one Marigold hoped to get to know better.

"James Johnson will be here in a bit to escort all of you to the ranch," Marlys told her. "He's a nice young man with a baby girl named Ava. His wife, Hannah, is a skilled seamstress. Her services are in such high demand, she's had to hire help in her shop."

Marigold uncovered the food tray and found oatmeal, toast and cooked apple slices that smelled like cinnamon. She scooped them into her oatmeal and perched on a stool near the doctor to eat. "I'm sure there are a lot of new people to meet."

"How did you come to teach—and to accept this position?"

"My mother was sickly and my father traveled a lot.

I had a teacher who took an interest in me, and when her husband went to fight, she and I spent a lot of time together. She helped me get my teaching certificate. Her husband didn't return from the war, so she moved to be with family. That's when I became the schoolteacher in our small town, Athens, Ohio. My older sister and I inherited our parents' home, so things were comfortable enough for a while."

None of that explained why she was here. She rested her spoon on the tray. She'd come here to put all of this behind her but for some reason she related her story to the woman. "We both worked and cared for my niece. It wasn't easy for a couple of years, but we had each other. Then Daisy got sick. I took care of her, but she got weaker and weaker until she died."

The doctor turned and gave her a sympathetic nod. "I'm sorry." Then she handed her a warm wet cloth covered in pungent-smelling leaves. "Press that to the bruise."

Marigold did as instructed. The soothing warmth felt good. "After that I just couldn't stay in that big empty house."

"And your niece? Where is she?"

A crushing weight pressed against Marigold's heart. She flattened her palm against her breast as though to relieve the ache. "She… Her father came and got her. She went to live with him."

"I didn't mean to pry."

Marigold shook her head. "No, it's all right. We all have our stories."

A sound alerted them to another's presence in the room. She turned to discover Seth Halloway's imposing presence several feet away. He'd dressed in his clothing, which had obviously been laundered and pressed since yesterday—brown trousers, a loose white shirt without a collar and suspenders. He had a worn holster with a revolver slung over his shoulder. She'd thought him imposing lying down, but he was an even more intimidating figure standing erect.

"Mr. Halloway experienced one of my mineral baths this morning." The lady doctor closed and locked her cupboard before walking toward him. "How does your side feel now?"

"Surprisingly better."

"Is your head hurting any longer?"

"No."

She reached up to move the hair from his forehead, and Marigold astonished herself by wondering what that lock felt like to the touch. Her fingertips against the poultice pack tingled, and warmth crept into her cheeks.

"The swelling has gone down," Marlys told him. "All you need now is rest. I'm going to warn you the ride home won't be pleasant with those bruised ribs. I want you to take a tincture for the trip."

"It feels better."

The business-like lady doctor put a hand on her hip. "Do you want to spend the entire ride in pain and pretending it doesn't hurt so you don't frighten the children?"

His lowered eyebrows showed he hadn't considered that. "All right. Just for the ride." His gaze traveled to Marigold and pinned her to her seat. "Are you all right?"

"Oh. Yes. Just a bruise." She took away the cloth, so he could see her chin.

Seth took a few steps closer and reached to pick a leaf from her skin. He set it on the cloth in her hand. His lashes were thick and black, his eyes revealing concern as he inspected her injury. Her breathing came shallow and ragged at his unsettling nearness.

The bell over the door chimed and Seth stepped back, breaking the tension. The black-haired young man who had taken Seth's supplies to the ranch the day before removed his hat. "Mornin', ladies. Halloway."

"Thanks for your help, James," Seth said to the newcomer.

"James, this is Miss Brewster, our new schoolteacher," the doctor said. "Marigold, this is James Johnson."

"How do, miss." He inquired about their bags and carried them outside.

The door opened again and a slender older woman wearing a small gray hat with red ribbons flowing down the back stepped in, her gaze darting to Seth. The hem of her red-and-gray plaid dress swished when she hurried toward him. "Are you all right?"

"I'm good. A little banged up, but I'll be fine."

The top of her head only came to his collarbone, but she rested her head against his chest and he gently hugged her with one arm. "I couldn't wait to see for myself. There were so many injured. Thanks be to the good Lord no one died." She stepped back and turned her attention to Marigold. "And you must be Miss Brewster."

"Yes." She stood, setting down the poultice, and let the older woman give her a brief embrace, the delicate scent of lilac water drifting to her nostrils.

"I'm Evelyn. Seth's mother. I'm so sorry about this difficulty and so relieved you weren't seriously injured."

His mother…of course. He had her dark hair and eyes. "Your son came to our rescue or it might have been much worse."

"I don't want you to worry about anything," she went

on. "I've made arrangements for you to stay at White Rock. We have plenty of room, and what with the news that we'll have three little ones, two in school, it will be convenient to transport you to town in the morning with the children."

"White Rock?" she asked.

"Seth's ranch," his mother explained. "You're coming to stay with us."

Chapter Three

Marigold rolled that announcement around in her mind for a moment. She was going to be staying with the Halloways? She'd had no idea where she'd be staying, except that her room would be at a student's home and likely change occasionally. But this arrangement had her thoughts spinning. Seth, too, looked every bit as surprised by his mother's revelation as she felt.

She had her reservations about going home with this family—especially with the children. She'd been drawn to them, felt compassion for them, offered them care and concern…as long as she knew this was a temporary occurrence. After today she'd believed she wouldn't meet them again until they showed up in her classroom. But now she would be living with them?

"When did you make this arrangement?" Seth asked, echoing her mental question. Marlys handed him a vial holding a clear liquid and a glass of water. He drank both and gave her a nod.

"After young James explained the situation and all the upheaval in town. I rode in early this morning and spoke with Will and Daniel," his mother explained.

The lady doctor turned to Marigold. "Will Canfield

and Daniel Gardner are two of the town founders and formed the city council," she explained. "They help arrange the bride trains to aid the establishment of Cowboy Creek."

"You'll be able to see Daniel and Leah Gardner's house from the schoolhouse," Seth's mother said. "He owns the stockyards. Leah arrived on a bride train, and she's a midwife and—" Evelyn Halloway shook her head. "Sorry, I got ahead of myself. You'll have plenty of time to know everyone in town." She gave Marigold a smile. "The important thing is, the city council took a quick vote this morning and agreed it was logical for you to stay with us. James located the rest of your belongings and has them loaded. The boys didn't bring much, I hear?"

Marigold experienced the sensation of being swept along in a swift-moving current. "No, only two small bags of clothing, and Mr. Johnson already took one, along with mine."

Marlys gestured to the window. "Sam took the other last night. He should be bringing the children any minute."

"How much do I owe, Dr. Mason?" Seth asked.

"I've been notified that all medical care, food and lodging for anyone involved in the train accident is being picked up by the railroad," she replied. "I imagine Will Canfield had some pull arranging that." She turned to Marigold. "Will has aspirations for the Kansas governorship, and has influential friends."

Marigold had much to learn and a lot of people to meet.

"Thank you for tending to me," Seth told Marlys.

"It was my pleasure. Do let me know if I can be of

any assistance with those boys. There is going to be an adjustment period for them."

"I must admit I was taken aback by the news," Evelyn said. "But now that they're here, I can't wait to meet them. Do they look like Tessa?"

"Like both she and Jessie, I'd say," Seth answered.

As though on cue, the bell over the door rang and Sam Mason ushered in all the boys. Little John removed his thumb from his mouth and ran straight for Marigold.

Seth and his mother looked as surprised as she felt. She kneeled and wrapped an arm around the three-year-old's sturdy little body. "Did you sleep well last night?"

Little John nodded. "Da book's in our bag."

Is it wise to be living with these children? The warning echoed in her thoughts, making her stomach feel a little shaky. She smiled at the little boy. "Thank you for taking care of it for me."

"We slept in a big bed in Mr. Mason's upstairs," Tate told her. "A comfortable one."

"Peony and I slept in a bed in Dr. Mason's back room," she told him with a smile. "A very comfortable bed, as well." Pausing over her last words, she released Little John and stood. "Mrs. Halloway, I've brought my cat with me. I understand that's too much of an imposition, and I'm happy to go wherever the council had originally planned."

The lovely woman blinked and gave her a smile. "We have cats and dogs at the ranch. I don't see one more as a problem. Cats keep the mice population down."

"Well, Peony is a house cat. I don't know what she'd do if she got outside unattended. And I doubt she'd know what to do if she encountered a mouse."

"I see. Well, I'm sure we can accommodate your Peony. I'm going to be thankful for your help." She patted Marigold's hand. "It's been a long time since I've had children around, and what with Seth laid up…well, I'll appreciate another hand."

As reluctant as she was to get any more involved, Marigold couldn't possibly decline to help. It was because of Peony that Seth had gone back into that debris, rather than immediately getting to safety. It was for her sake he'd been in that position in the first place. But all of this was more of the same—life was still happening *to* her, even though she was attempting to forge her own path. With a sick feeling in her chest, she resigned herself to going along with this family.

"It's the least I can do," she said and meant it. As soon as Seth was able to tend for himself, do chores and help with the boys, she'd make her excuses and find another place. Her meager salary wouldn't afford her the luxury of Aunt Mae's, and she didn't want to live off her savings, but food and lodging was in her contract.

"I've given Mr. Halloway herbs for pain," Dr. Mason explained to his mother. She picked up a small canvas bag from a nearby counter and extended it. "Mix a half teaspoon of this powder with water and give it to him with an additional glass of water every six hours." She cocked an eyebrow at Seth. "If he'll accept it."

"I'll take the herbs if I need them," he said.

"Thank you for all of your help and the good night's rest," Marigold told Marlys. She took her crumpled bonnet from her bag, nodded to the boys and led the gathering outside.

James had their belongings nestled in the back of a buckboard with wood sides, along with what looked like a few purchases Mrs. Halloway must have made. He'd formed a couple of makeshift stairs with crates and stood to the side while Seth made the climb into the rear. After only a few muffled groans he seated himself on another crate, which had a nest of blankets behind. James then ushered Seth's mother up to the wagon seat, while Marigold and the boys scrambled up.

"That's not ours," Tate said, pointing to their stack of belongings. "That train. It isn't ours."

The item he referred to appeared to be a small wooden train engine with a couple of cars attached.

"It belongs to the other children on the train," Harper agreed.

Marigold remembered seeing the toy during the trip to Kansas. "There were no other children on the train, Harper."

He nodded and gave her a wide-eyed look of sincerity. "There was. And that's theirs."

She glanced at James. "Are you aware of any other children arriving, Mr. Johnson?"

"No, miss. Only these here boys."

Marigold raised an eyebrow at Tate and Harper, but then she shrugged. If they'd made up imaginary friends to pass the time, she wasn't going to create a disturbance over their play. "Well, we'll take it along until someone else comes for it."

James loaded the makeshift steps and, with an agile leap, seated himself and clucked to the horses. "I'll take you in a roundabout way out of town, Miss Brewster, so you can see a little more of Cowboy Creek."

"That's thoughtful, James," Evelyn told him.

His route first took them east to Lincoln Boulevard, where he turned the team left and headed north past the schoolhouse and an elegant two-story home.

"That's the Gardner place," Evelyn said. She narrated the tour as they went as far north as Sixth Street, then turned south onto Eden, the main thoroughfare. She pointed out everything from the grand opera house to the bakery, where the enticing scents of cinnamon and yeast drew sighs from the boys.

Only once they passed Aunt's Mae's boardinghouse did Marigold get her bearings. Then, after a few more blocks of seemingly thriving businesses, they headed south, out of town.

"It's so flat here," Tate said. "Where are the trees?"

Marigold had thought much the same for days while the train crossed the prairie with little more than short grasses in sight.

Seth reclined against the blankets, his forearm crossed protectively over his side. "You're right. What you see for miles and miles is little bluestem and buffalo grass. They withstand drought."

"What's drought?" Harper asked.

"No rain," Seth explained.

Marigold studied the terrain from beneath the brim of her bonnet.

"A couple of horticultural societies started up recently, teaching Kansans about forestry," Seth told them. "It's possible to grow trees, but it's not easy. The dogged wind makes the soil all the drier."

Tate held onto his hat as a strong gust threatened to take it.

"You'll see a few trees when we get to the ranch."

His effort to talk to the youngster touched Marigold. She glanced at him, and when his gaze met hers, she quickly looked away. She'd thrust herself into the midst of strangers in a peculiar land, and now she had to make the best of it.

She hadn't known what she'd expected, but White Rock Ranch consisted of acres of spring grasses, freshly plowed fields and pastures with grazing horses. Barns, corrals and a dormered two-story house with covered porches along two sides came into view. A row of eight-foot elms stood to the west of the house.

"That's a big house," she said to no one in particular.

"It came with the ranch," Seth told her. "There's a soddy out behind where the previous owners lived until they built this one. My brother told us about the land as soon as the rancher came to him for help selling."

"Did you plant those trees?" Tate asked.

Seth sat forward and inhaled sharply. "I did."

James lowered the tailgate and jumped into the back of the wagon to assist Seth. He and Mrs. Halloway helped him down to the ground.

"Until we get more beds, I've given the boys your room with the bigger bed," his mother told Seth. "Miss Brewster will have the far bedroom, and you'll be sleeping in the room off the kitchen for now."

"Sounds busy."

She raised an eyebrow and smiled. "It's convenient."

"I'd prefer a bed out here." He made his way up the porch stairs to a rocker and sat.

"I'll arrange it." Evelyn reached the door and gave Marigold a resigned smile. "He's made up his mind. I'd be wasting my breath to argue."

"I'll help you with the beds and the cooking."

"There's plenty of room," she assured Marigold, "but the rooms aren't all furnished yet."

James carried in Marigold's and the boys' bags and left them as directed. Marigold carried Peony's carrier into the room she'd been assigned. She sat on the narrow bed, lifted the cat out onto her lap and squeezed her eyes shut. Only a year ago she was living in the comfortable home her parents had left to her and her sister, teaching in a well-appointed school, helping care for the niece she adored. Memories of her sister, Daisy, and her niece, Violet, assailed her. They'd been on their own because Daisy's husband had contracted gold fever and disappeared for months at a time, but they'd had each other. With both of them working, they'd been able to support themselves and care for Violet. Life would never be like that again. She might as well resign herself to the unfortunate fact.

She could have stayed in her family's home. She would have managed. But every room, every corner, every furnishing had held bittersweet memories. The reminder of her loss was too great to bear. She'd cared for her parents until their deaths, and because Daisy had never had a home of her own, Marigold had been thankful for her company and happy to help care for Violet. After Daisy's death, she and her niece had clung to each other—until Violet's father had come for her.

Marigold had no legal right to her sister's child. Violet had cried, and Marigold had encouraged her to be brave when all she'd wanted to do was cry herself. Later, she'd done plenty of that in the hollow house in which she'd been left alone.

It had been time to leave. Start over. Make her own decisions. The teaching position in Cowboy Creek had sounded like a grand adventure.

She glanced around. The room was clean, the quilt-covered bed comfortable enough, the pine chest of drawers and washstand adequate. She would meet new students and be up to the challenge of teaching them. Teaching brought her joy.

She had much to look forward to.

"Ain't neither caterpillars."

"Are so."

"No, they ain't. Caterpillars ain't brown."

"Some are. Go on, touch 'em."

Seth listened to the loud whispers, wondering what the boys were talking about. He'd been dozing on the narrow daybed his mother had instructed James to set up on the porch. She and Miss Brewster had made it up with crisp fresh-smelling sheets and a thick quilt, and he'd succumbed to Dr. Mason's herbal concoction and the rigor of the ride home.

His lip tickled, and he swatted at it. The tickle under his nose came again, and this time when he swatted, he came away with a skinny arm. He opened his eyes to find he'd captured Harper Radner. The boy's wide dark eyes stared back, but his fascinated gaze was fixed on Seth's upper lip—specifically his mustache.

"What are you boys up to?"

"Harper said you got caterpillars on your lip. I said nuh-uh."

Seth grinned. "Well, you're right smart, Harper. What fella would want caterpillars on his lip? What if they fell into his supper?"

The five-year-old scrunched his face into a mask of distaste. "Ewwww!"

From the other side of the porch Tate guffawed.

Seth released the boy's arm. Harper backed up, spotted an empty bucket, which he turned over for a stool, and sat a few feet away from Seth's bed. "I'm gonna sit here and watch for a while."

"I have a chore for the both of you. There's a shed out behind the house. Go back there, leave the door open for light and find me a couple of lanterns. I'll want them when it gets dark."

"To see your way to the privy?" Harper asked.

Seth nodded. "And to read. Where's Little John?"

"Inside with Miss Brewster." The two turned and darted around the corner of the house.

The screen door opened ten feet away, and Miss Brewster exited the house carrying a tray. Little John walked so closely beside her, Seth hoped he didn't trip her.

"We heard you talking to the boys. Your mother sent your lunch." She set the tray on an upended crate and moved it closer to him. "Do you want to sit up a little more?"

"I reckon one more cushion."

She leaned across him to tuck the padding behind him, and her citrusy scent enveloped him. The unique zesty scent suited her—it wasn't heavy or floral, but bright, like her hair and eyes. She wore a pale blue shirt-waist with lace trim down the front and an apron over a blue-and-white checkered skirt. The fabric rustled as she moved. Standing, she handed him a plate of food and smoothed her hand over her hip in an unconscious nervous gesture.

Looking at the bruise on her delicate jaw made him wince each time he saw it. Her face was flushed and her eyelids seemed pink. The day wasn't uncomfortably warm, which made him wonder if she'd been crying. The thought disturbed him more than he'd have liked. "Have a seat."

She glanced behind her and lowered herself onto a cushioned twig chair.

Little John immediately leaned against her knees, and she lifted him onto her lap. He stuck a thumb into his mouth and rested back against her. His untrusting gaze bore into Seth's.

She smoothed the little boy's hair from his forehead. The gesture made something in Seth's chest shift uncomfortably, and he questioned his reaction. No female had ever affected him the way this one did. In her presence, he felt appreciative, protective, uncertain, wary… and enchanted. All at once. The tumble of emotions confused and worried him. He didn't have time to think about perplexing feelings.

He said a silent blessing and ate the meat and potatoes his mother had prepared, his gaze moving across the landscape. Once spring had arrived, he'd inspected all the buildings and made repairs to stalls and corrals. He and old Dewey had ridden fence for weeks, mending and replacing. Dewey was most likely finishing that chore today. Seth's mother hadn't mentioned him, but she'd left for town early and probably set out a breakfast for their hand. Right now Seth should be checking wells and pumps, inspecting the troughs to make certain they'd hold rainwater. Once this rib quit hurting he'd be able to ride.

He glanced at Marigold, noting Little John had fallen asleep on her lap. "You can lay him at the foot of the cot here. I'll sit up while he naps."

She shifted the boy's weight so he was in a manageable position, then rose to place him on the bed. The child curled up and stuck his thumb into his mouth. Seth watched the boy slumber, his long lashes against his pinkened cheek. Glancing up, he noticed that Marigold hadn't moved away, but was studying Little John as well, her expression undecipherable.

"You're good with the boys," he said.

She came out of her reverie to glance at Seth. "Children fascinate me. I suppose that's why I became a teacher. They're impressionable and for the most part unspoiled. They don't resist change or new information, and unless they have cause not to be, they're accepting."

She moved back to the chair and smoothed her skirts.

"He's pretty wary of me." Seth set aside his plate. "I confess I don't much know what to do for youngins. I realize Tessa was desperate for someone to look out for them, but I don't know that I was the best choice."

"Apparently she trusted you."

He took a deep breath that shot a stabbing pain to his side. "I reckon." He shifted, trying to get more comfortable. "Aside from feeding them and giving them a place to sleep, what do I do with them?"

"They're curious. They're energetic. Give them room to play and discover. They need guidelines and routines, enforced with kindness. They need a sense of well-being and someone to listen to them."

Still feeling inadequate, he thought over her words.

"Not all that different from adults in that respect," she added and glanced away from his gaze.

Was she missing a sense of well-being? She'd come all this way on a train by herself. He'd heard talk about the hiring of a new teacher, but until now he hadn't put any thought into what kind of person would accept the position. All of the other women who arrived in Cowboy Creek were either already married to businessmen or ranchers, or had come seeking husbands. Marigold Brewster had apparently come to teach, but it was a long way to travel for a position.

"What brought you to Kansas?" he asked.

She glanced at Little John and then aside. "I lived in Ohio with my sister. We worked and took care of each other. And then she died. It was lonely living in my parents' home without them—without Daisy, I mean. I saw the advertisement for a teacher in a growing boomtown community, so I sent a telegram and once I heard back, I sold the house. I wanted to start over."

"Did you have friends there? Other family?"

She shook her head. "We had friends once. The war changed everything."

He nodded. "Indeed."

A moment passed and the cry of a hawk echoed in the distance.

"Where were you during the war?" she asked.

"We ranched in Missouri, so I guess that tells you something. We were battling over statehood from the start. Towns and families split over joining the Confederacy. My father had built up stock and my brothers and I helped out. The ranch was thriving, but when the war broke out, most of the ranchers had to set their cattle loose while they went to fight. We thought it would only be for a few months and we'd come back and round 'em up, sort 'em out and go on. We lost at Wilson's Creek early on, won at Pea Ridge, but the battles went on and on, and there was no law to be had."

"I followed the newspaper reports," she said. "What about your parents?"

He collected himself before speaking. "My father was killed in sixty. Before the war. Then between Quantrill, the James brothers, Bill Anderson and the like, it was too dangerous to leave my mother alone, so we sent her to her brother's family in Philadelphia, and she waited out the war with my aunts. I ended up fighting in Arkansas, was with General Steele during the Red River Campaign."

"You said 'we'?"

"I have two younger brothers." He spotted a trail of dust in the distance. "Looks like you'll be meeting one real soon."

Marigold turned in the direction Seth studied. Dust rose in the air as a rider approached. He reached the dooryard and slid from his sleek black horse. Dressed in a black waistcoat, black trousers and shiny boots, he approached the porch and removed his hat. He was as tall as Seth, but leaner. A neatly trimmed goatee made his face appear all the more angular.

The stranger turned his attention on Seth. "I just returned from Lawrence this morning and heard you got banged up yesterday."

"I didn't know you were gone."

"Last-minute trip." The man turned to Marigold. "You must be Miss Brewster, our new schoolteacher. Russell Halloway, miss."

"A pleasure," she said.

His gaze slid to the sleeping boy. "And this is one of Tessa's children?"

"That's Little John," Seth answered. "Did you look over the letter?"

"I did. She had it witnessed, and I sent a telegram to the witness who confirmed being present and that Tessa was of sound mind when she wrote it. If someone contested your custody of the children, the letter would be enough to sway a judge that you should have them. It's not a legal document, however, so no court could force you to take the boys if you were set against it."

"What other options would there be?" Marigold asked with concern.

"The records of disposition of desperate orphans have increased by thousands in the past five years," Russ explained. "There are orphan asylums across the country that take children from infancy to age thirteen."

"Desperate orphans," she repeated, glancing from his brother to Seth. A slice of panic rose in her chest. "An asylum sounds dreadful."

"I'm not refusing to take them," Seth assured them

both. "Tessa wanted them in my care, so that's where they'll stay. I just want to make sure everything is legal. There can't be any question about the authenticity of Tessa's will."

She took a deep breath and thanked the Lord for Seth's magnanimous compassion.

The brothers looked at each other, and Marigold sensed the tension barely below the surface.

"I wouldn't want 'em to settle in and then find there's a problem," Seth insisted.

"You can petition a judge and sign papers to adopt them if it's what you want," Russ told him. "Just remember if they carry your name that upon your death they will legally inherit your land and holdings—shared with any other children you might have, so you'll need to have a will in order."

The thought of leaving these children a share of his land didn't seem to bother Seth, because he replied immediately. "Get those papers ready to sign then."

Russell rested his hat on a small table. "It will take me a few days to put the papers in order, so you'll have time to think about it."

"I've thought about it."

"Russ!" Evelyn pushed open the screen door and hurried to give her son an energetic hug. "I was expecting to see you yesterday."

"Just returned this morning," he explained.

"Miss Brewster, you've met my second-born son? He's a lawyer and has his very own practice in town— the one you saw on Eden Street. Daniel Gardner and Will Canfield contacted him and suggested he come to Kansas. Russ is the reason we're here, too. He told Seth about this ranch when it came available."

Russ appeared uncomfortable with her lengthy introduction. "We've met, Mother."

Undeterred, Evelyn continued. "Russ is expecting a lovely young woman to arrive by train very soon. We're all looking forward to her arrival." She turned to her middle son. "Would you like some dinner? It's still hot."

"I am hungry," he said.

"I'll get it." Marigold stood quickly. "You sit and visit with your sons, Mrs. Halloway."

Marigold entered the house and busied herself making another tray, giving the Halloways time to talk. When she carried out the tray minutes later, Evelyn had moved the table near Russ's chair.

"Thank you, Miss Brewster." Russ picked up his napkin and settled it on his lap.

Evelyn gave her son an affectionate look. "After my husband died, we got into hard times back in Missouri. Russ was at university out East. He had to take a job and earn scholarships to finish his law degree. It took him a few years, but even with him going off to fight, he did it."

Marigold found a narrow space on the opposite side of the sleeping Little John and squeezed herself in. "That's quite an accomplishment."

"After the war, he earned himself a reputation fighting for veterans' rights," she went on, with pride in her voice. "That's how he came in contact with Daniel and Will."

Russ's harsh features showed his displeasure. Marigold imagined he was a force to be reckoned with in a judge's chambers. "I'm sure Miss Brewster doesn't want to hear about me."

"I'm captivated," Marigold said with a smile.

"I have another son, too," Evelyn added, lifting her

chin. "Adam is my youngest. After the army, he joined the Pinkerton National Detective Agency."

"And that's the last we've heard of him," Seth commented.

"He's written a few letters," Evelyn said quickly. "I'm sure he's very busy bringing criminals to justice."

Marigold had noted the vague information in Seth and his mother's stories about his father's death. Seth had mentioned he was killed. Marigold barely knew them. She didn't want to ask personal questions that would surely bring up a painful subject. After all, she had her own hurts she didn't want to talk about.

As they talked, an older man approached on foot from the direction of the barns. He was tall and slender, wearing bibbed overalls and a shirt with the sleeves rolled back. As he approached the house, he removed his hat and held it against his chest.

"Hello, Mr. Dewey," Evelyn called out. "Our morning was so busy, I didn't see you. Are you ready for some dinner?"

"Oh, no, ma'am. I fixed myself something. Didn't wanna be no bother. I just wanted to see how Seth was doin'."

"Well, come join us and meet Miss Brewster, the new schoolteacher we've been hearing about."

"How do, miss," the fellow said and stopped at the foot of the stairs.

"Come up here and sit with us. I'll get you a cup of coffee," Evelyn said. "Marigold, this is Mr. Dewey. He's Seth's friend and works here." Evelyn hurried into the house.

"Pleased to meet you, Mr. Dewey."

"Just plain Dewey, miss."

"Dewey and I drove cattle from Texas to Colorado and have more than a few scars to show for it," Seth said.

Dewey brought a chair from the far end of the porch and settled onto it. He was a lanky fellow, his body all sharp angles. He had a full head of silver-gray hair, but his big mustache was still shot with patches of black. "And a whole passel o' stories."

Tate and Harper came around the side of the house and set dusty lanterns inside the porch rail.

"How many did you find?" Seth asked.

"Four, sir," Tate replied.

"Fine work. Come close."

The boys glanced at the two strangers and moved beside Seth.

Seth introduced them to his brother and the ranch hand, and Evelyn returned with a tray of full coffee cups for the men.

"This is more people than we've had on this porch since we got here last fall," she said with a smile.

"Reckon you should get busted up more often," Dewey said to Seth, and Seth chuckled while holding his side.

It was the first time Marigold had seen a smile on his face, and she appreciated the relaxed expression. He and Dewey had obviously shared a long friendship.

"You rode the train all the way from Missouri?" Russ asked the boys.

Harper looked at Tate, and Tate responded. "Yes, sir. Part way we met Miss Brewster, an' she helped look after us."

"She has a cat," Harper added.

"Where do you live?" Tate asked.

"I have a place in town," Russ replied.

"A new house," Evelyn said. "I helped him with rugs

and furniture and the like. It will be a fine home for a family."

Russ gave his mother a tolerant grin. "Someday."

"Not long now." She glanced at Marigold. "The young woman Russ has been corresponding with is coming to Cowboy Creek in only a few weeks."

"Mother," Russ said by way of shushing her.

"Where do you stay, Dewey?" Marigold asked, to change the subject.

"I have a place in the rear of the small barn." He gestured over his shoulder with a thumb.

Evelyn tilted her head. "I've tried to get him into the house, but he won't have it—not even over the winter."

"Got ever'thing I need right out there, and I don't bother nobody when I get up to look at the stars of a night," he replied. "Ain't slept in a house my whole life, an' I don't have a mind to now."

It was clear they'd had the discussion more than once, and Evelyn wasn't winning.

Little John woke up, and his disoriented gaze went from person to person, until he found his brothers. He sat up and scooted close to Marigold. She patted his leg. "This is Little John," she told the newcomers.

The boy stuck his thumb into his mouth.

"Harper, will you please take him around back?"

"Yes'm."

Tate followed his younger brothers.

"Three children are a big responsibility," Russ commented.

"I know all about responsibility." Seth's voice held a depth of meaning.

Russ took a sip of his coffee.

"Miss Brewster is here to help us." Evelyn gave Marigold a warm smile.

"I'll see to those dishes now," she said. She got up and made her way inside.

There was more to this family than anyone had shared, but it was none of her business. None of this was her business, when it came right down to it, but here she was, embroiled in the care and feeding of three children and a wounded rancher.

Chapter Four

That evening she was putting things away in her room when there was a tentative knock at the door.

"Come in."

Tate entered and looked around. "Seth asked me to fetch you."

"Thank you. I'll be down in a few minutes."

She found Seth alone, propped in a sitting position on the narrow bed on the porch. As far as the eye could see the darkening sky to the west was streaked with vivid tones of orange and purple. Already a few stars blinked in the broad expanse.

"I thought we should talk some about how the days are going to work."

She seated herself on the twig chair. "All right."

"For now, Dewey will give you and the boys a ride to school in the mornings. The more efficient way to travel will be if you learn to ride and take a couple of horses. There's a corral and water troughs behind the livery and saddle shop. If there was a storm, Colton there would see to the stock. From there it's just a walk around the corner to the schoolhouse."

Horse riding hadn't been in her plan when she'd traveled here, but she understood the practicality. "I see."

"And then there's safety."

At his words, she looked straight at him.

"We'll start lessons tomorrow."

"Lessons?" she asked.

"Shooting, loading. I have a few revolvers, and you'll be able to find one you can handle well enough."

Alarmed, she balked at the plan. "Who might I have to shoot?"

"You may never have to shoot at all, but you need to know how." He paused and she continued to question him with her stare. "A snake, a bandit, a wolf."

The woman was obviously reluctant about the prospect of these lessons, but Seth felt as accountable for her as he did the boys. She'd be staying under his roof, on his land, and he had to look out for her.

"I'm just going to say this straight," he continued. "Cowboy Creek is a peaceable town, with lawmen and regulations, but it's a cow town and it's brimming with men. Lots of men, young and old, nearly all of them looking for a woman. The school is located near prestigious homes and close to businesses, so it's not secluded whatsoever, but sometimes things happen. Ruffians have been known to ride into town. You're there to teach the children, and they're in your care each day. Always be aware of your surroundings. Keep a gun in a safe place, just in case it's needed."

"Does the current teacher have a gun?"

"I can't tell you for sure, but if she was my wife, I'd be sure she had one."

Her focus skittered away and her face seemed a trifle paler than it had moments ago. She swallowed and rubbed her palms on her skirt. She was a city girl, raised in a comfortable home, educated and perhaps protected. He felt bad about delivering hard facts, but someone had to. She needed to be aware.

"Miss Brewster…" he began.

Her gaze flitted to his again.

He took a match and striker from the small stand beside his cot and held them out to her. "Will you light a couple of the lanterns, please?"

She did as he asked, her skirt pooling on the porch floor as she kneeled. Dust flamed inside the glass chimney and burned off quickly.

"You know more about me than I know about you, partly thanks to my mother. No one ever has to wonder what she's thinking." He shrugged. "But I'm curious. What was your life like in Ohio during the war?"

"Probably very different than the stories I've heard about lower states," she answered. "The men, young and old—except the very young boys—were off fighting. My father was a banker. His family had come to Ohio from New York when he was a boy. He took a job working for the governor just as the war started, and he spent a lot of time in Washington. Daisy married about that time. Her husband was wounded at Arkansas Post and later recovered and went back to his regiment. She wrote him daily, but rarely had a letter in return. He returned for a day or two now and then between assignments. My mother became sickly, so my sister and I cared for her with domestic help."

She adjusted the wicks on both lamps, stood and took a seat again. "We followed the news and corresponded with neighbors and schoolmates who were off fighting. When news came of men killed, the war seemed so far away. Daisy and I attended church and oyster suppers and gatherings and received callers. We made cakes for special occasions. We had ladies over and sewed quilts for sons and husbands, rolled bandages for the field hospitals, and all the while we prayed for the fighting to end."

The sky had darkened, and now the golden light from the lanterns glowed on her delicate features. "I'm sure my telling seems idyllic to someone like you, who was in the thick of things, getting shot and all."

"Thinking of scenes like that kept a lot of us going," he answered. "Knowing there was gentility to return to. Families, church suppers and cakes. Quilts."

His deep tone and heartfelt words betrayed his emotions, so he cleared his throat. "Did you write to someone special?"

"I was merely fourteen when the struggle over slavery began. My father insisted Daisy and I continue our studies. I hadn't time to grow into thinking about boys before they were all gone."

"But you'd become a teacher."

"Yes. And I got my father's affinity for numbers. I'd make someone a good accountant in a pinch, but I prefer working with children. I'll always find employment."

She was obviously smart and ambitious, and took pride in being able to support herself. "That's admirable."

"Thank you."

The breeze picked up her citrusy scent and carried it in his direction.

"What's that scent you wear?"

She looked at him with surprise. "Orange-flower and almond-oil toilet water. My father always gave it to me at Christmas."

"It suits you."

Marigold had lived a life very different from his,

from that of his family. It had taken courage and a desire for change to come this far alone. Quite a few brides had arrived in Cowboy Creek, and he'd heard some of their stories, but he'd never stopped to consider what the journey had meant for them. Until now.

"I don't want you to be afraid living here. I only want to make sure you're able to protect yourself and the children in your care."

"Truly, I never considered I might have to protect them."

"You will likely never have to. But you'll be prepared regardless."

She nodded. "Yes. Thank you."

"Thank you. For looking after the boys."

"It's my pleasure."

"You're likely exhausted."

"I am."

"Good night then. Sleep well."

"And you." On a delicate current of orange and almond, she departed.

Dozens of cowboys and business owners were going to appreciate Miss Brewster's delicate beauty and intelligence. The last teacher hadn't lasted six months before she was married. He suspected this schoolmarm would be temporary as well. Even Russ had shown covert interest when he'd thought no one was looking. And why not? Marigold Brewster was the prettiest thing Seth had ever seen.

Little John cried the next morning when Marigold and the boys prepared to leave with Dewey. She kneeled and gave him a gentle hug. "You're going to be just fine with Mrs. Halloway. She loves little boys. I'll bet she'll even read you a story."

Evelyn rubbed his back and smoothed his hair. "I have just the book, too."

Marigold had assured him he could come to school with them occasionally after her adjustment period had ended, but he didn't take kindly to his brothers going without him. She cupped his chin and wiped his tears, then joined Dewey on the wagon seat and didn't look back. Evelyn was the best person to care for Little John while his brothers were in school. She had been happy at the thought of having him with her during the day. It had, in fact, been her idea.

Dewey pointed out hawks and ground squirrels to Tate and Harper, and then answered a dozen questions on the drive to town. As they made their way to Lincoln Boulevard, the streets were already brimming with wagons; shopkeepers swept their stoops and opened their shutters. Dewey rolled the wagon right up along the curb before the single-story wood-frame building with a small vented bell tower, and helped Marigold to the ground. The boys grabbed their tin dinner pails and jumped down. As she'd noticed on their way past yesterday, the schoolhouse was larger than she'd anticipated.

"Looks like Mizz Aldridge is just gettin' here," Dewey said. "I'll be off now."

She thanked him and he drove the wagon away.

A dark-haired woman only a few years older than herself crossed the lawn and greeted Marigold. "Miss Brewster?"

"Miss Aldridge?"

"It was Libby Aldridge before I was married. I'm Libby Thompson now. I'm so glad you're here." The swell of Libby's belly indicated the arrival of a child in the next few months.

"I'm glad to finally be here. The trip was…eventful."

"Oh, my goodness, yes! Thank God you weren't injured in the train wreck! We were aghast when we heard the news."

"Some bumps and bruises, but I'm fortunate to have walked away. Mr. Halloway is the one with the most injuries."

"The tale of him being injured while rescuing you has spread all around town. The ladies are finding it quite romantic."

"Oh, no. No," Marigold declared. "It's not like that at all."

"Let's take our things inside. I suppose you have more supplies you'll be bringing?"

"Yes, another day. I wanted to meet you and the children and become oriented this week." She gestured to the two boys flanking her sides. "This is Tate Radner. And this is Harper. Gentlemen, say hello to Mrs. Thompson."

After they exchanged greetings, Libby led them into a tiny entryway below the bell tower and then further inside, where the smell of new wood, paper and chalk prevailed. To the right was a large empty classroom and to the left a smaller one with rows of double desks. "As you can see the building is only a year old. The council thought of everything. There's an entire half of the building to accommodate growth and eventually another teacher. Wood is delivered for the stove. There's a shared well on the next block north, and a lad brings water to us each morning."

"This is so much larger than I expected."

"The town founders firmly believe in education, and they built the school with expansion and exceptional learning in mind. Right now we use that room for activities and exercise when the weather is poor. We hold our school programs in there as well."

She pointed to a wooden chest along the side wall. "The children place their dinners in the pine box when they arrive. I assign two students to pass them out at noon. Leah Gardner will be here soon. She makes a few lunches every morning for the children who don't have much to bring. And her own isn't even old enough for school yet."

"I've already heard a lot about her." Marigold instructed Tate and Harper to stow their tin pails in the chest. "Are there seats available for these two new students?"

"Yes, of course. Right now I have the children arranged according to grade levels, and the open seats are in the rear. We will do a bit of rearranging today, and then you may want to reassign seats once you've done an assessment and know where to place them."

Libby showed her the supplies provided by the school board—books, slates, chalk, paper and pencils. There were maps and a globe and even a pianoforte under an Indian blanket in the corner. "I don't play, but occasionally Hannah Johnson comes to give a music lesson. Do you play?"

"I'm adequate, yes."

"That's excellent news. Hannah has a lot to do already, what with her dress shop and a little one, but she's been faithful to devote a morning to us every week. My biggest challenge has been the German children. August Mason has learned some basics, and he is quite helpful in our communication, but I'm afraid the students are sorely behind. I know how important it is for their parents to have their children in school, but truthfully,

I don't know how much they're actually getting out of the lessons. I do my best."

"I can't imagine how difficult it must be for them to be here and not understand what's going on."

There was a tap on the open door and a slender young blond woman in a stunning plaid dress with a lace collar and cuffs entered. She carried a basket over her arm and a chubby baby on her other hip. "Good morning!"

"I told Miss Brewster you would be here. Miss Brewster, this is Leah Gardner."

Libby hurried to take the basket from Leah and placed the contents in the chest.

"We've been looking forward to your arrival," Leah told Marigold with a bright smile.

She was lovely, fresh-faced and fair, with curling blond tresses down her back. Shiny pearls bobbed on each earlobe, and her dress had been made with fine fabric and obviously sewn to flatter her curvy shape. "You live just across the boulevard, and you're a midwife, I understand."

"I do, and I am. And this is my daughter, Evie." She glanced down at the chubby baby. "I'm just that close, so if you ever need anything, send one of the older children over to get me. I have help a few days a week, so most often one of us is available. Daniel and I will want to welcome you properly with dinner at our home very soon. Of course, the church will hold a welcome party for all the brides on Sunday, since you missed out on a proper welcome the day of your arrival. We're all so thankful there were no serious injuries."

"We were fortunate."

"I heard about the children," Leah told her. "And Seth? How is he?"

"His arm in in a cast, and he's in quite a bit of pain

with his ribs, but he's expected to heal quickly. Dr. Mason took good care of him. Of all of us."

"My husband said there were new arrangements made for you to stay with Evelyn and Seth. How do you feel about that?"

"I admit I'm a little overwhelmed. There are so many people to meet and so much to do."

"I understand completely. I was very much out of my element when I arrived here last year. Remember, you don't have to learn it all in one day."

The sound of children's voices reached them.

Libby handed Leah the empty basket. Leah leaned toward Marigold. "Make sure this lady sits down and puts her feet up for a while this afternoon."

"Yes, of course."

"Enjoy your first day." Leah turned to leave and greeted the children who were entering.

Coming to a Kansas boomtown, Marigold had expected a more primitive situation than this well-appointed school, and she was delighted to have been wrong in her imaginations. All of her communications with the superintendent and Will Canfield had been professional, and she'd been told the facility was new and the materials adequate, but still she'd had her doubts. Her living arrangements weren't what she'd planned on, but this school exceeded her hopes.

Nine-year-old August Mason recognized her and gave her a warm smile. She had a moment of uncertainty upon meeting seven-year-old twin girls, Abigail and Jane. Libby had apparently noted her expression of concern, because she said, "Don't worry. After a week or two, you'll be able to tell the Burgess girls apart."

Four children of various ages had the last name Ernst, three were Simmses, plus the students with German names. Altogether, including Tate and Harper, there were fourteen children. They took their seats and showed interest in the new teacher. Libby formally introduced her to the class and had each student stand and say their name and grade.

"While you instruct the children with their numbers this morning, I will evaluate Tate and Harper to see where they are academically." Libby took the boys to the side.

As Marigold taught, she noticed the German-speaking children misunderstood directions and obviously had trouble communicating. Libby had seated August directly behind them, and he did his best to help them, but he couldn't do his own work and help them with theirs.

After they had eaten lunch and the students went outdoors to play, she and Libby spoke.

"The Stirling and Willis children are obviously unable to communicate well enough to understand the lessons," Marigold said.

"It's been a problem since the first," Libby agreed. "They are capable, and they are learning minimal English by being here and watching the others, but their lack of understanding is a problem. August is a big help, but it's not fair to burden him with the responsibility of making sure these other children understand."

"You're right about that."

When school was dismissed at the end of the day, she followed August outside. "How have you and Marlys been learning to speak German? I could buy a book, but I'm not sure I'd be able to pick up a language that way."

"It is hard to learn with only books," he replied. "But Mrs. Werner has helped us. She's from Austria, and we have taught each other."

"Where might I find Mrs. Werner?"

August gave her directions, and she thanked him.

Dewey was waiting beside the wagon on the boulevard. The boys scrambled into the back. "Hello, Dewey. Do you think you could take me to the Werner home before we head back to the ranch?"

"Yes'm," he said and helped her up to the seat.

The Werner place was a simple two-story wood frame two blocks north of the livery. Beatrix welcomed Marigold inside. She was young, barely over twenty, with shining brown eyes and lustrous mahogany hair, a color Marigold had always wished for herself. "You are the schoolteacher?" Beatrix asked with a thick accent. At Marigold's nod, she welcomed her into a small informal parlor. "I will heat water for tea."

"No, thank you. That's kind, but Mr. Dewey is waiting for me, and I don't want to be any trouble. What I have to ask you won't take but a minute."

"Please. Have a seat."

"Thank you. Mrs. Werner—"

"Beatrix, please."

"Beatrix, August mentioned that he and Dr. Mason have been learning German from you."

"*Ja.* He is a very intelligent young man. Marlys speaks several languages. They help me with English—reading and grammar."

"Do you have children?"

Her smile would have been answer enough. "My baby, Joseph, is sleeping now."

"We have a few students at school who are struggling. The Stirling and Willis children."

Beatrix's expression changed to one of concern. "I know their parents. I am sorry to learn they are having difficulties."

"They're bright and obviously lovely children. The

problem is the language barrier. Mrs. Thompson has done the very best she can, but with so many students in various levels, there simply isn't enough time to teach them English."

"What can I do to help?"

"I was hoping you might have a few mornings or afternoons available to come to the schoolhouse and work with them."

Her cheeks pinkened charmingly. "I would be honored to help in any manner I can. Thank you for asking me."

Marigold sensed her heartfelt appreciation. "I feel fortunate that you're willing to give your time to the students."

"I have time, Miss Brewster. I do not have skills like many of the other women in our community, but I do know how to help your students."

"Perfect." Marigold stood. "I'm sure you'll want to speak with your husband before you decide on days and times, but we will be grateful for anything you spare us."

"My Colton will be glad for me to do this," Beatrix assured her. "I can come three days a week. Joseph sleeps in the afternoon, so I will bring his basket."

Impulsively, Marigold hugged the young woman and thanked her again.

"You are very welcome."

Little John was delighted to see them. He ran across the yard to meet the wagon, and held his brothers' hands as they all walked to the house. Marigold watched Tate and Harper climb the stairs with their brother between them, and she smiled.

"Tate! Harper!" she called out.

"Yes, miss?" Tate replied, and they turned on the top step and looked down on her.

"I want you to know how very proud of you I am. You are kind to each other. You look out for each other. I know how difficult things have been for you, losing your parents and getting on a train alone to come to this place you knew nothing about. You did something difficult today, too. It wasn't easy to go to a new school. But you did your best, and you made me proud. I'm happy to be your teacher."

"I'm proud of you, too, Miss Brewster," Tate said.

Harper nodded, but looked to his older brother to see what else he had to say.

"You did all those very same things. And you have to be a grown-up besides."

Marigold blinked back the sting of tears at the boy's sensitive words. It wouldn't be good to blubber in front of them when they were expecting her to be an adult. She cleared her throat before she spoke. "When we're not at school, I'd like it if you called me Marigold. It's the name of a flower. Did you know that?"

Harper grinned and Tate shook his head.

She reached up and ruffled their hair. "Why don't you go put Peony's leash on her and take her outside for a while? Hold on and don't let go."

"Okay!" They ran ahead of her to the door.

Seth stood from the chair where he'd overheard their conversation. "It sounds as though you had a successful first day."

She joined him in the shade and they both seated themselves. "No one cried."

Her face was flushed, and he'd seen her hold back tears at Tate's words. "But it was close," he said.

"I had no idea the school would be so well-appointed. It's as modern as the school where I taught in Ohio."

"You can have anything brought in by train if you can afford it, and Cowboy Creek has a thriving economy, what with the stockyards, ranches and prosperous businesses. The town founders saw the possibilities and enticed merchants, tradesmen, cattlemen, brides and families—and all those couples and families need schools and churches. Women and children turn houses into homes and towns into communities."

"What about you? You said your father was a rancher back in Missouri. What happened to that land?"

"That depends on who you talk to."

"You said your father was killed, but that happened before the war started."

"There was no body, but I believe he was killed. He was a leader in the community. Times were tough. There was drought, and a lot of the ranchers were in trouble and took out loans from a man named Zane Ogden, using their ranches as collateral. What they were unaware of were the penalties and ruinous interest payments they turned up owing. Several times my father tried to talk to Ogden on behalf of the ranchers. When my father turned up missing, Ogden produced loan papers with my father's signature, claiming he'd borrowed against our land. The sheriff agreed it was my father's signature."

"Was it?"

"I don't believe my father would have risked our land. Russ thought differently. And Adam got angry with both of us for not fighting harder to have the loan papers canceled."

"What happened?"

"I had to pay back the loans or leave. I sold off a section of land. Mother sold jewelry and furnishings, and we scraped together enough to save the ranch. Russ was in school at the time, and there wasn't enough left to pay his tuition."

"But you kept your stock?"

"Yes, but the war broke out. Army bought the horses. Nothing left for the ranchers to do but let their cows go to fend for themselves. We sent Mother to Philadelphia and then joined the army."

"What about the land? Your home?"

"There were so many cattle roaming Texas after the war that they were worthless everywhere but in the north and east. Dewey and I ran a few herds from Texas to Colorado and built up some savings."

He said it matter-of-factly, but the arduous and dangerous task had undoubtedly been rife with struggles. "And that's where you met Comanches."

He cocked an eyebrow at her. "I wouldn't say 'met.' They stampeded our cows and tried to kill us. We fought back and eventually got away. Had to start that herd all over again. Mother was safe and content with her brother's family during those years, but eventually she wanted to be near her own children again. When Russ sent word about this place, I sold the land in Missouri and sent for her."

"So you've known Dewey since after the war?"

"No, Dewey worked for my father. I've known him since I was a boy." With his arm pressed to his side, Seth stood. Apparently, the talk was over and he had a mission. "After supper we'll start lessons."

"Riding or shooting?"

"Shooting. Put on boots suitable for standing in a field."

She stayed seated and looked up at him. "I'm guessing there's no use arguing?"

"You got that right, teacher."

Chapter Five

Dewey had gathered tin cans and old bottles, and lined them up on stacks of crates on the east side of a pasture.

Marigold looked over the revolvers lying on the piece of canvas Seth had unrolled. "Have you given your mother these lessons?"

"My mother was a rancher's wife before I was born. I'm guessing her father taught her how to ride and use a gun. If not, my father surely did. You can ask her."

She wiped her palms on her skirt.

"Pick up each one and find one that feels right in your hand," Seth instructed. "Your hand should fit up high on the grip, and your knuckle needs to wrap over the trigger."

The revolvers were heavy, and none of them felt right, but she chose one.

"Does your knuckle joint bend over the trigger?" he asked.

"I think so."

She showed him and he approved of her choice. "It's a Remington army revolver. First, I want you to learn to plant your feet and hold the gun steady. Lean forward slightly to counteract the kick of the gun. You're going to look down the barrel and find your target."

She leaned too far forward and he corrected her with a gentle alignment of her shoulders. "That's good. Look along the top of the barrel, and get your target in line. Your goal is to pull back the trigger so smoothly that the firing mechanism ignites and fires the bullet. If you jerk or move, the bullet won't go where you want it to. Focus on releasing the trigger as smoothly as you pulled it back. Go ahead and fire a few shots so you know what it feels like. I don't expect you to get your first shots on target until you know what I'm talking about."

She glanced at him. He gave her an encouraging nod. She held up the revolver, hoping she remembered everything he'd told her. Her hand trembled, and she lowered the gun. "There's so much to think about. How can you remember all this? When those Comanches were shooting arrows at you, did you think about all this?"

Behind them Dewey chuckled. "Purty sure he was thinkin' 'bout shootin' 'em faster before they put any more holes in 'im."

"Shooting becomes like anything you've done hundreds of times," he assured her. "It's like putting on your boots or signing your name. Once you've done it repeatedly, it's second nature."

She couldn't imagine shooting a gun would ever be second nature, but she understood the importance of learning, so she lifted the revolver again. Once she had a shiny bottle in her sites, she pulled back the trigger. The gun jumped in her hand. A plume of dust spat far to the right of the crates, and the explosive sound startled her.

"That's good. You have five more shots before you have to reload, so just get the feel of it. We'll work on aim as we go."

Seth patiently taught her how to load bullets into the chambers, and after reloading several times, she asked, "Are you sure there's not something wrong with this gun?"

He took it from her, raised it, cast and all, and fired six times in a row. A neat line of tin cans flew back into the weeds. He turned the butt toward her. "Reload."

She met his eyes, and couldn't suppress a grin. "Apparently it's not the gun."

Dewey cackled and found himself a spot to perch on a fallen log well behind them.

She opened the cylinder and loaded the chambers.

"You're doing just fine," Seth told her in an encouraging tone. "You'll get the feel of it."

"Even if I get good at hitting cans, I don't know how I'd be able to shoot a person."

"Might be a snake you need to shoot. Or a coyote. But if someone was a threat to you or to the boys, you'd be able to shoot. You can shoot to wound without killing."

Her arms grew tired after several more rounds, and Seth apparently recognized her fatigue. He rolled up the guns, and they headed back to the house. "Tomorrow you'll learn to saddle a horse."

Yes, because this has gone so well, she thought, and resigned herself to another challenging day.

"There's a reception planned for Sunday afternoon," Evelyn told Marigold when they were preparing the evening meal the following day. "You and the other new women will be officially welcomed to Cowboy Creek."

Marigold finished peeling potatoes and started them boiling. "What do you do with the peels?"

"There's a pail outside the back door. Scraps go into

the compost pile for the garden." She set plates on the table. "You can let your cat out of your room if you like. She can have her freedom in the house."

"You wouldn't mind? She doesn't shed terribly, but she does lose a little fur."

"I have to sweep every day anyway, what with those two men and now three boys. What's a little cat hair?"

"I'll try letting her out of my room for a little while and see how she does. Thank you."

Once the meal was ready, Seth came inside and Dewey showed up freshly washed. They seated themselves and Marigold ushered the boys to their places on benches. It was the first time they'd all sat around the table together and Seth had joined them inside.

Seth and Evelyn sat with their hands in their laps. "We're going to say a blessing over our meal now," Evelyn said.

"Bow your heads like Seth is doing," Marigold told the boys.

Tate and Harper obediently lowered their heads, but Little John watched wide-eyed as Seth prayed.

It had been many years since Marigold had heard her father's deep voice lifted in thanks to the Lord, and Seth's prayer vividly reminded her of the many good years during her childhood.

She'd helped provide the same safety and comfort for her niece, creating a little family for the child whose father had rarely been around. She had wonderful memories of Violet as a toddler and a small girl. She'd doted upon her, felt important and needed. But all that had come to an end. When Daisy had died, she'd written letters and sent telegrams to her brother-in-law because she'd known it was the right thing to do, but she'd secretly been relieved when he hadn't responded. She'd let herself fall into the hopeless dream that she and Daisy would be a family forever. But then—

"Marigold?" Evelyn, holding a bowl of beets, brought her out of her reverie. She quickly put a small portion on her plate and passed the bowl.

Evelyn cut Little John's chicken into bite-sized portions and stirred his potatoes. The child sat on a wooden stool Dewey had cleaned up and brought in from the soddy.

The meal and their conversations all seemed so commonplace, but she knew better than to take anything for granted or get used to these familial occasions. Seth and his mother and Dewey had been together for years, and now the Radner children were officially in his care and part of his family. She was an outsider, here for a brief stay before moving to another student's home.

"You're getting around well now, Seth," his mother said to him.

"I'm feeling better."

"Do you want to sleep inside tonight?"

"No. I get up during the night, and I don't want to disturb anyone."

"Is sleeping uncomfortable?" Marigold asked.

He nodded. "Some." He glanced at Tate on his left and Harper between Dewey and Marigold on his right. "We're going to saddle up tonight."

"We getta ride the horses?" Tate asked. "I want a big black one."

"The mares are the gentlest," Seth told him, "and they're mostly brown."

"What about Marigold?" Harper asked. "Is she gonna ride, too?"

He met her glance. "Yes, and I have a special horse for her."

"Is this like the revolvers?" she asked. "I pick the one that feels the best?"

"No. I picked one for you."

Her arm and shoulder were sore from yesterday. "I can hardly wait."

"Peony is going to have her freedom in the house," Evelyn told them.

"Please watch that she doesn't get outside," Marigold asked. "I only take her out on a leash. I don't know what she would do."

"She'd be a barn cat," Seth replied. "We have several of those around here."

"She hasn't even seen another cat since her brothers and sisters," Marigold reminded him. "And she's never seen a horse or a chicken. She'd be terrified."

"Don't worry so much," he said. "Animals are smart." He placed his napkin on the table. "I'll have coffee later. We'll get to our lesson."

"I'll help with the dishes," Marigold said.

"No, you go on with your lesson," Evelyn told her. "I can clean up the dishes."

"Are you sure?"

Evelyn got up and waved at her. "Shoo."

Dewey, Tate and Harper hurried ahead. Marigold and Seth followed, Little John between them, and reached the corral. Seth opened the gate with one hand.

"What's that horse, Seth?" Tate asked.

"She's a paint. I brought her from Missouri."

"She's purdy," the lad replied.

Dewey caught the multicolored horse and walked it toward the rail Marigold hugged. With his good arm, Seth reached for the animal's halter and brought her close. "This is Bright Star. Go ahead and let her get your smell."

Tentatively, Marigold reached out, but when the massive animal nuzzled her hand, she jumped back.

"She likes her forehead rubbed here. And you can stroke her neck. She's a fearless and gentle girl. Don't be afraid."

With her heart beating in terror, Marigold did as he asked. The beast stood silent and still, occasionally flicking her ear.

"Get her used to your voice," Seth said with a nod.

"Oh. All right." She focused on the beast in front of her. "Well, hello. We don't know each other, but Seth thinks we should fix that." Bright Star's ear twitched again. "I, uh, I guess we're going to be friends. Do you like poems? 'High waving heather, 'neath stormy blasts bending, midnight and moonlight and bright shining stars. Darkness and glory rejoicingly blending, earth rising to heaven and heaven descending…'"

Seth didn't know whether to be amused or impressed by the schoolteacher's bravado. She stepped up and met every challenge presented to her. He'd chosen Bright Star for her because the mount had seen him through difficult times. It was sure-footed and built for endurance, while also being trustworthy, calm and gentle. Bright Star trusted him, and therefore would make an excellent first horse for this first-time rider, because the animal would sense the importance of this responsibility.

"'Man's spirit away from its drear dungeon sending, bursting the fetters and breaking the bars.'"

Marigold was feminine, but she was no wilting flower. Seth was relying upon her height, her untapped strength and innate desire to learn and prove herself. "I think she likes poetry. Who wrote that?"

"Emily Brontë."

Definitely more charmed than amused, he nodded. "Now she knows your voice." He instructed her to stand on a stool and flatten the hair on the horse's back, then throw a blanket over and smooth it out. "It's important there's not the slightest wrinkle under that saddle. Even if a gentle mount suffers in silence, pain will keep it from listening to your commands. Your horse depends on you to use a good-fitting saddle and make it comfortable. None of my animals fight the bridles or saddles. A horse that knows the tack is painful will fight letting you put it on."

He had Dewey demonstrate how to lift the saddle and use his hand to protect the horse's withers as he settled it. Marigold got the saddle on right the first time. He leaned back and raised his eyebrows in appreciation, and she gave him a half smile. Seth showed her how to tighten the cinches and check the straps.

While Bright Star stood saddled and waiting, he instructed her on mounting. After several awkward hops, she figured it out and sat atop the horse. A sheen of perspiration glowed on her forehead, and tiny corkscrews of red-gold hair formed at her temples. Her hazel eyes were bright when she glanced around, looked at the horse beneath her and then down at him. "I did it!"

"Yep, you did." He held the reins and led her around the corral at a walk.

Tate sat atop the fence and waved. Across the enclosure, Dewey led Harper and Little John on the back of a spotted gray mare named Frances.

"You're going to walk her around yourself now," Seth said and handed Marigold the reins and instructed her how to use the reins and her knees to guide Bright Star. "In a few days, you'll be riding outside this pen."

She walked the horse around the interior a couple of times without a problem and reined in beside him. He instructed her how to swing her leg over the horse's back—the same way she had when getting up—and then step to the ground. "She'll stand right there for you."

She got her leg over, but lost her confidence and started to slip off. With his good arm, Seth caught her from behind and eased her to the ground. The delicate orange-blossom essence that was part of her hair and clothing stirred his senses. She was strong and soft and trembled ever so slightly in his one-armed embrace. Her feet reached the dirt, and she turned to him, her face inches from his, her eyes wide with surprise.

He took a step back.

She handed him the reins, their fingers brushing. Her cheeks flushed, making her all the prettier. She gave a breathy half laugh. "That probably wasn't my most graceful moment."

"You caught on more quickly than anyone I've ever taught."

"So, you've never taught anyone before?" she teased.

"No, I have. I was serious."

"Well, after yesterday's lesson, that's encouraging. If someone starts shooting at me, I won't bother shooting back, I'll just ride like the wind in the other direction."

He laughed out loud and lifted the reins to the front of the horse, putting distance between them and bringing a sharp pain to his ribs. "It's good to know our strengths."

"You'd better rest," she said.

The boys joined them, and Dewey took the horses into the barn.

Seth watched her take Little John's hand and guide

the boys out the gate. Tate and Harper chattered as they walked across the grass toward the house, and she replied in soft tones. For the first time, he truly regretted not having time for a woman in his life. As soon as he was able to ride and work, his days would once again be filled with horses, planting and chores. If he decided to take a wife once things settled down, he didn't want to make one feel as though she was second fiddle to a ranch. He wouldn't want Marigold to—

He stopped that thought right in its tracks. Marigold Brewster hadn't come here looking for a husband.

He wasn't husband material anyhow. He already had three youngins he hadn't been prepared for. They were all he could take on now.

She disappeared into the house but her scent hung in the air, an elusive reminder of regrets he hadn't been aware of until now.

The congregation was abuzz Sunday morning. Marigold was thankful for the Halloways flanking her as their little group made their way up the center aisle.

"Miss Brewster!" Leah Gardner, towheaded baby on her hip, made her way to greet her. "This is my husband, Daniel."

The tall, brown-haired man beside her gave Marigold a friendly smile. "I've heard a lot about you already. I hope you're getting adjusted at the school."

"Yes, thank you. I'll be on my own this coming week, and I'm confident it will go well. Beatrix Werner is going to be an important help. She'll be working with the German-speaking students."

"That's good news," Daniel said. "And these are the young ones, Seth?"

"These are the Radner boys," Seth said from over her shoulder.

"How's the arm?"

"Arm's good. It's these ribs that have kept me down."

The first strains of the organ threaded though the building, and the people made their way into the rows of pews. Evelyn had gone in first, guiding Tate and Harper ahead of her, leaving Seth and Marigold together with Little John.

"We have much to be thankful for this beautiful April morning," the reverend said from the front of the church. "I see several new faces, so I'll introduce myself. I'm Reverend Taggart. Playing the organ is my daughter, Hannah Johnson."

"That's James's wife," Seth whispered.

Marigold spotted James holding a toddler on his lap on the other side of the aisle.

"We came to Cowboy Creek the same way so many of you did, after seeing advertisements in the newspaper and traveling by train," Reverend Taggart continued. "Fortunately, our train did not derail. Today we are thanking God for His provision and protection. With us we have several newcomers who were involved in the train accident, and we want to welcome you. If this is your first Sunday in Cowboy Creek, please stand and introduce yourself."

Several young women stood, and Seth nodded encouragement to Marigold to stand as well.

Reverend Taggart indicated a young woman to Marigold's far left. She turned hesitantly to face the people. She had a full curvy figure, and lustrous brown hair. Her face was heart-shaped, and Marigold found her lovely. "Good morning. I'm Sadie Shriver. I'm from Philadelphia. Thank you all for the warm welcome."

"Miss Shriver," the reverend said. "I understand you've already found employment."

Sadie smiled, making her features all the more stunning. Some fellow was going to snap up this bride-to-be. "Yes, I'll be starting work at the telegraph office."

Congratulations rose here and there from the church members. Sadie sat again.

The reverend smiled at a petite young woman with jet-black hair in perfect waves, and she turned toward the congregation. She was thin and delicate-looking with porcelain skin. Her ebony gaze flitted uncomfortably from person to person. "I'm Deborah Frazier. I want to thank those who came to help the day we arrived. It was frightening, and several people were hurt, but we were treated kindly and taken care of. So, thank you."

Two other prospective brides, including a brunette named Molly Delaney, introduced themselves, and then the reverend's attention lit on Marigold. "And you, miss?"

Her stomach dipped, and she glanced down at Seth beside her. He gave her a reassuring nod. It wouldn't do well for the new schoolteacher to tremble or faint, so she took a deep breath. "Good morning. I'm Marigold Brewster, the new schoolteacher. I was teaching in Ohio before seeing the advertisement for the position in Cowboy Creek. After corresponding with Mr. Canfield and the superintendent, I was delighted to accept the council's offer. I've already met your school-age children. Mrs. Thompson graciously stayed on this past week to help me become oriented and get to know the students."

She glanced around at the faces and expressions, most of them encouraging. "The children are bright and well-behaved, and I'm excited to work with them and to get to know the families—to get to know all of you better. Thank you for this opportunity."

Her introduction was met with a smattering of applause and smiles from the parents.

She seated herself, and Little John climbed onto her lap. She sensed Seth's gaze and glanced to the side, finding him studying her. He gave her a quick smile and glanced away. Evelyn smiled broadly over the boys' heads.

Hannah was an accomplished organist, and Marigold looked forward to her coming to her class for music lessons as well as having her play for programs.

She got to her feet with the congregation, and Little John stood on the pew beside her so she could keep her arm around him as they all sang.

"'Holy, holy, holy! Lord God Almighty! Early in the morning our song shall rise to thee—holy, holy, holy! Merciful and mighty, God in three persons, blessed Trinity!'"

The familiar melody and words lifted her spirits and comforted her. Voices rose in song around her. How amazing to think people had been singing this same song of praise in homes and churches for many years. People were not so different. No matter where they lived, they had hopes and dreams, lived through troubles and trials, loved their families, loved the Lord, worshipped.

After the songs, Little John climbed back onto her lap as Reverend Taggart read a passage from the first letter to the Corinthians. Little John's weight against her breast and his soft hair under her chin reminded her of many, many Sundays with Violet. She longed for the child she adored, and the ache brought quick tears to her eyes. Fumbling for her handkerchief, she blotted her eyes and held back the sobs that rose in her throat. She could see her, feel her, as real as the child she now held. Marigold closed her eyes and silently prayed for Violet's safety, petitioned God to help her niece feel safe and at peace. She prayed for her comfort and well-being. Knowing Violet was with a stranger—even though he was her father—broke her heart.

Seth couldn't miss the pain on Marigold's face. At first he thought perhaps Little John's weight was too much for her and that he should take him, but then at the tears she quickly wiped, he realized the weight was on her heart. Like so many of them, she'd lost family, but maybe there was more.

Tate and Harper were surprisingly well-behaved during the service. He told them so after the reverend ended with a prayer and invited everyone to join the welcome celebration outside. Makeshift tables had been set up along the church and covered with an assortment of tablecloths. A bevy of women set to work arranging dishes and trays, his mother among them. He was glad to see how she'd joined in and made herself part of the community since they'd been here, making friends and joining the ladies' circles.

Several parents surrounded Marigold, introducing themselves and asking her questions. She set down Little John, and Seth took his hand and led him a short distance away. "She's talking to the parents of her students now," he told the boy. "We'll wait over here, okay?"

A straw hat shaded her face, and the blue ribbons on it matched the trim of her gauzy white dress. A cascade of red-gold curls hung down her back under the hat and caught the sunlight. She'd camouflaged the pain he'd seen earlier, and was now smiling and nodding. She rested her hand on the shoulder of a child who joined them.

"Looks as though our new schoolteacher is making friends. The parents seem to like her."

Seth turned to Will Canfield, who'd come up beside him. The man wore his usual shirt and vest with a black tie, the chain of a pocket watch visible. Seth extended his broken arm and Will gave his hand an easy grasp. "She's great with children."

"I hope we made a good choice," Will added.

"Why do you say that?"

Will nodded, indicating the cowboys standing to the side, hats in hands, waiting for introductions. "A man or a mature woman might have been a better choice. Young women don't last long at the job."

Will was probably right. As the parents and students moved away, the fellows vied for Marigold's attention. She spoke to each one, still smiling.

A brunette wearing a green plaid dress was receiving as much attention as Marigold, though her smile had worn thin, and she glanced around as though searching for an escape. Seth recognized her as one of the brides who had introduced themselves. She noticed him and Will, excused herself from the cowboys and made her way over, skirts swishing. "Hello, gentlemen."

"Welcome, Miss…" Will began.

"Delaney. Molly Delaney."

"Miss Delaney. I'm Will Canfield. My wife is that little spitfire at the end of the dessert table over there."

Molly glanced in the direction he indicated. "She's lovely, Mr. Canfield." She looked up at Seth and then down at the toddler at his knee.

"This is Seth Halloway."

"And which one is your wife, Mr. Halloway?"

"I don't have a wife."

She had long-lashed dark brown eyes that lit with a new fire at the news. "But this little one? You're a widower?"

"No, miss. I've recently become a guardian."

"It's a pleasure to meet you. Both of you."

Will smiled and excused himself from the conversation, leaving Seth and the brunette standing together.

"What do you do, Seth?"

"Raise horses. Have a spread to the south."

"Is there a house on your farm?"

"Ranch. And yes."

"Of course. I traveled with Deborah, Sadie and the others."

She'd introduced herself in church that morning. "But you're not from Philadelphia?"

"I only boarded the train there. I'm from Sullivan, actually. I'm staying at Aunt Mae's boardinghouse."

The brides always stayed at the boardinghouse. He glanced over her shoulder to find Marigold in yet another group of men, this one including one of the barbers, Jake Osborne, and Freddie Simms. Freddie had been with him when they'd discovered Marigold and the boys under the rubble in the train car. "I trust you're comfortable."

"Oh, yes, quite. Have you had a chance to sample any of Deborah's desserts yet? She fancies herself quite the baker. I don't eat sweets myself."

"No, I haven't."

"I understand you were injured in the train wreckage. Are you all right?"

Marigold appeared to be laughing at something Freddie said. He answered Miss Delaney without looking her way. "Yes. Good."

Little John tugged at Seth's pant leg, pulling his attention away from Marigold. Seth glanced down. Little John motioned him nearer, so he leaned over. "Are you thirsty? You want water?"

The child whispered in his ear.

"Oh!" Seth straightened and looked around. Marigold was still surrounded by admirers, his mother was serving casseroles and Tate and Harper were nowhere to be seen. The task was his alone. "All right. Let's go. Excuse us, Miss Delaney."

He took the boy's hand and led him out behind the church, where there was a row of outhouses shared by the church, Booker & Son, the dressmaker's shop and Godwin's shoe shop.

Several minutes later they exited a privy with Seth feeling quite accomplished. "We avoided a calamity, didn't we, little man?"

Little John merely returned his stare.

"Let's find the wash barrel and then we'll get something to eat. You're probably hungry after your busy morning, what with all the singing and talking to the ladies."

Little John reached toward Seth with both arms in the air.

"Oh." Seth didn't take time to rationalize his next move or the repercussions. The child was showing not only a yearning to be held, but also acceptance. "Okay."

Seth used his good arm to scoop him up and hold him against the side that didn't scream in objection. Just the exertion of the movement made jagged pain shoot through his side. He paused a moment and breathed slowly, then got his bearings and headed for the wash area. Little John patted his cheek. He looked into the boy's eyes, and his heart expanded in his chest. He'd never been around children, especially any this young. Providing a home, food on the table, schooling and taking them to church was all well and good. What he hadn't thought about was the rest. Being an example, showing them acceptance and love, guiding them in the ways of the Lord, teaching them to be men. How would he know how to do that? His mother was a help, of course, but she'd already raised her children.

The sound of iron clanging echoed across the lawn. Dewey had joined Gus and Old Horace at their favorite spot behind Booker & Son. When the two weren't on their benches in front of the building, observing the comings and goings of the townsfolk, they were back here playing horseshoes.

"What are you doing?" Marigold showed up and reached to take Little John from him. "You could hurt yourself."

"I'm fine. We're going to wash so we can eat."

"I'll help." She set down the boy, soaped his hands and lifted him to rinse. He and Seth shared a towel. She smiled. "Let's go get some food."

He'd thought about what Jessie would have wanted for his boys, why Tessa had chosen him, of all people, and figured she'd trusted him. He aimed to live up to her faith in him. Seth didn't want to let anyone down.

But he was in over his head, and he knew it.

Chapter Six

They arrived back at the ranch in time for a riding lesson. While reciting another poem to the horse, Marigold saddled Bright Star herself. "'Riches I hold in light esteem, and love I laugh to scorn. And lust of fame was but a dream that vanished with the morn. And if I pray, the only prayer that moves my lips for me is—'leave the heart that now I bear, and give me liberty.'"

She stroked the animal's neck and rubbed its forehead. After checking the cinches, Seth approved her work. She rode the mare around the interior of the corral. Marigold had removed her hat and tied up her hair. The red-gold tresses shone like golden fire in the evening sun.

With Dewey's help, the boys took turns on the black-and-gray mare.

"I'll show you how to hang up the saddle and brush the horse." He waved her into the stable. She guided Bright Star to where he stood, and he helped her down. "You'll want to ride her in close to the rack," he told her. "The saddle's heavy, and you'll be more tired than before you saddled her."

He gestured to the empty rack and showed her how

to lift the saddle off the horse. "If the horse has been run, the blanket will be damp or downright wet. Throw it over a rail to dry. Dry the animal with some clean feed sacks. The brushes are in this chest."

She took a brush and worked on Bright Star's coat.

"What about these tangles here?" she asked after a few minutes. "Her mane is so pretty, with the black streaked into the white."

He opened the chest and handed her a wide-toothed comb. "Some wranglers cut the mane short so they don't have to work out the knots."

She worked the snarls from the long, coarse hair. "That would be a shame."

They passed a few minutes in quiet, until Seth's remark split the silence. "You got a lot of attention today."

"As predicted."

"Did you enjoy yourself?"

She continued brushing. "It was nice to meet my students' parents and talk to them about curriculum."

"I meant did you enjoy meeting the cowboys. And Freddie."

"Everyone is friendly, so that was nice."

"Freddie's a nice fellow."

"Yes," she agreed. "He's nice."

"He and I were searching cars together when we found you on the train."

"I can't remember that day very well," she admitted. "I was confused and everything is a blur."

"He didn't mention it?"

"No, he didn't."

"Hmm. Modest, too, I reckon."

She stopped combing and looked at him. "You know I didn't come here to find a husband."

"I know. But you're young. Don't you want to be married someday?"

She tossed the comb and brush into the chest and closed it. "I suppose so. I haven't really thought about it. Does Bright Star go out into the pasture or stay in the stable at night?"

"She has a stall back here." He took the horse's lead, and Marigold followed, her hand on the paint's hip. He led the horse into the stall and closed the gate. "She has feed and water." He turned to face Marigold. "Is there more to that poem?"

A tiny line formed in her forehead as though she didn't remember what he was talking about.

"The one you were reciting for Bright Star."

"Oh, yes. "'Yes, as my swift days near their goal, 'tis all that I implore through life and death, a chainless soul with courage to endure.'"

Seth glanced at her. "That's it?"

"It's one of Brontë's short poems. Some are so long I don't have them memorized."

Dewey met them, leading the gray into the barn. "I'll put 'er up," he said.

"I'll take the boys into the house and get them something to eat." She turned to Seth. "You can join us for their story."

He nodded and watched her go. She was young and full of life. Obviously, she loved children. Marigold would change her mind. Someday she would want a husband and children of her own.

Marigold didn't sleep well that night, knowing she would be on her own with the students the following day. At her school in Ohio there had been other teachers nearby whenever she'd needed advice. Emergencies were no concern because the school was in the middle of the city and help was a shout away.

Not all of the children had spoken English well. The frustrated expressions of Ludivine and Jakob Willis, Helene, Arnold and Louis Stirling kept coming to mind. Beatrix was going to be there, she reminded herself. Thank God Beatrix was willing to offer her time. Marigold should have picked up a gift for her. Perhaps she had something that would be meaningful.

She'd known she was coming to Kansas, of course, and this school was better equipped than she'd imagined, but she was solely responsible for the students' education and safety. She assured herself she had Libby Thompson's previous assessments and notes to help guide her. Still, sleep was elusive. Even Peony must have picked up on her unease. The cat meowed loudly enough that Marigold was concerned she'd disturb the boys or Evelyn, and then she jumped on and off the bed. Only when she finally settled down on Marigold's shoulder was Marigold able to close her eyes.

The school day got off to a rocky start, with miscommunications between herself and the German students. Thankfully, Beatrix arrived at nine, but time was lost in the translations. Marigold gave them their assignments, and Beatrix worked with them, though she occasionally stopped to tend to the baby she carried in a sling on her back.

As helpless as Marigold felt with the German students, she felt more inadequate with August. He was the brightest child she'd ever known, immediately grasping each and every concept he encountered. At first she'd found his gift incredible and had been excited to teach him, but as realization sank in, her confidence waned. She was concerned she didn't have enough to offer August, didn't have the skill and wasn't equipped to offer the advanced level of learning of which he was capable.

She took extensive notes and made a list of possible topics and books. She would send telegrams to her former teacher friends in Ohio, to a professor friend, and see what recommendations they might have.

Midmorning, a new student showed up, a tall broad-shouldered young man who didn't appear happy to be there. He slumped into a desk at the back of the room. The few children who looked his way were met with glares.

Surprised and unprepared, Marigold walked back to where he sat. "I'm Miss Brewster."

"Yeah."

"What's your name?"

"Michael Higgins. My ma made me come."

"Well, I'm glad you've joined us. Have you been here before?"

"Coupla times. Didn't like it then, neither."

"Did Mrs. Thompson assign you a primer? Our primers are on the back table."

"Don't need one. Ain't gonna read those dumb stories."

Marigold glanced at Beatrix. The woman lifted her eyebrows and shrugged. Marigold went to a shelf and got a slate and a piece of chalk for Michael.

The boy sat with his arms folded across his chest the rest of the morning. When she gave the older students assignments, she included him, but he wrote nothing on his slate. At dinner break, he sat on a stump in the yard and ignored the other children.

She carried out one of the lunches Leah had provided. "We always have extra lunches in case someone forgets. Mrs. Gardner brings them every day."

"Ain't hungry."

"All right. Well, I'll just leave it here in case you change your mind. You can take it home if you don't want to eat it now."

She made her way back inside and peered out the window. With furtive glances at the other children, Michael had opened the wrapping and tasted a sandwich.

"Is he eating it?" Beatrix had taken the baby out of the sling and laid him on a blanket near Marigold's desk.

"Seems to be."

Marigold took a seat and the two women ate their lunches. "What do you know about the Higgins family? I'm going to need to speak with someone about Michael."

"I don't know everyone, and there are always so many new people," Beatrix replied. "I'm sorry. I will ask Colton, though. He meets many people as the farrier."

"Don't be sorry. You're a big help with the Stirling and Willis children. Thank you for taking time to be here. It's helpful to me to not be alone as well. I feel so inadequate."

"You are an excellent teacher, Miss Brewster. I am learning, too."

Marigold grinned. "Call me Marigold, and I imagine the only thing you've learned is how ineffective I've been today."

"That is not at all true." She folded her brown paper. "You are, how do you say…*wirksam*? Your efforts have positive consequences."

"Thank you."

"Once the children return, I will help you with the next assignments, and then it will be time for me to leave."

"Thank you, Beatrix."

"Bitte."

Marigold had noted that across the boulevard from the schoolhouse someone had dug a well and planted a few hackberry and walnut trees. They were not yet tall, but provided a small amount of shade. She decided this was a good afternoon to venture out of the schoolhouse and read in the shade of those trees. She assigned older children to carry blankets she'd found on a shelf and others to bring a pail of water and a tin cup. The children spread the blankets and made themselves comfortable on the spring grass.

"Imagine we're sitting by a riverbank," she told the children, "daydreaming, as is Alice, the character in this story we're going to read."

"Is it *Alice's Adventures in Wonderland*?" August asked.

"Yes, it is. Will you take turns reading it aloud with me?"

August agreed with an enthusiastic nod.

Two of the younger children fell asleep as she and August took turns reading, and the remainder listened with rapt attention. Even when a wild turkey swooped low and strutted several feet away, the children's attention remained on the story. The turkey lost interest, however, and flew off.

August read until the end of chapter two, and Marigold announced it was time to go back to their desks and tidy up before the end of day. She woke the two sleeping children, folded the blankets and followed her students across the boulevard.

"Will you be back tomorrow?" she asked Michael when the day was over.

He shrugged. "Dunno."

No one was waiting for him outside, but many of the children walked home on their own. He took off at a lope down the street, and she watched until he was out of sight.

That evening she asked Seth and Evelyn if they knew the Higgins family, but neither had heard of him. If he returned, she would find out more about him.

Michael didn't return, but a few days later, Marigold discovered one of the primers missing. She suspected he'd taken it when no one was looking.

One morning, when Leah brought lunches, she asked, "Have you heard the news?"

Marigold paused in her preparations for class and turned to her new friend. "What news is that?"

"Will Canfield has declared he will run for Congress instead of governor. We're so proud. Our very own town founder and friend will be a senator. Isn't that exciting?"

"Indeed, it's very exciting."

"I've known Will since we were in a schoolroom like this one. He and Daniel and I grew up together in Pennsylvania. He always had big plans and dreams. Daniel is so proud of his friend."

"But I thought you were one of the first to arrive on a bride train."

"I was, yes. I had been married previously, and then widowed. I was in a desperate situation when I answered one of the advertisements. And who should I see when I stepped off that train into the crowd, but both Will and Daniel? Daniel asked me to marry him soon after that. It took me a while to warm to the idea, and then to work through my past, but eventually I did."

"I'm happy for you, Leah."

"Thank you." She closed the lid on the box holding the lunches. "Would this Saturday be a good time for you to come for dinner? I'll invite a few others, so you can get to know more people."

"That sounds nice. You're very kind."

She headed for the door. "It will be my pleasure."

"Before you leave, Leah, do you know a family by the name of Higgins?"

"It doesn't sound familiar. Why do you ask?"

Marigold explained to her about Michael, who had come to school only one day.

"I'll ask Daniel. He may know something. Have a good day."

After Leah left, Marigold went to work on her music lesson preparation. Opening the lid on the pianoforte, she was pleasantly surprised by the sound and quality of the instrument. She shouldn't have been, she reminded herself. The school had been generously equipped. She had time to draw five straight even lines for the staff on the blackboard and add a chart of music notes before the students arrived.

"We're going to begin with a music lesson today," she told them once they were settled at their double desks.

Garland, one of the older students, raised her hand. "Is Mrs. Johnson coming?"

"No, I'm going to teach the class. Are you familiar with what notes are?"

Thankfully Hannah had gone over notes with them. Marigold did a quick quiz and then asked, "Does anyone know who Stephen Foster was?"

The students shook their heads.

"He was a songwriter who died a few years ago. You may not know his name, but you've probably heard some of the songs he wrote. We're going to sing a few of them. The first one is 'Old Dog Tray.'" She took a seat at the instrument and played the opening measures.

Ivy raised her hand.

Marigold nodded to her. "Yes?"

"My pa plays that song on his banjo."

"Do you know the words?"

Ivy nodded.

"Will you come up here beside me and help me sing?"

Ivy joined her and they sang. "'The morn of life is past, and evening comes at last. It brings me a dream of a once happy day, of merry forms I've seen upon the village green, sporting with my old dog Tray.'"

A few others knew the words and the chorus was easy to learn. As they finished the song, Michael Higgins showed up and dropped into his seat in the back row. A few children turned to look, but Marigold didn't draw attention to his late arrival. She had prayed for wisdom to know how to handle the boy and to teach him, so she was going to trust God to work it out today.

As usual August finished all his work early that day and asked if he could help her with anything. "What would you like to do?" she asked. "Are there subjects you'd like to learn more about?"

"I'd like to study maps," he replied.

She opened a long low cabinet and found an atlas. "How about this?"

He reached for it, his eyes open wide with interest. "Thank you, Miss Brewster!"

He was absorbed with the book the rest of the school day. After the children had gone home and Dewey arrived to pick up her and the boys, she asked if he minded taking her to one of the mercantiles.

Dewey drove the wagon to Booker & Son and he and the boys waited while she went in. A bell rang over the door as she entered. The enormous building was on a double-wide lot and the interior was laid out in sections. The proprietor came from behind a wood-and-glass counter, his spectacles pushed up on his balding head. "G'day, miss. What can I help you find?"

"I'd like to see your catalogs, please."

"We have everything from flour and salt to hardware and jewelry," he said. "I might have what you need."

"Do you carry maps and atlases?"

"No, miss. I'll find the catalog you want."

Before he walked away, she said, "I didn't ask if there was a library in town."

"No, but I've heard talk of building one."

He came back with a fat book and she carried it closer to the front windows so she could read the small print. When she'd found the maps and atlases she was looking for, she carried the catalog back and pointed out what she wanted. "I'd like one of each of these, please. How long will it take?"

Order completed, she bought a small bag of licorice for the boys. "Do you have a customer by the name of Higgins?"

"Don't believe so, but I don't know everyone by name." He smiled at her. "Don't know your name."

"I'm Marigold Brewster, the new schoolteacher."

"Pleasure to meet you. Abram Booker."

She returned to the wagon and shared the licorice with Dewey, Tate and Harper.

That evening she wrote a letter to Violet. She had asked her sister's husband for an address, and he'd given her one in Dahlonega, Georgia. After some study, she'd learned gold had been mined in that area for years, so that explained why her sister's husband was there. He'd also been in Colorado and Montana, so who knew where he'd be taking Violet next? She prayed for her niece's safety and that she'd be able to go to school. The memory of her misery and tears as her father carried her from the house kept her awake many nights.

She got out her Bible and, with Peony purring in her lap, thumbed through to several of her favorite verses. In Deuteronomy, she found one in chapter thirty-one.

Be strong and of a good courage, fear not, nor be afraid of them: for the Lord thy God, He it is that doth go with thee; He will not fail thee, nor forsake thee.

She pondered the verse and prayed. "Lord, help Violet be of good courage and not to be afraid. Help her to remember and know that You are with her all the time."

Flipping through to the words of Isaiah, she read aloud. "'So do not fear, for I am with you—do not be dismayed, for I am your God. I will strengthen you and help you. I will uphold you with my righteous right hand.'

"Thank You, Father God, for strengthening Violet and giving her peace and comfort. I ask Your best for her, in Jesus's name."

Peony's fur was soft under her fingers, the feline's weight and gentle purring a comfort. Truth to tell, Marigold was comfortable in the Halloway home. Teaching was what she'd always wanted to do, and she certainly had enough challenges to keep things interesting. Missing Violet was completely natural and expected, so that could explain why she felt empty and lonely. She'd always believed her students were enough for her. She shared her love of learning with them and taught them so much. That was enough. She'd always believed teaching was all the satisfaction she needed. So why was she so unsettled tonight?

The house was dark and silent as she closed her Bible and put it away. In preparation for bed, she put the ribbon leash on Peony and carried her downstairs and out the front door. Marigold tugged her shawl around her shoulders and waited for the cat to explore the grass and dirt in the spot it had selected. Then she carried her back up the porch stairs.

"Couldn't sleep?"

Startled, she turned toward the voice and saw Seth. "I didn't realize you were still sleeping out here. I'm sorry to disturb you."

"I wasn't sleeping." The moonlight revealed his outline on one of the chairs. "Have a seat."

She seated herself, but Peony didn't want to remain on her lap. The cat jumped down and rubbed its face against Seth's pant leg.

"Are things going well at school?" he asked.

"I think so. There's certainly no lack of materials. The children are bright. Everyone I've met has been helpful."

"You'll get to know others at the Gardners' gathering."

"You'll be going?" she asked.

"It's hard to say no to Leah."

Marigold mulled over that statement. Leah intended to invite the females who had arrived, so she would likely ask unmarried men as well. Seth was young, unmarried, a ranch owner. And he certainly wasn't hard on the eyes. No doubt there were women who would not be put off by the three children who had recently fallen into his care.

She was thankful she was not dependent on a man

to provide for her. There were no guarantees when it came to husbands or fathers. Seth's own brother was one of those men who disappeared and left his family wondering where he was.

"You know more about youngsters than I do," Seth said. "I need to get some beds and furniture and get the boys settled. There are plenty of rooms upstairs, but maybe we should keep them together. What do you think?"

She laid her head back a moment, deep in thought. Night was silent in Kansas, compared to the city, where she'd always lived. Then she looked toward Seth. "After what they've been through I'd suggest keeping them together until they're older. Perhaps Tate might have his own bed, but Harper and Little John could share one."

He nodded. "All right. I was wondering if you'd be willing to help my mother select furniture."

"Yes, of course."

"Are they smart, Tate and Harper?"

"Yes, they're very smart. Harper makes friends easily. He's the one always talking or playing with another child at recess. Tate, though, is more focused and serious. Probably similar to you as a child, do you suppose?"

"We all helped alongside my father. He expected a lot, and I can remember not wanting to disappoint him. Adam got away with more, of course. He's the youngest. I looked forward to spring roundup with the hands, sleeping under the wagon and eating off tin plates. It was an adventure. The men told stories, showed us how to snare and skin rabbits. My father played his old violin and sang. Russ came along, but he had his head in a book at every opportunity."

She liked hearing these stories of his family, and was hungry for more. "What was your father like?"

"He had a good head for business. He could be stern, but he was fair and kind. He had a sense of humor. He and my mother laughed a lot. He taught us faith by example."

"I would have liked him."

"Everyone liked him."

A question echoed in her mind, one she probably shouldn't ask but couldn't stop. "Do you think your mother would ever find someone and marry again?"

"She says he was the love of her life. No one could ever measure up."

Marigold smiled at the notion. "You know, I believe this is the best place the boys could have ended up," she told him. "Their mother knew you, knew your family, believed you would be influential in their lives. I have no doubt she was right."

"You have more confidence in me than I have in myself," he answered. "I've been thinking, though…" He shifted his weight on the chair. "Thinking I won't want to do this alone."

Marigold glanced into the darkness. "Meaning you will need someone besides your mother to help."

"She has already done so much, but she has raised her own family. It's not fair to her."

"She doesn't seem to mind, but you should probably ask her."

Silence expanded between them for a few minutes and Marigold couldn't help but think of the lovely women who had arrived on the bride train.

"Seems now there might be some interested candidates," she said at last. "And from what I hear, more arriving all the time."

He looked at her, but in the darkness she couldn't read his expression. "Yes. I suppose so."

Try as she might, though, she couldn't think of one of them suitable for Seth Halloway.

Chapter Seven

On Saturday Evelyn had attended an afternoon tea with a few friends earlier in the day, so she was happy to stay home and put the boys to bed while Seth and Marigold went to the Gardners'. Since they were going to the same event, Dewey readied a wagon and Seth drove it into town.

"The little park is lovely," Marigold remarked as they passed the schoolhouse on Lincoln Boulevard. "We've begun reading in the shade."

"Do you suppose more trees would be a good addition?" he asked. "I found a stream where those hackberry trees are growing from seeds along the banks. I was planning to bring a few to the ranch, and I could dig more to plant here."

"Why don't we ask Daniel this evening?"

The Gardner home was an impressive structure set at an angle on the corner of Third and Lincoln. Marigold saw it every day from the schoolhouse, so she was fascinated to finally see the inside. As they pulled up, a young man greeted them.

"I'll be taking care of the horses this evening," he told Seth.

Once inside, Leah greeted them. She was beautiful—
her shiny pale gold hair was gathered in loose curls at
the back of her head, and she wore an exquisite dress
that matched the blue of her eyes. A glance into the room
proved the other ladies who had arrived were dressed
in their evening finery as well. Marigold's white crin-
oline with blue and silver embroidery felt out of place.
While she'd been looking in the mirror in her room,
she'd thought the open-shoulder neckline had been too
much, but now she was thankful for the added drama
of the gown. Unconsciously, she touched her bare collarbone and noted Leah's stunning teardrop gemstone
necklace.

"Marigold!" Sadie Shriver approached with a smile.
"I haven't had an opportunity to speak with you since
we arrived. Everything was so chaotic that week. I
heard you were trapped and required a dramatic rescue."

"It was frightening. Mr. Halloway was among the
men who found me." She turned, but Seth had already
been drawn into a conversation. "You remember the
little boys aboard the train? I was with them at the time
of the accident." She explained how their mother had
sent a letter asking Seth to take her children.

"Are you staying with a family of one of your students?"

"I'm staying with the Halloways right now. Until
Seth is well enough to handle chores and help with the
boys. He was injured."

"Oh, I pray he is doing well. I did see you with them
at church. I'm staying at Aunt Mae's with the other
soon-to-be brides. Aunt Mae truly is like family to all
of us. Between her cooking and Deborah's baking, we're
all watching our waistlines so we don't grow out of our
clothing. Today Deborah baked some little meringues

with blueberries and candied bacon to bring this evening. Wait until you taste one."

Marigold experienced a moment of panic. "I didn't
bring anything."

Sadie rested her hand on her arm. "No one else did,
either. Deborah is making an effort to show her skills
to the community."

They were joined by a young man and then another,
until they didn't have further opportunity to talk.

"Pleasure to meet you, Miss Brewster."

She studied the gentleman dressed in dark trousers,
a white shirt and vest. He had thick umber-colored hair,
combed back in tight waves, and friendly blue eyes.

"I'm Buck Hanley. I know who you are. I heard some
of the fellas describe your hair. It's as pretty as they
said."

Her cheeks warmed and she stopped herself from
reaching up to make sure her hair was in order. Someone had talked about her hair? "I, uh—thank you."

"Didn't mean to embarrass you. I'm not very good
at this. I work with a bunch of men all day."

"I'm not good at this, either. I work with children
all day."

They smiled at each other, breaking the ice. His skin
was sun-darkened with white creases radiating from the
corners of his eyes, and he had a wide friendly smile.
She liked his smile and felt more at ease already.

"What do you do, Mr. Hanley?"

"I've been in Cowboy Creek for a few years now,
doin' this and that. This last year I partnered with a
friend and started a construction company. Hanley and
Ewing Construction Company. Our office is on First
Street, close to the land office and town clerk, near the
lumberyard."

Daniel and a couple joined them, and the host made the introductions. "Will, Tomasina, this is Marigold Brewster. Marigold, these are the Canfields."

She shook Will's hand and his wife, a pretty woman with curly bright red hair and a friendly smile, stepped forward to give her a hug in greeting. When she stepped back beside her husband, he rested a hand protectively around her waist. Tomasina glanced up at him, and the look the two exchanged caused a flutter in Marigold's chest. Was that what love looked like? The question created an ache deep inside, a longing for something she'd never thought to dream for.

"I've heard only good things about you from Libby Thompson and the parents." Will drew her back to their conversation.

"That's nice to hear," Marigold replied. "As soon as you answered my letter and told me about this town, I knew I wanted to come. It's everything you said it was."

"We're proud of Cowboy Creek." Will nodded in his friend's direction. "Daniel and I were friends from our childhood days. Our friend Noah, who we met during the war, settled here first and wrote us about the opportunity to buy land along the new railroad. Our investment has paid off for sure." He nodded toward the man beside them. "I see you've met Buck, our former sheriff."

She gave Buck another long look, and he met her eyes. "He didn't tell me he'd been a sheriff."

"Sad to see him move on, but he's got a good business going now."

"Welcome to Cowboy Creek, Marigold," Tomasina told her. "You just let one of us know if you need anything... ever."

"I will, thank you." After they'd moved on, she turned to Buck. "The sheriff?"

He shrugged. "I said I'd done other things."

"Anything else you're holding back?"

He thought a minute. "My partner, Owen, is the undertaker, and I've helped him out a time or two."

"Is there anything you don't do?"

"I'm not a doctor, so don't come to me with a boil."

She cringed, but laughed. "I don't plan to ever have to go to anyone with that malady."

Freddie Simms joined them, followed by a couple of other men, who introduced themselves. Buck disappeared for a few minutes, and she watched him thread his way through the gathering. He returned with a glass of lemonade for her, and she rewarded him with a smile. She liked Buck Hanley.

Seth could feel his thoughts wandering. In front of him, Molly Delaney was talking nonstop about the meringues one of the other women had spent the afternoon making. She wore a green dress again, this one with gold ribbon sewn around the neckline and on the sleeves. She was pretty, in a flamboyant sort of way. She knew she was pretty, and she knew men admired her. She didn't seem the type to thrive in a cow town, even one with as many amenities as this one.

Seth's attention was drawn across the enormous drawing room the Gardners used for entertaining to Marigold and her flock of would-be suitors. She was polite and talked to each person, but when she had a moment to breathe, her attention went to Buck Hanley. She smiled at him. And why not? He was a nice-enough-looking fellow. Seth knew him to be a hard-working entrepreneur, having gone after investors and then developed his own company. No reason he wouldn't soon have a house to rival the Gardners'. Maybe very soon if he found someone to marry.

He spotted his brother talking to Will and excused himself from Molly's company to join them.

Will reached to shake his hand. "You've heard the news that I've decided to throw my hat in the ring and run for congress?"

"You'll have my vote," Seth assured him. "Will you move if you're elected?"

"We can live half the year here," Will assured him and grinned. "But that leaves the mayoral position open. I've been talking to your brother about him becoming Cowboy Creek's next mayor."

Russ glanced at Seth as though uncertain of his reaction.

"Russ is honest and trustworthy," Seth said. "He's a worthy advocate for those things he feels strongly about. If it's something he wants to do, I'm sure he'd be an excellent candidate."

"Quite an endorsement from your brother," Will said to Russ.

"On the other hand," Seth said, deadpan, "if that should happen, I'd have to hear my mother boast nonstop. For that reason, I don't know if I could vote for him."

The two other men laughed.

"Excuse me," Will said. "My wife has that look that says she needs rescuing."

"You were only half joking," Russ said to Seth once they were alone.

Seth shrugged. "Some things never change."

"I may not have agreed with you about our father, but I admire what you did to pay back those loans." Russ believed their father had signed those papers and had hidden the loan from them. He and Seth had engaged in many heated arguments, because Seth was convinced someone had killed Gilbert and then forged his signature on the documents. Neither had proof. But Adam was the one who'd been angry enough to leave and not look back. Seth didn't feel bad for doing what he'd believed was right, whether or not their father had signed the papers. Having to pay that money was an injustice, but he couldn't prove different.

Russ's gaze moved beyond Seth's shoulder.

"I had no idea there was another Halloway as handsome as the first one I met."

Molly's honeyed voice identified her before Seth even turned. He exchanged a look with his brother. "Miss Delaney, this is my brother, Russ. Russ, Miss Delaney."

"You may call me Molly," she said and extended her hand for Russ to take.

He grasped her fingers briefly and released. "It's a pleasure."

"Are you a rancher as well?" she asked.

"No, I'm an attorney."

Her eyes opened wide and her big smile grew even bigger. "Ooh, a lawyer. Now that's impressive."

Seth imagined Russ's expression would rival that of a man facing a hungry lion. "If you'll excuse us, I promised Leah we'd help her with something."

He jerked his head to the left and Russ quickly followed him through the gathering of people and into the Gardners' kitchen. They stood in the well-appointed room, the sounds from the crowd muted on the other side of the door.

"Thanks for not leaving me there." Russ lifted the

napkin covering a tray and helped himself to what must have been one of Deborah's meringues. "Interesting," he said as he tasted the confection.

The door opened and Leah carried in an empty tray. She stopped and tilted her head. "Are you two hiding in here?"

Russ answered, "No."

"Yes," Seth replied.

She grinned. "Shall I guess?"

"Your prize is one of these sweet things," Russ told her, pointing to the meringues. "Is that bits of bacon?"

"Candied," she replied. "Miss Delaney is exceptionally friendly, am I right?"

"Exceptionally," Seth agreed. "Perhaps she can be distracted. Buck would be a good catch."

Her amused expression indicated she saw everything. "Buck would make anyone a fine husband."

Russ chuckled.

"You two are not funny."

Russ clapped Seth on the back. "He's making a good impression, but you have the upper hand, brother. She's staying at your ranch."

"She didn't come to Cowboy Creek for a husband," Seth said.

"Maybe not, but the teaching job may lead to more."

"I'm not the one who sent for a wife. I have enough on my plate."

Leah's surprise was evident. "Russ, you sent for a bride?"

"Your husband and Will thought it would be good if I was settled down and married before I run for office. I've been communicating with a young lady from back East. She'll be arriving soon."

"Well, I'm happy for you."

"I'm happy for you, too," Seth said honestly.

"You might mention that to Miss Delaney," Leah suggested. "She'd likely take her friendliness elsewhere." She uncovered the tray of meringues and handed it to Russ. "You might as well look as though you're helping."

Seth followed them out of the kitchen. He'd told Marigold he'd been thinking he didn't want to raise the boys alone, and he didn't, but marrying Molly Delaney wasn't an option.

The moon was high and bright on the way home. "The Gardners are a nice couple," Marigold said. "Did you know Leah brings a couple of lunches to the schoolhouse every day so there is food for the children who don't have anything to bring?"

"I didn't know that. Are there children who don't bring a lunch?"

"Occasionally. I ate one once because I forgot my pail in the wagon. Often the lunches are still there and the children share them at recess."

"We forget how fortunate we are," he said.

"Life is good in Cowboy Creek," she agreed.

"I heard talk that there have been things missing around town. One of the women thinks someone is taking eggs from her coop. Another said she had clothing missing from her line last week."

"Has theft been a problem in the past?" Marigold asked.

"I don't think so."

Her thoughts went immediately to the primer that was missing from her school. She remembered it happened right after the Higgins boy had come to class. He'd been to class twice but she wasn't entirely convinced he could read, because he hadn't written on his slate or completed any assignments. He was certainly a puzzle. For a moment she wondered whether he was alone and had made up the story about his mom making him come to school.

She kept her thoughts to herself, choosing instead to enjoy the balmy spring evening.

Seth took off his hat and set it behind the seat. "Buck appeared attentive tonight," he said.

"He's nice. He invited me to supper at The Cattleman."

Was it her imagination or did Seth seem to bristle at her revelation? "Did you accept?" he asked.

"Yes."

That response seemed to halt any further conversation. Seth didn't speak for the remainder of the ride home. Marigold didn't find his silence surprising. Seth was often quiet, but tonight was an uncomfortable quiet.

"I'll help put up the horses," she offered when they got to the White Rock..

"No. Not in your pretty dress. I'll manage. Likely Dewey will hear and join me."

He extended his good arm and wrapped it around her waist to help her to the ground.

"Thank you for the ride," she said.

She'd learned enough about him to understand he felt responsible for her. It was his nature to take responsibility. When she'd shown him the letter from the boys' mother, he hadn't even questioned assuming care of Tessa Radner's children. And after his mother had arranged for her to stay with them, he'd taken it on himself to teach her how to protect herself.

It stood to reason, then, that he felt a duty to be vigilant about any men who might come courting, as well. Undoubtedly he—

A high-pitched scream split the silence of the dark yard. Startled, Marigold turned and ran toward the house. Seth's boots pounded behind her. He was faster, hitting the porch first and throwing open the door. She followed him up the stairs.

A lamp was already lit in the room where the boys slept. The screaming had turned to childish pleading. "No, I want Mama! I want Mama! No, I want Mama!"

"I know, sweetheart," Evelyn said, perched on the edge of the bed. She tried to smooth Little John's hair, but he pushed away her hand. The little boy's pale hair was damp, standing in disarray. His face had turned red from crying and obvious panic.

Evelyn moved back, making room for Marigold to sit beside him. "What's wrong, darling? What's wrong?"

Sobs broke the words until they were barely distinguishable. "I—I—I wa-a-ant Ma-maaa. Pwease, pwease."

Beside him Harper was crying now. Seth strode to the other side of the bed and reached one arm toward the boy. Harper lunged against his chest and clung to him, Seth's cast across his back. Seth sat so Harper was in his lap and used his good arm to grasp Tate's hand.

"Little John had a bad dream." Tate's voice trembled.

"Dreams can be very real," Seth said somberly.

Evelyn went for a wet cloth and Marigold washed Little John's face, neck and arms, cooling him. Finally his sobs subsided. Marigold wanted to cry, too. She'd been devastated when her mother had died, and she'd been an adult. How difficult it must be for children to comprehend. The person who'd always been there for them, loving them, making them feel safe, the person they loved most in the whole world was gone.

"Little John, your mama is in heaven now. Do you know that?" Seth's deep resonate voice was gentle.

"I told 'im," Tate said.

"Well, it's not easy for a little fella to understand," he said.

"I wanna go, too," Little John said.

Marigold's chest ached and she felt impossibly helpless.

"We'll all go to heaven someday," Seth told him. "The Bible says Jesus is in heaven making a place for us. Until then your mama and daddy want you to be happy here."

Seth knew the perfect things to say in beautifully simple language. Tessa Radner had indeed chosen well. Marigold felt all the more inadequate, but her heart was filled with gratitude.

Little John climbed into Marigold's lap and stuck his thumb into his mouth. She held him close, felt his heart beating against hers. From her seat on the bed behind them, Evelyn laid her hand on Marigold's shoulder and stroked it affectionately.

Having let go of Seth's hand, Tate pulled up the covers, made himself comfortable and closed his eyes. "I bet it's pretty in heaven."

Seth shifted Harper's weight, and the five-year-old released him and stretched out alongside his brother.

Little John had grown slack in her arms, and she laid him on Tate's other side, then leaned down and kissed his forehead. Evelyn motioned for Marigold and Seth to move toward the door, then she turned down the wick and doused the lamp.

The three of them stood in the hallway, the silence of the house reassuring.

"Poor little fellows," Evelyn said. "I think they'll sleep well now. Did you have a nice evening?"

"Yes," Seth answered. "Thank you for watching after them. All the time."

"It's almost like having my three boys little again," she said with a soft smile.

"Good night," he said and embraced her.

She padded down the hall to her room and the door closed.

Seth shifted his weight and a floorboard creaked.

Marigold faced him in the dim light that filtered through a window at the end of the hall. "Their mother couldn't have made a better choice selecting someone to care for her children."

He was silent for a long moment before he spoke. "I hope I can live up to her confidence. And yours."

Much as she wanted to stay right there and bask in his gaze, she knew what she had to do. "Good night, Seth." She went into her room and lit a lamp, then closed the door.

Marigold met Beatrix's husband, Colton, at church on Sunday. She held Joseph and admired his pale blue outfit. "Did you sew his gown?"

"Yes. He's wearing short clothes now because he's almost ready to crawl."

"He seems to like being in the school," Marigold told Colton. "He naps during the afternoon. Your wife is a blessing to me and to the students. I'm so thankful for her help."

"She's grateful for the chance to help," he said. "She talks about you and the students all the time." He took

Joseph from her, and Beatrix gave Marigold an impulsive hug.

Hannah Johnson threaded her way through a group of parishioners to talk to Marigold. She carried a rosy-cheeked baby. "This is Ava."

"Hello there, pretty girl."

The child grinned and tucked her head against her mother's neck.

"It's already come to my attention that you play the piano," Hannah said.

"I've had lessons, yes, but I'm not near as accomplished as you. Libby told me you taught the children's music class before I arrived, so I hope I'm not stepping on your toes. You're welcome to come to school anytime."

"Goodness, no. I did it because she needed the help, and I believe it's important for the students to be exposed to music and its history. But I have so much work of my own, it was something I truly didn't have enough time for, so I'm thankful to step aside. I did want to prepare you, however, that once Pippa and the committee who put together plays and pageants at the opera house learn your skill, they will approach you to rehearse and play for them." She spoke in a low tone. "I'm quite honestly grateful for another person to take part of the burden."

"Oh. Well, I've never done anything like that before."

"Even if you helped them out at their rehearsals and weren't comfortable with performances, it would be a blessing."

"I'll think about it if someone comes to me."

"Pippa will approach you. She's about as big as a minute, but she's not shy."

Marigold laughed. "Thank you for the warning."

James approached, looking very different with no hat over his forehead, a pressed white shirt and his long black hair tied back. "Miss Brewster."

"Hello, James. I wanted to thank you for all of your help after the accident. You were such a help to me and to Evelyn. We appreciate it very much."

"Glad to be useful," he said with a grin.

"He's more than useful," Hannah remarked. "He's Daniel's right-hand man at the stockyards. He's a mighty fine father, too." Hannah was tall enough to look right into James's eyes. They smiled at each other with such a look of warmth and love that Marigold's eyes teared. She blinked the moisture away quickly.

Ava reached for James and he took the tiny girl from his wife and kissed her round little cheek. The picture of him with his daughter would melt the hardest heart. Hannah looked at him with adoration in her eyes.

Their affection for each other touched her so deeply that Marigold was still thinking about them, along with Daniel and Leah together, and the glances of love between Will and his wife, as she walked toward the open church doors and was greeted by Reverend Taggart.

She'd never experienced a similar connection with a man before. Her sister had been her best friend, and she'd adored her niece, but she'd never seriously considered having a husband to share her life. She wanted to teach, and she wanted to make her own choices, but why couldn't she do all those things and still be married? Hannah had her own business, a husband, a child, and seemed busy but happy.

Looking for Evelyn or Seth, she glanced across the churchyard at the groups of people in conversations. The boys had found friends from school and stood with them, Tate holding Little John's hand.

"What are you thinking about that has you so serious on this beautiful April morning?" Buck Hanley held his hat to his chest and the sun shone on his head of russet waves. He looked handsome in his black trousers and white shirt this morning.

"Good morning, Buck. I was watching the boys with their new friends."

"I was wondering if this would be a good day to take you to dinner at The Cattleman. We could go for a ride afterward, if you liked."

Evelyn had said something about preparing a chicken after church, but no special plans. She and Seth could get by without her for the afternoon. And why not? Hadn't she just decided she'd like to have more than work in her life?

"That's sounds nice. I'll let Evelyn know."

Chapter Eight

The Cattleman hotel and restaurant was a short walk from church. On the corner of Eden and Second Street, atop the third story of the hotel, was a bell tower. Buck instructed Marigold to look up. "That bell rang the day the train overturned. I was east of here at the site of a new house when we heard it."

"So, it's for emergencies?"

"Yep. I've only heard it a few times. Once when a bunch of rowdies rode through town and shot out the *O*s in the sign over Abram's mercantile. Another time when there was an accident digging a well, and once when a cyclone was spotted. The sound gets attention pretty fast."

She'd noted the tree in front of the hotel was the only one on the main street. They stepped onto the wide front porch, with its numerous windows and green shutters. He held the door and she entered into the lobby ahead of him. Buck navigated them toward the restaurant and they were seated.

The tables were draped in pressed white linen, set with white china and gleaming silverware. Each table

Dear Reader,

IT'S A FACT: if you answer 4 quick questions, we'll send you **4 FREE REWARDS!**

I'm not kidding you. As a leading publisher of women's fiction, we value your opinions... and your time. That's why we are prepared to **reward** you handsomely for completing our mini-survey. In fact, we have 4 Free Rewards for you, including 2 free books and 2 free gifts.

As you may have guessed, that's why our mini-survey is called **"4 for 4".** Answer 4 questions and get 4 Free Rewards. It's that simple!

Thank you for participating in our survey,

Pam Powers

held a small vase with a blue lily. Marigold found the décor elegant. "This is a very nice place."

"It's one of Will Canfield's businesses."

She studied the menu. "What is a *jambon*?"

"It's kind of a glorified ham sandwich. I think it's something French. Ham, cheese and pastry. Pretty good actually. I always order fruit with my meal, because they have fresh brought in by train every couple of days."

"Do you eat here often?"

"Here, the Cowboy Café, The Lariat, and sometimes Aunt Mae asks me to breakfast. And truthfully, those are the best meals, like Mama used to make."

"Well, I believe I must try the *jambon* and have fruit."

Marigold wasn't disappointed with her selection when their server brought them each a small plate of cress, crisp radishes, strawberries, melon balls and sweet plum halves.

She had grown accustomed to Seth saying a blessing over their food. Buck placed his napkin in his lap and waited for her. "Do you want to pray?" she asked.

"Go ahead," he answered.

She bowed her head and said a brief prayer.

The flavors of the cold fresh fruit and vegetables burst on her tongue. "Thank you," she said to Buck. "This is a treat."

"You're welcome. It's a pleasure to share a meal with you. Now if you want meat and potatoes or a good stew, Aunt Mae's is your place. If you're hankerin' for a stack o' flapjacks, Big Robbie over at the Cowboy Café makes the best. We could try them all if you like."

"The flapjacks sound tempting. Maple syrup?"

"Of course."

The *jambons* were hot, with fresh buttery dough and pockets of tender ham and melted cheese. The meal was a treat, and she told Buck so as they left and walked toward the livery.

"We'll see what Colton has left to rent today," he said as they strolled up Eden. The sound of iron clanging reached them. "Sounds like Gus and Old Horace have finished Aunt Mae's dinner and started on their horseshoe game."

"I've never played."

"We'll have to fix that. There's a tournament at the church picnic next Saturday. Winning team gets a bundle of prizes, like a week of bread and rolls from the bakery, shirts from Mrs. Johnson, Dr. Mason's mineral baths, a pair of Godwin's boots and I don't remember what all."

"Who is your partner?"

"I don't have one yet."

Colton Werner had a one-horse buggy to rent, so he hooked the horse to the traces and Buck helped Marigold up to the seat.

"You take care of our schoolteacher," the liveryman said. "My wife is plenty attached to her in one piece."

Buck laughed. "So am I. Don't you worry about that."

Buck took them west, past fields and across a bridge that crossed a flowing stream. "This is Cowboy Creek, where the town got its name."

He followed the stream for a few miles to a place where it got wider and more shallow and large flat rocks lined the banks. The area was mostly flat and bare except along rivers and streams, where trees had managed to sprout and send roots down into the water table. Grasses also lined the banks.

Buck stopped the buggy in shade for the horse and helped Marigold down. He led the way through knee-high grass, prompting frogs to jump from the weeds into the stream. They reached the rocky bank, and she walked over the large flat rocks, where water gurgled. Tiny fish darted in the shallow depths and shiny rocks gleamed in the sunlight. "How did you know about this spot?"

"I come here sometimes."

She flattened her skirt under her and sat. The rock was warm beneath, the sunshine relaxing. Buck took a seat beside her. "You really like it here? Cowboy Creek, I mean. You're planning to stay?"

She glanced at him. "Yes. I like it a lot. I'm looking forward to teaching the children." She thought a minute. "It might sound odd, but when I see the babies, like Ava and Joseph, I think that one day they'll be in my classroom. And I imagine what the older children will do with their lives. Some will become ranchers and others might want to teach... August will do something great, I just know it." Feeling a little sheepish, she shrugged. "I feel as though I have a contribution to make, and it's a good feeling."

"What if you decide to get married?"

Was he being bold or merely curious? "I'd still teach."

"Have you thought about it? Getting married?"

She studied the sunlight reflecting on the rippling water. "A bit."

"I like you a lot, Marigold."

Her face got warm. "I like you, too."

"I don't know much about how this is done. I don't know if it needs to be official..." He hesitated and swallowed hard. "Am I courting you? Is this courting?"

"I don't know, either."

They sat in silence a few minutes.

"I won't decide anything quickly," she told him.

"Which is good. You have a lot of options. There are plenty of eligible men who'd like to make you theirs. I hadn't considered a bride until…well, until I met you."

"Could we…?" she asked hesitantly. "Can we be good friends until I have a better idea of what I want to do?"

"Of course."

They sat in companionable silence, listening to the water and enjoying the sun until he eventually stood and extended a hand.

Marigold took his hand and he helped her to her feet.

Her thoughts were whirling as he drove the buggy to White Rock Ranch and they said their goodbyes. She watched him go, leaving a trail of dust behind the horse as it trotted back toward town.

Evelyn had spread a blanket under the narrow shade of the hackberry trees, and she and the boys were playing with wooden soldiers when Marigold approached.

Little John got up and ran to take her hand. She sat with them, and he gave her a bright smile.

"I found these in one of the trunks I had shipped from Missouri and hadn't bothered to open yet," Evelyn said, holding out a handful of wooden soldiers to her. "They belonged to my boys when they were small."

Marigold lined up a few soldiers in the fold of the blanket.

"How was your meal?" Evelyn asked

"It was very good. And the company was nice as well."

"Buck Hanley is a nice man."

She glanced at the porch. "Where is Seth?"

"He had some chores and couldn't be persuaded to let them go."

"I'll change out of my dress and help."

Marigold changed clothing and found Seth in the near pasture with Dewey and a slender young man. They seemed to be watching a cow as it stood a distance away.

Seth glanced at her and back at the cow.

"What are you doing?" she asked when he didn't volunteer any information.

"Waiting for her to calve."

"That'un over there dropped hers this mornin'," Dewey said. A small black-and-white calf was lying on the ground, and its mother stood protectively near. "Most were born last month, but there's still a few late calves."

"This is Hayden Kluver," Seth told her with a nod to the young man. "He works here part days."

Hayden tipped his straw hat. "Miss."

"I came to help," she said. "What can I do?"

"You can help Hayden drop hay if you like. Should have had it done earlier."

She looked to the youth. "What do I need to do?"

"You can either drive the wagon or throw the hay."

"I've never driven a wagon."

"I'll show you how."

It took a while to get the hang of it, but she did a passable job of leading the team, slowing so as not to pitch Hayden off the back of the hay wagon. "I could never keep my balance and fork hay at the same time like that," she called back to him.

"You could," he said. "Come try."

She pitched hay until her back and shoulders ached, and her skin itched from head to toe. She only fell off the wagon once, and Hayden jumped down to assist her, but he laughed the whole time he brushed her off.

She'd never been so glad to see the bare wood of a wagon bed as she was once all the hay was gone. Hayden shoveled out the stalls in the barn and she helped him lay fresh bedding for the horses. He finished for the day and headed out on a mahogany horse with a black mane. Marigold thought of a poem and recited it to Bright Star before heading out of the barn.

Seth was hanging tools inside the door and paused to give her a nod.

"Are you all right?" she asked.

"I'm fine."

"Ribs doing okay?"

"Yes, I'm fine."

She watched him a minute and went on to the house, where she washed up at the dry sink on the back porch. Evelyn had shown her how to pump fresh water for the pail, and she filled it a couple of times a day.

Evelyn met her at the door and held out Marigold's hairbrush. "I went and got this when I saw you on the porch. You'll want to brush your hair before coming in."

Marigold took the brush and Evelyn followed her. She bent over at the foot of the stairs and brushed out her hair. Bits of hay fell to the ground, and she laughed. "Oh, my."

She proceeded to tell Evelyn how she'd fallen off the back of the wagon, and the two women laughed like schoolgirls. "I've done that plenty of times myself."

Seth walked past them and up the porch stairs, where he washed at the dry sink.

Marigold exchanged a look with his mother.

He dried his hands and went into the house without a word.

"I asked him if he was feeling well, and he said he was fine," Marigold said.

"He's been quiet ever since we left church."

Marigold looked at her again.

"I think his mood has something to do with your dinner with Buck Hanley."

"Oh." She glanced out into the yard and toward the sun lowering in the sky. "Oh," she said again. "You think…?"

"I think he feels…protective."

Marigold didn't know how she felt about that. "I appreciate that he's teaching me to ride and shoot and protect myself."

Evelyn pursed her lips and looked as though she wanted to say more. Instead, she made for the stairs. "It's time to get the boys some milk and then prepare them for bed."

"I'll read their story," Marigold offered.

Evelyn told the boys good-night and left the room as Marigold brought a book and perched on the side of their bed. They'd finished *Jessica's First Prayer* and started on *Hans Brinker, or The Silver Skates* the previous evening. Before she even started reading, Seth joined them, and pulled a chair close to the other side of the bed.

"Look, Seth!" Harper got to his knees and leaned so Seth could see his tongue moving his front tooth. "Thith toof is wiggly."

"You're right. Your tooth is going to come out."

"Why do teeth fall out?"

Seth glanced at Marigold and then away. "Don't really know."

"Do you know, Marigold?" Harper asked.

"Well, we might ask Dr. Mason, but I suppose it's

because a baby's jaw doesn't have enough room for adult-size teeth, so God gives babies little teeth. When kids get bigger, the little teeth fall out and bigger ones grow in."

"Tate has big teeth in front," Harper said.

"God's pretty smart." Tate's expression was serious.

"So is Marigold," Seth added.

"You can read to us, Seth?" Harper asked.

She handed him the book and he opened to the place where they'd left off. "'Holland is one of the queerist countries under the sun. It should be called Odd-land or Contrary-land, for in nearly everything it is different from other parts of the world. In the first place, a large portion of the country is lower than the sea…'"

"Is Holland on the map at school?" Tate asked.

"Yes, and I've ordered new maps, as well," Marigold answered.

Little John's eyes had closed and he was already fast asleep.

Seth continued to read to the end of the second chapter. Together they tucked in the boys and said goodnight.

"I'm going to bathe and wash my hair before bed," she told him. "I'm still itchy from the hay."

"I'll carry water for you."

"You don't have to do that."

"But I will," he insisted. He hurried down the stairs ahead of her, carried in several pails of water and started a fire in the stove.

After bathing, she dressed and dried her hair in front of the stove as it cooled down. Seth showed up to bail water from the tub, which sat in a small room behind the kitchen. He only used one arm to carry, since he still had a cast on the other, so it took him twice as long, but all her objections had been ignored, so she let him.

She heated him coffee and made herself a cup of tea, and pointed it out when he returned. He sweetened the brew with a spoonful of sugar and thanked her.

She sat at the table.

"How was your dinner?"

His question surprised her and she glanced up at him. He stood there, holding the cup in his long fingers without using the tiny handle. His gaze drifted over the hair that fell over her shoulders.

"It was nice. The Cattleman has an interesting menu and fresh fruit."

He sipped his coffee. "How was the company?"

"Buck? He's nice. We went for a ride afterward."

"Did he kiss you?"

She blinked at the question. "That's none of your business, but no."

"Did you want him to?"

She didn't know how to answer or if she should. His questions made her uncomfortable. She got up from the chair and reached for her cup. "I'm taking my tea to my room."

In one stride, he set down his coffee and stopped her with a hand against her neck and jaw, his fingers threading into her hair. She raised her chin to look up at him, placing their faces inches apart. Marigold's heartbeat increased, and she was compelled to raise her hand to the front of his shirt. Beneath her palm, his heart thumped in an erratic pattern.

In the light of the lantern, her eyes moved from his intense gaze, along his lean jaw with its evening shadow, to his full lip beneath his dark mustache. He lowered his head and blood pounded through her veins in anticipation.

When he touched his lips to hers, the caress was tender, more tender than she'd expected, though she hadn't known what to expect. He wasn't holding her there; with one strong but gentle hand, he cupped her shoulder, while his other arm, with its cast, rested at her hip. She could easily move away. She could easily end the kiss.

Seth Halloway was kissing her.

And she was kissing him back.

Her head felt light, and her breath came in quick bursts. She stood, enthralled in the moment. She'd never been kissed before. She raised her other hand and pressed both against his chest, easing herself away and separating them by several inches.

He looked at her lips, into her eyes, his gaze intense.

The air around them crackled with tension and expectation. He was large and brawny, his chest and shoulders muscled under his shirt, but his size and strength didn't intimidate her. She wasn't afraid of him.

She lowered her hands and he released her.

No, Seth didn't frighten her. She was afraid of how he made her feel.

She was afraid of herself.

Consumed by her citrus scent, her shiny hair, by the look of surprise and confusion on her face, Seth gathered his thoughts. He wasn't sorry he'd kissed her. He'd wanted to for some time.

She didn't move for a moment, and when she did, she turned, picked up her cup and left the kitchen without a word. She liked people and got along with everyone, had laughed with young Hayden today, though she'd just met him. His mother loved her, the boys loved her, apparently students and parents and everyone else appreciated her. Buck Hanley had taken a real shine to her.

What was not to like? She was smart and thoughtful… lovely, actually.

He wasn't fooling himself. He'd been steadfast in his ambition to start a stable life for himself and for his mother, and even for Dewey, who was like family after all these years. His focus and energy had paid off and landed them here. White Rock Ranch was shaping up to be all he'd worked for.

He went out to check the horses in the barn, came back and extinguished the lanterns. The Radner boys had been unexpected. After the initial surprise, he'd quickly determined they belonged here with him and he'd do everything in his power to give them the life his friends would have wanted for them. His injury was frustrating, but the boys weren't a burden.

Marigold's presence, on the other hand, had chafed his hide from the beginning, and the condition had only worsened with the passing days. Evelyn claimed she needed her help, and Marigold was indeed a big help. She was kind and patient and knew all the right things to say to the children. She held herself aloof, at times more aloof than others, and that was likely a good thing. She didn't plan to be here forever.

But he was not unaffected. He went to his temporary room and backed up to the bootjack to remove his boots, then sat on the edge of the narrow bed. He liked to think she was unsuited to this land, to ranch life, but she gave everything her best and was learning to thrive. He'd told himself he was too busy, had too many other concerns and didn't have time to think about a book-smart female who recited poetry to horses. But instead of his self-admonitions helping, he thought about her all the time.

And the thought of her spending time with Buck Hanley—or any other man—put a burr under his saddle.

So he'd kissed her.

Seth stretched out, rested his arm with the cast at his side and stacked the other hand under his head. He hadn't wanted it to happen—hadn't expected it to, but the city girl with the red-gold hair and big hazel eyes had gotten under his skin.

Chapter Nine

Michael Higgins arrived midmorning, making a production of stomping to the front to drop a pail into the wooden lunch chest, and then he took his seat. Marigold gave the students assignments and stepped to where he sat. "May I see you outside for a few minutes, please, Michael?"

She continued to the door and stepped out into the sunshine, then waited, unsure of whether or not he would follow.

The boy opened and closed the door behind her and dragged his feet to where she stood waiting. He was nearly as tall as she, with wide shoulders. He was quickly growing into a large man. "You gonna kick me out?"

"No. I just wanted a moment in private with you."

"About what?"

"I was wondering why you don't attend every day, and why, on the days you do attend, you're late arriving."

"I got chores."

"I see."

"My ma makes me come anyhow."

"I'd like to speak with your mother. Where is it you live?"

"My pa don't like strangers comin' around."

"Perhaps she could meet me here after school one day."

"I'll tell 'er."

"I like to work with families to learn the best studies and an education plan for each student. It's helpful when everyone is involved."

"Ain't nobody gonna be involved."

"All right," she said. "Well, we'll see after you speak with her. Tell her I'm available any afternoon."

He shrugged.

"Michael, did you take one of the primers home?"

"No. Told you I ain't gonna read them stupid stories."

"All right. Thank you."

"Can I go back now?"

"Yes, of course."

Michael wasn't disruptive the remainder of the day, ate his lunch alone and took off as soon as she dismissed the class. Hopefully, a talk with his mother would shed some light on his strange behavior.

At supper that evening, Seth behaved as though nothing out of the ordinary had happened between them. Marigold, however, had barely slept the previous night, thinking about the kiss. Now whenever she looked at him she got befuddled and couldn't get it out of her head.

"We're going to saddle up tonight," he said before leaving the kitchen. "You and the boys meet me in the corral in ten minutes."

Evelyn smiled at her. "Go ahead, dear. Change and join them for a ride."

Evelyn had given her a split skirt, so she changed and headed for the corral.

"You saddle Bright Star while I get the other horses ready," Seth told her.

She touched the horse's neck and forehead as Seth had taught her, while reciting Henry Longfellow. "'The day is done, and the darkness falls from the wings of night, as a feather is wafted downward from an eagle in his flight. I see the lights of the village gleam through the rain and the mist, and a feeling of sadness comes o'er me that my soul cannot resist.'" She smoothed the animal's hair over its back, then laid the blanket over it and smoothed out every wrinkle. "'A feeling of sadness and longing, that is not akin to pain, and resembles sorrow only as the mist resembles the rain.'"

After lifting the saddle down from the rail, she settled it on Bright Star, fastened the leather straps and checked them.

Seth had three horses waiting when she led hers from the stable. He helped Tate and Little John on the back of one and Harper on the other. "Can you get up?"

She put her foot in the stirrup and hoisted herself. Her arms and shoulders complained from the previous day's hay throwing, but she muffled a groan and eased herself into the saddle.

Dewey and Hayden stood near the corral fence, and Hayden opened the gate.

"Where are we goin'?" Tate asked.

"You've been doing all your lessons in the corral, and now we're going for a ride," Seth told him.

"Just like real cowboys!" Harper yelled.

"Real cowboys are careful," Dewey said to him. "You hold those reins loose and guide the horse gentle-like."

"Yessir."

"Have you ridden since your ribs were hurt?" Marigold asked Seth as they walked the horses.

"Tried a couple of times. This is the first it didn't hurt." He nodded toward the oldest boy. "Tate is a natural. Takes after his father."

"You and Jessie were close?"

"Friends as boys. He lost his mother when he was young, but our fathers were friends."

"And Tessa?"

"Her father was a Texas Ranger, settled in Missouri. She could keep up with us boys, when it came to ropin' and ridin'. She set her sights on Jessie right off, and there was never a doubt those two would marry one day. They'd no sooner married, started their ranch, had a couple babies and the war came. We enlisted together, he and I."

"They'll always have you to tell them about their parents."

"Doesn't seem like enough." He pointed to a few scattered trees and bushes. "There's a stream ahead. We'll stop and water the horses." He rode ahead and directed Tate and Harper to guide their mounts toward the stream. The horses didn't need any encouragement. They smelled the water and lightened their step.

Marigold slid from the saddle and held the reins as Seth did, then led Bright Star to the water.

"You can loop the reins around the pommel. She won't go anywhere."

The boys walked along the bank, tossing pebbles and sticks into the current. Seth kept an eye on them and the horses.

"Do you ever resent being the responsible one?" she asked. "You said you paid off the loans for your father's ranch, even though you didn't believe he signed the papers."

"It was that or lose the land altogether. I couldn't let that happen."

Marigold nodded, understanding. "You feel a responsibility to your mother."

"She's helping *me* right now."

She looked toward the children, then back to Seth. "I know their parents were your friends, but you didn't ask for responsibility of three children. Do you feel like you'd rather make your own choices?"

He studied her for a long minute before turning his gaze back to the boys. "Is that how you feel?"

"Yes. That's why I came here. So I could make my own choices."

"I respect that."

She should be thinking about leaving the Halloway ranch. That's what she told herself she'd do. Seth would get better and she would board with one of the other families. The longer she remained here, the more difficult it would be to explain her departure to the children, to Evelyn. The more difficult it would be to resolve herself to going. If she was going to make her own choices, she needed to be quick about it. How much longer until Seth was fit to do all the chores? "When will you see Dr. Mason again?"

"Why do you ask?"

"I wondered how long until your ribs were healed."

"They're better. They were only bruised."

"But you have a few more weeks with that cast on your arm."

"Only two more weeks."

She could stay two more weeks.

Seth rubbed his upper arm. "The first thing I'm

going to do when this cast comes off is ride up Cowboy Creek a ways to the deepest spot and get into the water."

She arrested her thoughts and stayed focused on the next two weeks. "Do you suppose the boys and I might be able to ride to school without Dewey soon?"

"Seth! Marigold! There's little fishes! Come see!"

Little John was in the water with his boots on, hunkered down and leaning forward, attempting to catch the tiny fish that darted in the shallow water. Seth gave a hearty laugh at the child's splashing attempts. Getting his own boots and pant legs soaked, he leaned over and, with his good arm, joined the challenge. Tate and Harper were next, trudging in beside them and scooping handfuls of water.

The sight of the four of them heedlessly splashing and giggling lightened Marigold's heart and she laughed at their antics. Seth's big spotted gray gelding, shied and moved several feet from the bank. Marigold followed him and spoke soothingly. "Those fellas are making a lot of commotion, aren't they? You stay put, all right?"

The horse nickered a reply. She patted its neck and rubbed its bony forehead. It snorted and bobbed its head.

Seth and the boys approached, leading the other horses. "What's Hank saying to you?" he asked her.

"I'm not sure. I think he likes me."

"Maybe he just likes poems."

She reached for Bright Star's reins. "For your information, I didn't recite him a poem." Grabbing the pommel, she placed her foot in the stirrup. "Are you poking fun at me?"

Squinting, he used his thumb and forefinger to show her a half inch of space.

She pulled herself up onto the saddle. "You're the one

who told me to talk to Bright Star. I couldn't think of anything to say the first time. And she liked the poetry."

With one strong arm, he helped the boys onto their horses' backs and mounted Hank. When he glanced back at her he was grinning.

The expression disarmed her. "What do *you* say to the horses?"

"That's between me and them." He nudged his horse forward with a heel and the others followed obediently.

Michael's mother didn't show up the next day. When Marigold questioned him, he claimed his mother had too much work to do. At day's end, she informed Dewey that she wanted to follow one of her students home after school, and asked him to let her down and to follow her at a distance. He agreed and stopped the wagon outside town to let her climb down, and he and the boys stayed well behind as she trudged through a field and came to a sod house with a small barn and a few raggedy tents. Animal skins hung on stretchers made of tree limbs.

Marigold had seen Michael run ahead and dart into one of the tents. She followed, and her heart leaped into her throat when a dirty black-and-brown dog ran toward her, barking and snarling. She stood in her tracks and stared at the animal.

Michael came out of the tent and took only a couple of steps toward her. "What are you doin' here?"

"I came to speak to your mother."

"I told you my pa don't take kindly to strangers."

"If I could just speak with her for a moment."

"Hush up, Dutch!"

A man's gruff voice startled her as much as the barking had, and she swung to see the man standing in the doorway of the soddy. He had an unkempt beard and wore trousers with suspenders and one empty pant leg folded back. He stood on his one leg with the aid of a crutch. "Who're you?"

"I'm Miss Brewster, Mr. Higgins. I'm Michael's teacher. I didn't want to bother you, but Michael said his mother was too busy to come speak to me at school, so I thought it might be more convenient if I came here."

The man's scowl swung to Michael, whose face had grown pale. "He said that, did he?"

"I don't want to cause a problem. I just wanted to speak to Michael's family about his placement and lessons."

The man had no problem using the crutch to navigate across the doorway and toward where she stood. "Did he tell ya his ol' man was a cripple?"

"No, sir. He said you didn't like visitors."

"Did he tell ya his ma was dead nigh on two years?"

Marigold's stare moved to Michael. He dropped his gaze to the ground.

"No, sir. He didn't."

"He's got no time for book learnin' when there's work to be done here." He turned a contemptuous eye on his son. "So that's where you been runnin' off to when I cain't find ya. Why they ain't no skins or stew to show for a day's trappin'. Our bellies are rubbin' our backbones an' you ain't got the sense God gave a chicken. Ain't no rabbits to be caught in that schoolhouse."

Michael's neck and face flushed red, and his gaze darted from Marigold back to his father. "No, sir. But Ma wanted me to get learnin'. She made me promise I'd learn to read."

The situation became crystal-clear. Michael had made a promise to his mother. The gruff man's expression crumpled and he jerked his gaze away from both of them.

"What if Michael attends half a day, Mr. Higgins? I could teach him to read in half days."

The man pursed his lips and shook his head. "Waste o' time."

"What if I come here and teach him? In the evenings?"

"He was right about one thing. I don't like no strangers comin' 'round."

"All right."

"I found a book of Ma's," Michael said. "I wanna read it."

His father's gaze moved across the dirt yard, toward the west where the sky was ablaze with color. The dog sat and whined. A bee buzzed around a single clover near a well.

"He's a bright boy," she told him. "He'll learn quickly, given the chance."

"He can come half a day. That's it."

Michael was so surprised his jaw dropped. "I can? I can go?"

"How'd you get 'ere?" Mr. Higgins asked Marigold.

"Wagon, part of the way. Walked the rest. Mr. Dewey is out there waiting for me."

"Why?" the man asked.

"I became a teacher because I care about children, and I think education is one of the most important things we can give them, besides love, and food, water and sharing our faith in God."

"Where you from?"

"Ohio," she replied.

"You came all the way to Kansas in your fancy clothes to teach people to read and write?"

"And appreciate music and history and learn to figure numbers and think for themselves."

"Girls do all them things too?"

"Girls just like me," she answered.

He looked at her for a long time, then he rubbed his nose with one finger and spat in the dirt. "Michael's ma would've liked you."

She nodded. "I'm sure I would have liked her, too."

He looked toward Michael. "You still have to set your traps in the mornin'."

"I will, Pa. Every day."

"Very well." Marigold glanced at her student. "I'll see you tomorrow, Michael."

He actually grinned. "Yes'm."

The following day Michael arrived midmorning and took his seat without disrupting the class. He paid attention when she spoke, and he took one of the primers and followed along with Dwight Simms's unobtrusive help. She didn't want to single him out or embarrass him, so she waited until everyone had left the schoolroom before she praised him. "You did a fine job today, Michael."

"Thank you, Miss Brewster. Thanks for talkin' to my pa."

"You're the one who convinced him. He knows what you're capable of."

Instead of Dewey coming for them after school, Evelyn brought the team and wagon. "I thought we'd do some shopping for furniture today."

Marigold settled the boys in back and climbed up to the seat. "Where will we go?"

"Over on First Street, Mr. Irving has a fine furniture store. Makes most of it himself, but purchases pieces as well. What we don't find, we can order—and we can look through the catalogs at the mercantile as well."

"Do you think the boys need a few toys?" Marigold asked. "After seeing how they enjoyed the soldiers, I realized they must have left most everything behind when they came here. I have plenty of books for them, but perhaps we can purchase some things boys like." She glanced at Evelyn. "What do boys like?"

"Horses, animals of all sort, marbles."

Irving Furniture was a well-stocked store on the northeast corner of Grant and First. There they agreed on a bed for Harper and Little John to share and a narrower bed for Tate, as well as bureaus and a washstand. Marigold paused in front of a desk.

"Do you think they need a desk?" Evelyn asked. "We could make do with a table."

"I'd like to buy them one," she replied.

Evelyn cast her a curious glance.

"I'm not impoverished," she told the older woman. "It's something I'd like to do."

"We certainly have room," Evelyn replied. "The rancher who built the house before Seth bought the land was well-to-do. He and his wife had several children."

"Are we set?"

"I think so. Let's talk to Mr. Irving about delivery. We'll have to go over to Hagermann's for bedding."

They rode to the mercantile a few blocks east, and selected bedding and pillows from one catalog. "We can make curtains," she told Evelyn.

"Remmy has a better selection of cloth than Abram, so we'll buy it here." Evelyn led the way to the bolts, and they selected cloth for two bedrooms.

While Evelyn chose thread, she browsed through another catalog and found a set of miniature horses and building blocks to make a fort. She added it to their order. Remmy had marbles inside a glass case, so she selected a bag full.

After the past two days Marigold couldn't help thinking how fortunate they were. Ever since she'd seen where Michael and his father lived, she'd thought of it often, wondered about their circumstances. She didn't know how she might help, or if she should, but the boy and his father were in her heart.

She was determined to think of ways she might make a difference for them.

Rather than embarrass Michael by putting him in a lesson group with the youngest children, she made a group for him alone. As much as possible, she worked with him privately, so as not to draw attention to the fact that he was learning basic skills, but the others didn't seem to think anything of his elementary training.

Beatrix ingeniously suggested they group the German children with Michael, since they were all learning to read and write the alphabet and simple words. The plan worked beautifully, and by the end of that week Michael even knew several German words.

Bright and early on Saturday morning, she and Evelyn fried chicken and baked cookies for the church picnic before scrubbing the boys in the tub, dressing them in new shirts and trousers and telling them to stay put on the porch while they washed their own hair and got dressed for the picnic. She dressed in a cheerful blue skirt and matching checked shirtwaist, and found her small-brimmed straw hat and added a cluster of paper flowers to the ribbon band. Dewey helped them load the food into the back of the wagon, and Evelyn and Seth

ode on the seat with Little John between them while
Dewey and Marigold sat with the older boys in the back.

She'd kept busy all week, but she hadn't forgotten
Buck's question. She'd given it some thought. Courting
him would take her mind away from the boys and the
ranch, but it was a commitment as well, and one she
wasn't sure she was ready for.

It became apparent she'd already made a lot of
friends in Cowboy Creek. The minute they arrived at
the church grounds, she was drawn into the circle of
women clustered around the tables, as they set out and
arranged the food, but soon discovered she didn't have
an opinion on where the pickled beets should go, so she
eased away from the tables.

Beatrix and Marlys Mason stood off to one side,
not venturing into the throng. Marigold joined them.
"Where is Joseph?"

Beatrix pointed to a row of folding chairs and baskets along the side of the church in the shade. "Napping.
Ludivine is keeping an eye on him for me."

"She's a sweet girl. She spoke to me in English yesterday."

It wasn't long until Tomasina Canfield produced a
bell and asked one of the cowboys to ring it. "Mothers
with children first!" she called.

Lines formed on either side of the tables. A young
fellow in a pressed chambray shirt with a red bandana
around his neck approached Marigold. "Would you do
me the pleasure of sharin' dinner with me, Miss Brewster?"

She glanced from his neatly parted and combed hair
to the two smiling women beside her and back. "I'd be
delighted, Mr...."

"Lawson. Kip Lawson. I barber with my pa. You've

probably seen our place." He smiled as though she'd gifted him with a pair of diamond-studded shears, and gestured for her to go ahead of him. "What did you bring, Miss Brewster?"

"I fried chicken with Mrs. Halloway. And I helped bake cookies."

"Show me which ones. I'll be sure to try them."

They filled their plates and he led her across the grass, where their neighbors had spread out blankets and tablecloths.

"My mama sent me with this blue-and-white cloth and her lemonade in jars."

"It's very nice. Thank you." She settled on the corner of the spread and tried a flaky biscuit.

"Have you been a teacher long?"

"For the past five years," she replied.

"I went to school in Illinois," he said. "That's where we came from. I sure never had a teacher as pretty as you."

"Thank you. Your father taught you to cut hair?"

"Yes'm. When we're slow, I help Sam Mason at the *Webster County Daily News* office. At first I just cleaned up, but now I set type. Sometimes, when I hear something interesting, I let him know and he looks into it for a piece in the paper."

"Which job do you prefer?"

"Barberin' is a sure way to earn a living. Men constantly grow hair and beards. But the paper is a lot more interestin'."

"Newspapers will always be needed as well. You're certain of a job in either case."

"You heard Will Canfield is running for congress?" he asked. "He had his hopes set on the governorship, but the party leaders thought he'd be better in congress."

He built that big house and all. But this will be even better for him—for us. He's a fine leader."

"If he wins, he and Tomasina won't live here year-round, I heard."

"No." He pointed north behind the church. "That's the back of their house, right there."

Even from the back, the grand house was impressive.

"I hear they'll build a smaller home," he said.

"Wonder who will buy a house that big?" she mused.

They finished their meal and Kip complimented her cookies. Marigold shook out the tablecloth and folded it up. She handed it to him just as Buck approached.

"Good afternoon, Miss Brewster. Kip."

Kip greeted him, but didn't look pleased with the interruption.

"I've signed up, but I still don't have a partner for the horseshoe competition." Buck's hat shaded his eyes, but they still appeared bright blue and friendly. "I know you said you've never played, but I'll help you. It will be fun. What d'you say?"

"If you don't mind losing," she answered with a cheerful shrug. She turned to Kip. "I enjoyed sharing lunch with you."

"The pleasure was all mine," he replied.

He and Buck exchanged a look before Buck offered his arm and Marigold tucked her hand into the crook of his elbow.

"It's not time yet, so I can show you how the game is played and let you take a few practice throws."

Two pits were obvious. Wide, flat boards had been set ground level to form rectangles from end to end, opposite each other, and inside them the ground wasn't simply dirt. "What is that? Not just dirt?"

"It's sand, gravel and dirt. We keep the ground in side the pit loose."

"Why it that?"

"So the shoes don't bounce."

"Bouncing isn't good?"

"No, you want the shoe to land where you throw it."

"Okay." She removed her hat and set it on a folded blanket. "Show me how."

He picked up two iron horseshoes with red paint on the tips. "There are a few ways to pitch, and you do i however it feels right. You can hold it right back here at the curve and toss with a bit of a lift, so you get the shoe to spin, or you can hold it more from the side and throw it so it hooks around the pin."

"Around the stake there?"

"Yes. It's a pin."

"How do *you* do it?"

He stood clear back at the opposite pit and swung shoe a couple of times before getting it go. It flipped i the air and landed with a clang beside the pin.

"That was good, right?" she asked.

"It was one point unless someone gets closer or get a ringer. Here, try a few throws to get the feel of it."

She took the shoe and tested its weight, then stood the way he had, swung and let go. It didn't reach all the way inside the pit.

"That's all right," Buck said. "Now you know you have to pitch a little harder."

She nodded and took another shoe. She swung it keeping her eye on the stake, and let it go. This time it went inside the pit and landed up against the wood.

"Better," he said. "Keep your arm straight as you re lease it." He handed her another and this time he stood behind her, his arm along the length of hers, showing

er how to swing, how to extend the shoe straight and
ot let her arm turn to the side. "Try it again."

She'd let him coax her into this, so she was going to
ive it her best.

Chapter Ten

Leah got Seth's attention and led him to where a few people stood watching Buck Hanley coach the new schoolteacher in pitching horseshoes. "She seems to be doing pretty well. I wouldn't be able to get that close."

Marigold's hair was a bright nimbus in the sun. He imagined he could smell orange blossom and almond, and his gut tightened. Seeing the former sheriff standing so near to her gave him a sick feeling. "Whatever she puts her mind to, she does well."

"Buck is respected in town," she added.

"She could do worse."

A few others ventured over to the other pit and threw practice pitches. Old Horace and Gus showed up and stood watching.

"Think Horace and Gus will be a team?" she asked.

"Those two spend as much time arguing as they do playing," Daniel said from behind them.

Leah turned and slipped her arm around her husband's waist. "Did you sign up?"

"No. Did you want to join?"

She shook her head. "Seth would make a fine partner, though."

Daniel glanced at him. "Want to compete? The prizes re good. We could get fortunate. Win a couple of Hanah's shirts."

"I forgot about your arm," Leah added.

"Dr. Mason wouldn't be happy with me using it, but I an try with my left arm. I've been forced to use it a lot."

"We'd better sign up and get in a few practice throws hen," Daniel suggested.

Seth joined Daniel at the makeshift sign-up table, and hen they waited in a line to do a little practicing. He oted Marigold and Buck had relinquished their shoes o others and stood together on the sidelines. She looked o be having a grand time.

"Seth! Are you competing?"

He glanced over and found Molly on her toes, waving. He gave her a polite nod.

"I'll be cheering for you!"

Daniel raised an eyebrow, and Seth ignored the unpoken question. His partner only took a couple of hrows and let Seth do more practicing. Seth didn't get ringer, as he likely would have with his other arm, but e didn't do too badly. They joined the crowd gathering to watch the games.

At last the bell rang and Reverend Taggart called for he teams to line up. They drew straws for positions, nd Marlys Mason and Hannah took over the scoring osition from chairs at a safe distance.

"How has it gone with Miss Brewster staying at your lace?" Daniel asked him as they waited their turn.

"She and my mother get along," Seth told him. "She's ood with the children, and they're attached to her."

"We don't seem to keep teachers in that position ong. We've talked about a man next time."

Seth remembered Will expressing the same concerns. "I don't see her giving up her teaching position," Seth reassured him, as he had with Will. "She's devoted."

"Even if she marries one of these suitors?"

"I can't speak for her."

"Well, Buck's a terrific fellow. He seems to have earned her favor."

Seth glanced along the line until he spotted Marigold listening to something Buck was saying. "Can't fault him for the attention."

Buck and Marigold's turn came after a few rounds and they took their places. She appeared nervous, but he spoke to her.

"I reckon Buck has a few things to teach Miss Brewster!" one of the men called out, heckling from the sidelines, drawing laughter.

"We'll see if she's been studying her lessons," another replied.

Marigold paused in her preparation and set a hand on her hip. "Give me a couple of turns here, and I'll teach you how to spell 'winner'!"

A cry went up from the crowd, and the jester gave her a dismissive wave, but joined in the laughter.

Beside Seth, Daniel laughed, too.

Seth didn't know the first thing about impressing or courting a woman. He was a rancher, spent his days with horses and his nights exhausted from the day's work. He wondered what Buck said to her, what kind of things they talked about. Seth hadn't missed her cozy lunch with Kip Lawson, either. The barber wasn't a ladies' man, but obviously he'd invited her, shared the meal with her. Perhaps it was to Seth's disadvantage that she was living with his family. He didn't feel right about intruding on her free time.

What he knew about women he could fit on the head of a pin. But he'd barged right ahead and kissed her. How coarse did she think him now?

Buck threw his horseshoe first and it landed against the pin. Marigold took her time with a few easy swings and let her shoe fly. It didn't sail smoothly, but it landed within a shoe's width of the pin.

"One point!" Reverend Taggart called.

The crowd cheered.

Marigold laid her hand on Buck's sleeve and jumped up and down, her red-gold curls bouncing.

Seth didn't do poorly when it was his turn. He landed a few shoes near enough to earn points. After several rounds, however, he and Daniel were eliminated and watched those still in the final competition.

Marigold and Buck were holding on in third place. One team fell out. Timothy Watson landed a ringer that earned him applause, but Buck landed a shoe on top, which canceled both their points and made Marigold's shoe leaning against the pin the winning point.

They accepted their prizes amidst the shouts of their friends and the good-natured teasing from their opponents. Marigold was so lovely, so bright and effervescent, the sight of her smile took Seth's breath away. Her scent was in his head, and just looking at her from this distance, he could smell citrus and almond. His chest ached with suppressed feelings for her.

Before he could obsess on her another minute, the tables were uncovered, and the bell rang to invite townspeople to help themselves to the remaining dishes and desserts.

His mother brought him a slice of apple pie, which was his favorite. Little John followed closely at her side.

"You did very well for being at a disadvantage," she told him.

Which disadvantage did she mean? Yes, his arm, of course. He took the pie. "Thank you."

With Tate and Harper in tow, Marigold found him. Each of them carried a plate of food.

Tate looked up at him with an eager expression. "Will you teach us to play horseshoes?"

"You want to learn to play, do you?" He picked up on their excitement. "Maybe Marigold would be a better teacher," he teased. "She's the winner after all."

Marigold's face was prettily flushed, her eyes bright with good humor. "I think it was just a fluke."

Tate looked from her to Seth. "You can both teach us."

He grinned. "That sounds like a grand idea."

"The boys were hoping we could all sit together for a while," she told him.

Evelyn gestured for them to follow her. "I'll unfold our blankets." She spread two blankets, giving them all room to sit. She gave Little John half a buttered biscuit. "I'm going to get myself a little something."

She was immediately sidetracked by one of her friends and stopped to talk.

Tate situated his plate on his lap. "Are them real honest-to-goodness horseshoes, Seth?"

"Yep."

"Like what's on the horses?" Harper asked.

He swallowed his bite of pie. "Yep."

Tate picked up a drumstick. "They sure sound loud when they hit together."

"You should hear the sound when the blacksmith is pounding the iron into shape."

Tate's eyes got wide. "He *bends* that iron into a shape?"

Seth nodded. "Holds the iron with tongs, gets it glowing hot over a forge and hammers it until it bends to the shape he wants."

"I wished I could see that."

After finishing his pie, Seth picked up the crumbs surrounding Little John. "I'll take you boys one day soon and you can watch Colton Werner."

Harper jiggled where he sat, showing his excitement.

"That's Mrs. Werner's husband," Marigold told them. "Little Joseph's daddy."

"I can't wait to see that," Tate told them with a serious expression.

"I grew up on a big ranch with a lot of horses," Seth said. "I remember being your age and watching the farrier shoe them."

Little John got up and tripped on the wrinkles in the blanket, picked himself up and backed up to sit on Seth's lap. Seth adjusted him more comfortably. "Did you have enough to eat?"

The child looked up at him and nodded. His imploring face and solemn eyes grew more dear each day. Immediately, he stuck his thumb into his mouth and leaned against Seth's chest. His outdoorsy little-boy scent held a touch of soap and a splash of sunshine. His solid little body relaxed until he was sound asleep. Seth ran his fingers through his silky pale hair, threading the locks away from his face. With three boys and himself, they would soon become very good customers at Kip's barber shop.

Running a thumb over the boy's soft cheek, he imagined these children growing up, turning into strapping youths and eventually young men. He had a big responsibility ahead of him. Perhaps bigger than any other that had come before.

He glanced at Marigold, finding her watching him, studying his expression. He wished he knew the thoughts behind those wide hazel eyes. He wished he was a smooth talker, comfortable with initiating conversations, a man with the ability to be charming…or at the very least agreeable. He wanted to make her smile, take her hand, win her favor. He wanted to kiss her again.

Her gaze fluttered across his face, to his mouth, as though she knew his thoughts—as though she was thinking about that kiss, too.

Evelyn returned, disrupting his reverie. "Have you heard anything about a coal-mining operation around here?"

"No. Why?"

"Seems they put up a sign on a building yesterday. Mitchell Coal and Mining Company, it says."

"Where at?"

"On the corner of Lincoln Boulevard, across from the lumber yard. All the way south of Remmy Hagermann's store."

"By the railroad there? No, I've heard nothing about it."

"I'm sure we'll hear news of it soon."

The dinner bell rang again, garnering the attention of everyone in the wide churchyard and those still around the horseshoe pits behind Booker & Son.

"Gather around, if you will!" Will Canfield called. "We have something more we want to do before this day ends." He and Daniel stood near the corner of the church, their wives and children with them. The townspeople gathered to learn what was happening.

Seth stood with his family and Marigold, Little John

still sound asleep over his shoulder. Eventually a hush fell over the people.

"Daniel, you go ahead, please," Will said.

"You all probably know that this community started out as a dream. Our friend Noah Burgess moved here and staked a claim. He saw the potential in the land and the location and, after the war, sent word to Will and me, asking us to come and see what he'd discovered. It was a small quiet town with a stage stop and a few scattered homesteaders. And then the Union Pacific approached, bringing Texas cattlemen looking to ship beef east. Before long this spot was chosen for a terminus.

"Will, here, ever the entrepreneur, knew we needed to buy up land, so we did. Obviously, he bought more than I did."

The people laughed.

"I built the stockyards and lured in the cattlemen. It wasn't a year until Cowboy Creek went from a few storefronts and settlers with sod houses to the town the newspapers back east were calling the next boom town."

A cheer went up.

Little John roused and looked around. Seth patted his back.

Daniel gave Will a nod.

"This town wouldn't be anything without all of you," Will told them. "Without the merchants, the ranchers, farmers, businessmen. Without the families who left everything behind and took a chance on a little Kansas town. Without the women who have traveled all this way to meet husbands and start families."

Whistles and whoops prevented Will from talking for several minutes.

"And this town would be nothing without the sense of community and family and the sacrifices each of you has made. Aunt Mae takes in these ladies, watches over them and makes them feel at home. Thank you, Aunt Mae!"

Aunt Mae waved an apron in the air and smiled from ear to ear.

"Each one of you had a part in helping out recently when the train carrying our newest brides and our schoolteacher derailed just outside our town. The town council wants to show our appreciation. If you helped search cars for trapped or injured passengers, if you housed a passenger, if you doctored someone or had a part in the rescue that day, please come up here."

Men hesitated at first, and then slowly made their way forward, encouraged by their friends.

"Go on up there, Seth," someone behind him said.

With an encouraging smile, Marigold reached to take Little John from his arms.

Someone else gave him a little shove. He joined a growing line of men and one or two women, including Marlys Mason, until Will and Daniel thought the line was complete. At least thirty people stood with the two founders.

Will studied the men and women standing with them. "This isn't nearly enough to say thanks, but the council has a little something for each of you. We want you to select six of these, and any remaining are going to the park across from the school."

"Come on, James!" Daniel shouted.

Dressed in buckskins and a dun-colored hat, James Johnson drove a team from the other side of the church, the wagon behind coming into view. In the back was a forest of young trees, all tall sturdy saplings.

A collective cheer went up, and everyone applauded.

"Fruit trees," Will said. "Shipped from Vermont. There's enough for each of you to choose half a dozen."

The generous gift took Seth by surprise. Freddie Simms slapped him on the shoulder. "How long will it take to get fruit?"

"Couple of years, I suppose."

The men good-naturedly chose their trees. Aunt Mae just laughed and told Will to plant hers over at the park. "And then send someone to pick apples for me!"

"We'll do just that!" he replied.

Seth selected three apple trees, and one each of peach, cherry and walnut. He loaded them in the wagon and told Evelyn what he'd chosen.

"I knew you'd get those apple trees," she said with a laugh.

Six trees and rope to steady them took up a lot of room. On the ride home Marigold rode on the seat with Little John beside her, as Evelyn led the team. Seth had squeezed into a corner of the wagon with Dewey and the other two boys.

"Who's going to help me keep these watered?" he asked, as the boys watched Dewey help him unload them into a spot where they'd be shaded near the house for now.

All three shouted and jumped in their willingness to help.

Marigold joined his mother in corralling them into the house for their bedtime ritual. Seth waved them on. "I'll be there shortly."

As Evelyn opened the door, Peony shot around her ankles and darted across the porch. "Oh, Marigold, I'm sorry. I didn't see her there."

"Peony!" Marigold turned to run after her.

Chapter Eleven

At Marigold's sharp cry Seth ran toward the house.

The orange cat stopped in her tracks and sat on her haunches, looking around, apparently confused over her sudden freedom.

Seth stopped as well, hoping not to further frighten the animal. He crouched low and spoke softly. "C'mere, Peony. Here, kitty. Here, girl."

Marigold gathered her skirts and descended the porch stairs, moving slowly and quietly.

Peony's head swiveled to look at her.

"Hello, sweetheart," she cooed. "Be a good kitty and stay right there."

Peony lowered her head and flattened her body in a crouching position. She glanced around and got back on her feet.

In the distance, the sound of the stable door sliding open startled her, and she darted off at a run.

"Peony!" Marigold chased after her.

Seth joined her and ran ahead. With both the cat and Marigold fraught with fear, he didn't hold much hope of catching the feline. He stopped at the corner of the barn.

Marigold ran up beside him. "Which way did she go?"

"If we keep calling and chasing after her, she'll only run farther. I think the best thing is to wait her out. She'll come back."

She grabbed his upper arm with both hands. "But how? She doesn't know her way around. She's never been outside alone. She could get lost. Or a bigger animal could get her."

"Did you see how fast she is? And she has instincts. The only thing faster is probably a fox or a coyote, and she can climb or hide."

Marigold released his arm and promptly burst into tears. "A coyote?"

He turned to face her. "No. No. I haven't seen a coyote in weeks. She won't go far. She was cooped up alone in the house all day and probably needed to go out. She'll do her business out there alone, and then she'll come back."

Tears streamed down Marigold's cheeks. She turned those anguished hazel eyes up to him.

He felt dismally helpless. "Have you seen the barn cats? They get by just fine. We'll set out food for Peony."

"Those other cats will eat it, won't they? Or a raccoon or something will take it. She'll be afraid if she sees those other animals."

Her anguish seemed out of character. She was always so poised and optimistic. This was a side of her he'd never seen—or she'd never allowed him to see. Seth pulled a bandana from his rear pocket, shook it open and blotted the tears on her cheeks. She reached for the cloth and he took her hand in his. "Peony will come back. I know she will."

Marigold grasped his hand. Hers felt slender and small within his. She looked into his eyes. Her lower lip quivered. "She's all I have."

In that moment, he understood. She'd lost her family, even her niece. She'd left her home and traveled across the country. Everyone and everything here was new and strange. That cat was the one thing that tied her to her home and her former life.

"I'll make a trap to safely catch her," he promised. "I'll put food inside it and keep an eye out. She's not used to catching her own food, so she'll come when she's hungry."

"Do you think that will work?"

"Yes."

Her glistening gaze moved across the pasture and the field beyond. She took a deep breath, as though collecting herself—or resigning herself, he wasn't sure which—and released his hand with a nod. "All right. I'll go help Evelyn with the boys."

"I'll be right behind you for their story."

He helped Dewey finish with the horses and asked him to keep an eye out for the cat before washing up. When he reached the boys' room, his mother had gone to bed and Marigold was sitting at the foot of Seth's mattress, where the children had lain down, their complexions pink from their day in the sun.

"We waited for you!" Harper declared.

"Wait for *you*, Seff," Little John said, mimicking his brother.

"Which chapter are we on?"

Marigold handed him the book, and he read until Little John was asleep and both Tate's and Harper's eyelids were drooping. She fussed with their covers, though they were already tucked in and comfortable, and he gave each one a hug.

She went downstairs ahead of him. "I'm going to heat water for tea. Would you care for a cup?"

"No thanks. I'm heading out to the barn. Sleep well."

He exited the back door and lit a couple of lanterns around his work area in the barn. He found a crate and set to work making a trap to capture Peony. He got it ready and set it up near the back door, where Marigold most often took the cat out on its leash.

He'd actually used the arm in the cast several times today, so it ached, besides the infernal itching inside the plaster of paris. He was of a mind to cut the thing off himself then and there, but didn't want to suffer Dr. Mason's scorn or that of his mother, or Marigold.

He had as good as promised Marigold her cat would be safe, and he'd catch it, so he dragged a comfortable chair and a blanket to the very end of the porch, where he could see the place where he'd left the trap, and settled in. He lit one of the lanterns and read for a while, but the light prevented him from seeing out into the darkness, so he extinguished the lantern. He fell asleep after a while and woke up as light was breaking across the eastern sky.

He'd started chores when Hayden showed up to help. He cleaned stalls, then helped get the wagon and team ready to go to church.

"Thanks for coming to help," Seth told him. "I'll see you at church."

"Not today. Pa wants me around. Has some people coming to dig holes."

"Wells?"

"Nah, some fella named Jason Mitchell came around, interested in coal. Guess he thought we might have a deposit. So Pa gave 'im permission to check our land."

"That must be the company that hung a sign in town."

"Dunno. Just know he's checking around."

Seth waved him off.

The sky turned overcast. Marigold's countenance showed she hadn't slept well, and the way she checked the sky often showed she was imagining lost Peony in a downpour.

"If it rains, she'll find shelter," he assured her.

She gave him a half smile. "Does Dewey ever attend services?"

"On occasion."

After church, Marigold wasn't her usual friendly self, politely dodging conversations and friends to arrive at the wagon in anticipation of heading back to White Rock.

"Would you ladies enjoy a meal in town today?" Seth asked. "We might try The Lariat that's just opened. I'll go find Russ and ask him to join us."

"That would be delightful!" Evelyn agreed with a smile. "Don't you think, dear?"

"Yes," Marigold replied without much enthusiasm. "That would be nice."

"There's room to leave the wagon down on Sixth Street. I'll stop at the livery for water for the horses." They took their places in the wagon, and Seth stopped as promised to bring the horses water.

The Lariat, farther north on the east side of Eden Street, was every bit as impressive as The Cattleman. It was a long two-story hotel and restaurant, painted dark green with a boardwalk and porch over a row of tall narrow windows with white shutters.

Russ, dressed in his waistcoat and holding his hat, stood in the shade on the boardwalk. Their mother was first to reach him, and he leaned his six-foot frame down to hug her. Then he nodded toward Marigold. "Hello, Miss Brewster."

"Please call me Marigold," she answered.

Near the door positioned against the outer wall was a six-foot-tall carving of a rearing horse with a rider, the cowboy swinging a rope above his head. The boys touched the grooves and bumps in the horse's rear legs and the wood-curved spurs and boots.

"Have you eaten here?" Evelyn asked her middle son.

"Of course, Mother. We unmarried men are keeping these restaurants in business. The kitchen in my house has barely been used to make coffee a few times."

"Why don't you just hire someone to cook and clean for you?"

"In case you haven't noticed there are more men with hungry bellies than there are women who can cook."

"Well, your little bride can't get here soon enough. I hope she can cook."

"If not, we'll eat here together."

His mother laughed.

The inside was lavish for this Western setting, with dark wood tables and chairs with red-cushioned seats. The man who arrived to seat them brought a tall youth chair for Little John.

"We need one like this," Evelyn said.

"Check Remmy's catalog," Seth suggested.

"Mr. Irving will be delivering furniture for the boys' room tomorrow," his mother told him. "Marigold bought them a desk."

Seth's gaze swept to Marigold's.

"They'll need it for schoolwork." She cast her gaze aside.

From a few tables away, Sadie Shriver gave Marigold a wave. She was having dinner with a thin blond-haired gentleman. "Sadie's friend looks familiar."

"That's Walter Kerr," Russ replied. "The photographer Will sent for. You've probably seen his photographs or photos of him in the newspaper."

They ordered and Russ took out his pocket watch for Little John to play with. He surprised Seth by talking to the children. The boys handled themselves surprisingly well, sitting patiently as they waited for their meals, and eating without incident. Harper left his peas untouched on his plate, and no one mentioned it. He hadn't complained, and to Seth that was well-mannered. They could talk about vegetables at home.

"Where's your black horse?" Harper asked Russ.

"He's at the livery. He has hay and water, and they let him out for exercise."

"Does he gots shoes on?"

"Yep, he does. New ones in fact."

Tate laid down his fork. "Seth told us how Joseph's pa gets the iron hot and bends it."

Seth met Marigold's gaze across the table. She smiled, as though she was pleased with their dinner and how the boys were interacting. He felt a strong connection to her, a connection that grew and matured each day. What was she feeling?

"I'll have the paperwork ready for you to sign this week," Russ said to Seth. "You can stop by my office anytime. If I'm not in, my assistant knows where they are and what to do."

"Thank you for handling that." Seth looked to his mother and then to Marigold. He lowered his voice and asked the women, "What shall we tell the boys about the adoption process? Will they understand?"

Evelyn looked to Marigold.

"I don't know that they'll understand the legality or all the details, but what you can tell them is that they're safe and they belong with you for good." A look of pain crossed her features, but she covered it quickly and managed a stilted smile. "No one can take them away. They'll understand security."

Seth nodded. When their waiter came, he asked for pie for each person. This was a good opportunity, with his family gathered at the table and other diners absorbed in their own conversations, to bring up the adoption. Over dessert, he set down his fork. "I have something to tell you, Tate." He glanced from boy to boy. "Harper. Little John."

"What is it?" Tate asked with a frown.

"It's something good. My brother Russ here is a lawyer. He takes care of legal things. He has written up papers that I'm going to take to a judge. The papers say that I'm going to adopt all three of you. That means I'll be responsible for you. I'll take care of you. You won't ever have to go away, and no one can take you away. Russ says as soon as the judge signs them, the adoption is legal, and you will always belong with me."

"Will you be our pa?" Harper asked.

"Well, that's the thing. That's something we can decide whenever we want to. Your father was a good man. He was my friend. I appreciate all the good things about each one of you that remind me of him—and of your ma. I know how much you loved him, and I'm not him. I'll take care of you. You'll always have a home with me. You'll be like my own sons. If someday you want to call me Pa, well, that'll be fine with me. If you don't, that's all right, too."

"What about Missus Halloway?" Tate asked. "Will she be our gramma?"

Evelyn was quick with a reply. "I certainly will be."

Tate's gaze slid to Marigold, but he didn't speak the question that Seth saw in his eyes. She'd been holding her fork in the air over her pie during the whole conversation. She set it down quickly. The last thing Seth wanted to do was make her uncomfortable.

"Marigold is your teacher." He spoke before anyone could ask. "She'll be your teacher until she's taught you everything you need to know."

She placed her napkin beside her plate and got to her feet. "Excuse me, please."

With a rustle of skirts and on a wisp of orange and almond, she'd gone.

"Is Marigold all right?" Harper asked.

Little John turned to watch her go. "Mawidold awight?"

"She probably needed some air." Evelyn wiped Little John's hands and face and told the others to use their napkins. She brushed Seth's cheek with a soft kiss. "Thank you for dinner, Seth. It was a lovely occasion. Thoughtful of you to think of it."

Her approval pleased him immeasurably. He only wished Marigold had been half as happy about the dinner.

Marigold was happy for Seth and she was delighted for the Radner boys. Their sense of security and their happiness were more important to her than it should have been. She'd resolved not to become attached, but she'd done all the wrong things to keep that from happening. She'd been attempting to fade out of the picture at bedtime so that the boys became dependent on Seth and not on her. She'd forged other friendships in town and, as much as possible, spent time with others at the church functions. But time and again she was drawn back into the Halloway circle, into caring about those children, into thinking too much about Seth.

She'd made up her mind that she was leaving White Rock as soon as his cast came off. One week ago tonight he'd kissed her. She'd thought a lot about that kiss. She was nothing to him—only someone who'd needed rescuing. Someone who knew about children. Someone convenient.

She didn't want to be convenient.

Caring made her weak, and she didn't want to be weak.

The Halloways came out of the building and joined her on the boardwalk.

"Are you all right, dear?" Evelyn asked.

She nodded and gave the kind woman a smile.

Russ gave his mother a hug and said to Seth, "I'll see you this week."

Seth settled his hat on his head. "I'll come by. Thanks."

The ride home was a quiet one. Little John fell asleep on Marigold's lap. When she got overly tired or distraught, the fears creeped in around the edges of her carefully constructed and guarded shield of protection. What if this was all there ever was, and she did nothing but teach and care for other people's children until she was an old lonely woman? Sometimes she was afraid to admit she even wanted more, because wanting made her vulnerable. But God knew her heart. He heard her silent pleas and her prayers. She was too practical to feel sorry for herself. It wasn't foolish or selfish to want something more for herself. If she was precious and beautiful in God's eyes, surely she could choose her own path and achieve her own destiny.

Little John awoke as Seth stopped the wagon. Seth jumped down and reached over the side for the three-year-old. "We still have plenty of daylight for a ride."

The boys cheered.

"I believe I'll read in my room for a while," she told him. "You fellows go ahead. Enjoy yourselves."

From her window, she watched Seth and Dewey saddle horses and get the boys mounted. Seth climbed into the saddle of his big spotted gray, and led them away from the stables. Once they were gone, she ran downstairs and out the back door, where she stood in the vast expanse where the yard blended into fields, and called for Peony. She checked, and the trap Seth had made, as promised, still had fresh food in it, so she went back to her room.

The impending adoption of the Radner boys brought up all kinds of confusing emotions in Marigold. The children were Seth's, as had been decided by their parents. That's why she'd tried to hold herself at an emotional distance from the beginning. She knew firsthand what it was like to have a child she loved taken from her. And now she didn't even have Peony.

Settling into the comfortable chair in the room she used, she picked up her Bible and held it. Opened it and read a few verses in Proverbs. She loved Proverbs because they were so practical—sometimes so blunt the verses made her smile. She loved the psalms of David in which he proclaimed his love and trust in his Lord. David always trusted God no matter the circumstances. She had to keep those verses fresh in her mind. God's Word was always true, and she could trust it—despite her situation.

God loved her and gave her His Spirit and He was working in her life even when it didn't feel like anything was happening or improving. Marigold closed her eyes. "I remember, Lord. I remember You're working in my life. You love me and care about me. I'm not alone.

You want what's best for me. Show me how to get past the loss and how to be a whole person."

She chose, in that moment, to be thankful for the good things she'd been given and her blessings. Her parents had left her a house worth quite a bit of money. She had nearly all of that money in the bank, and her physical needs were met. She had enough to buy additional supplies for the school and the children. Her life had been spared in the train accident, and she'd come through the ordeal with only a bruised chin. She had the privilege of instructing the children of this town. She had the children's respect and their parents' trust.

Leah, Hannah, Beatrix, Evelyn—so many women had befriended her and made her feel welcome. She even had the attention of several nice men, who wanted to court her—probably marry her. She wasn't alone. She could still choose her future path.

As evening arrived, Evelyn tapped on her door, bringing her bread and ham with a glass of milk. "I thought you'd be hungry since you haven't eaten since lunch."

"It was a big lunch, but yes, thank you."

"Little John was asking for you."

"I'll be down in a few minutes. I hear them playing outside."

She joined the others and watched Seth chase the boys until he caught them and tickled them. Dewey joined them on the porch for coffee, and told the boys stories about Seth and his brothers when they were young.

"Where's your other brother now?" Tate asked.

"We haven't heard from Adam for a while. My mom thinks he's off catching bad guys and making the world a better place."

"Like a Texas Ranger?"

"Like that, yes."

"Is he fighting Indians?"

"Well, I don't know about that."

"Did you ever fight Indians, Seth?"

"Comanche shot us full of arrows and killed our horses right out from under us," Dewey told them. "Seth caught a dead Indian's horse an' came back for me. We outran 'em and hid in a forest for two days."

Tate and Harper's eyes were wide as silver dollars. "Why did they shoot you with arrows?" Tate asked.

"Comanches don't hanker to anyone bringin' cows across their land," Dewey answered.

"Did they kill all the cows, too?" Harper's forehead wrinkled in concern.

"Nah, they stampeded 'em and run 'em off in half a dozen directions. Iffin we didn't get 'em when we started that drive over, those ornery longhorns are probably still grazin' in New Mexico."

"Do you got arrow holes?" Harper asked.

"I have scars."

The two boys bounced up and down, begging him to show them his scars, and Little John joined in.

"Go ahead, Seth. They won't let up until you do," his mother said from her seat on the porch.

Seth glanced at Marigold. "Apologies."

She couldn't suppress a grin. "You probably saw those scars when we first visited Seth at Dr. Mason's," she told the boys, "but you didn't know what they were."

"I didn't see 'em," Harper insisted.

Seth unbuttoned his shirt with his left hand, opened his collar to show them his shoulder, and sat on the top step. Three pale-haired boys crowded around him.

"Did it hurt?"

"Why did they shoot your horses?"

"This one, too?"

"That'un's all shiny and funny."

They talked at once, and Dewey cackled with pleasure.

Evelyn and Marigold exchanged a look.

"I hope you weren't laughing when my son had arrows sticking out of his arm and shoulder," she called to Dewey.

"I weren't laughin' on account of I had a few stuck in my own self."

"You want to show off those scars?" Seth asked.

Dewey waved away Seth's question and ambled away toward the stables. "I got work to do."

Seth stood and buttoned his shirt.

After giving the boys biscuits and milk and seeing that they'd washed, Marigold went to her room, leaving Seth to read their story. She fell asleep early, but disjointed dreams gave her fitful sleep. At first the soft tapping sound was part of her dream, but then she roused enough to realize the knock was actually at the bedroom door. She got up and found her wrap on the end of the bed and shrugged into it.

The hallway was dimly lit by one long window, but Seth's broad form was unmistakable. "Seth?"

She heard the sound before she could make out what he held against his chest. A very loud, very angry meow...

"Peony?"

She reached for the cat and the bundle of fur leaped into her arms.

Seth fumbled to find the matches for the lamp on the wall just inside the door and lit it. "I caught her in the trap."

Marigold petted the cat's long matted fur, finding twigs and bits of grass, but she didn't care that they fell to the floor. Peony's heart was beating fast, and she meowed as though telling her harrowing tale of nights in the wild unknown. The relief Marigold felt was immeasurable and she probably looked foolish to the man who stood watching. She wiped a tear from her cheek with her sleeve. She glanced at him. "It must be the middle of the night. What were you doing outside?"

"I've been keeping an eye out."

"From where?"

"I saw her last night. She didn't go into the trap. I think she saw me and ran, and I couldn't get to her in time. Tonight, I stayed in the shadows next to the house and waited."

"You've been staying awake and watching for her? You told me not to worry."

"You didn't have to worry. There she is. Safe and sound. I knew she'd come looking for food."

"You figured out how to catch her."

"I grew up with two brothers. I've set a lot of traps."

"But you were watching all night for her to return."

He paused a moment, watching her stroke the cat's fur. "It was important to you."

Those words, spoken in his deep, soft voice, created a fluttering sensation in her chest. She couldn't speak for a moment, could scarcely breathe. He'd waited outside in the dark, waiting for her cat because it was important to her. Because she'd cried over Peony's escape. She settled Peony on the bed and pushed Seth out of the room into the hall, closing the door behind them.

"That's the nicest thing anyone's ever done for me."

"Likely she won't try to run again." Moonlight from the window framed his head and shoulders.

She stretched up on her tiptoes and wrapped her arm around his neck to kiss his cheek. He leaned toward her willingly, his cast against her back, his other hand flattened behind her shoulder, but he turned his face to hers and their lips met.

Chapter Twelve

This was no peck of gratitude, but a kiss that stole her breath and made her heart pound. She wished life was as sweet and simple as this kiss. She wished kissing Seth made sense. It didn't make sense, though, because feeling anything for him didn't fit into her plans. He held her as though she was fragile when she wanted to be strong and brave.

She rested back on her heels, knowing she was cowardly. Denying what she felt was safe and self-protective and Marigold was not strong or brave.

She moved away. "Thank you, Seth."

"I don't want your gratitude."

Fear rested its head on her chest. She'd intended only to show her appreciation. He was the one who'd turned into the kiss. She searched his eyes. He'd gone to a lot of trouble and lost sleep, but for what reason?

"I only want to make you happy."

His words touched her. She was tempted to kiss him again, but that would be wrong. Instead, she twisted the doorknob and let herself into her room. "Good night, Seth," she said and closed the door.

For minutes she stood with her forehead against the

amb, her thoughts racing. Behind her came the sound
f Peony's paws hitting the floor, and a moment later the
at weaved around her ankles. She kneeled and picked
ıp the feline. "You're a naughty girl. I'll give you a bath
nd brush you in the morning."

Seth did make her happy.

And that frightened her even more.

Sam Mason was waiting for her when she and the
ıoys arrived at school the next morning. A whistle
ounded as a train neared the station a few blocks away.

"Mr. Mason."

"I was hoping I'd get here early enough to have a few
ninutes of your time."

"I should have a few minutes. What is it?"

"You've been here three weeks now—"

"Is that all? It's seems like so much longer. Sorry.
ou were saying?"

"I mentioned doing an interview for the newspaper.
Iopefully you've had time to settle in, develop a rou-
ine, get to know your students. Could you answer a
ew questions for me?"

"Yes, certainly. You won't mind if I get the room
eady while we talk?"

"Go right ahead."

He asked her questions about her teaching back-
ground, about why she'd chosen Cowboy Creek and
iow she liked it here, and she gave him explanations.

"Can you tell me more about teaching the children
vho don't speak English?"

She explained how well that was going. "And I can't
ell you what a help August is. I've come up with plans
o challenge him, and I want to talk about those with
ou and Marlys soon. He's an incredible young man."

"Yes, he is," Sam said with a smile. "Is there any
thing else you want people to know?"

"I'd like people to know I appreciate everyone wh
has donated time and effort to the school and the stu
dents. I'm not doing this alone." She explained abou
Leah and Beatrix's contributions, told him how ade
quately the council had supplied all the books and ma
terial needed, how Libby Thompson's efforts as sh
resigned had been beneficial.

"And I'd like people to know how important thei
children are to me. I'm honored to be teaching then
and I appreciate these bright young people more an
more all the time. What I want to do is have a part i
their education and an influence on their lives. I am in
vested in helping each one of them have a better future.

"I can assure you the parents and everyone else ap
preciates your dedication."

She glanced out the door, noting Tate and Harpe
were playing with a few other early arrivals. "Are w
finished? I want to talk to you about another student'
situation."

"Yes, of course. What is it?"

She told him about Michael Higgins and how she'
followed him home. "Apparently before her death Mi
chael made a promise to his mother that he'd go t
school, but his father keeps him home to help set trap
and do chores. The man's missing a leg. I don't kno
if it's a war injury, but he has difficulty getting aroun
They don't have much at all. I don't even know why I'r
telling you this, except you know a lot of people, an
you've seen a lot during and after the war. If I knew
way to help, I would."

"The man's hanging onto his pride."

She nodded. "I don't even know what kind of wor

e'd be suited for, but anything seems better than noth-
ng to me."

"How do you think he'd react to me if I paid him a
visit?"

She shrugged. "He didn't shoot me."

"I'd be interested in hearing if he was in the army,
and if so, maybe he'd be willing to tell me his story.
That might be an opening."

"Maybe. Thanks, Sam."

"Thank you."

"Now I'd better ring the bell."

The day went well. Michael arrived with the rest of
the students, and for the first time raised his hand when
a question was asked of the class. Marigold called on
him, and held her breath, but he gave the correct an-
wer. She rewarded him with a smile, and he blushed.

The maps and atlases she'd ordered from Booker &
Son arrived, and Abram sent a lad over with the brown-
paper wrapped packages. She had August and Ludivine
carefully help her unwrap them and save the paper for
a future project. Marigold cleared a table so they could
inspect the books and maps. Most of the children went
back to their seats, but three, including August, were
enthralled and went over page after page of the color-
ful illustrations.

Marigold assigned the three of them—August, Garland and Jakob—to design a map on an enormous roll
of paper. The map would show all the countries of the
world and which languages had originated in each one.
The children were enthusiastic and worked on the project all day.

When they got home from school later that day, Evelyn met them on the porch. She told the boys, "Wipe
your feet, young men, and then come upstairs with me

to see your new room." She motioned to Marigold
"You, too."

The door to the room beside Seth's stood open, and
Evelyn extended an arm. "You have two beds in you
own room now. Tate, the single bed is for you."

Their new bedding hadn't arrived yet, and she'
made their beds with blankets and quilts of her own
She explained they'd have new ones as soon as they ar
rived on the train.

Tate stood beside the narrow bed, made up with
simple wool blanket. "I have my own bed?"

"You'll have to make it yourself in the morning, too,
Marigold told him.

"Seth will be able to sleep in his own room again,'
Evelyn said.

Harper ventured to the simple dark oak desk Mr
Irving had made without fancy carving, but with fou
dovetail drawers on the right side.

"That's for studies when you're older. Marigol
bought it for you," Evelyn told them.

Perhaps he was too small for such a desk right now
but they would all use it in the years to come. Mari
gold wouldn't be here with them, but she could imag
ine them here, reading, studying. The thought brough
her pleasure.

That evening, she joined the boys as Seth took then
on a ride and gave them the lead. Afterward, once th
children were tucked into bed, Evelyn excused hersel
and Marigold made a cup of tea. She set up the boar
and heated the iron to press a few of her shirtwaists
Seth joined her with a ledger, and worked on calcula
tions at the table. He rubbed at the skin at the edge o

he cast. "As soon as this cast is off, I'm going to Wich-
ta to buy horses."

"I thought you had plenty of horses."

"This is breeding stock. You'll help my ma with the
boys while I'm gone?"

She paused and set the iron on the stove.

He noticed something in her face. "What is it?"

"I was planning to leave once you got the cast off."

"Leave?"

"Yes." She smoothed the fabric on the board. "Stay
elsewhere."

"Why?"

"It's not a good idea for me to be the boys' teacher
and live here, too." She didn't look at him. "It's complicated."

He laid down his pencil. "Is this because of the
kisses?"

"Only partly."

"What's the other part?"

"I told you. The children."

He stood, pushed back the chair and moved to where
she stood. "You were hired as the teacher. The boys
were unexpected. They take a lot more time than you
signed on for."

"That's not it."

He nodded. "I'm sure my mother will be able to
handle them for a couple of days. Dewey will come
with me, but I could ask someone to check in on them.
James, perhaps."

She said nothing.

He went back to where he'd been working and closed
the ledger. "The last thing I want is for my family or my
decisions to be a burden on you. You've already done a
lot for us, and I'm grateful."

Her heart was beating so fast, she thought it might burst.

"I have to check the horses." Seth left the kitchen, and his boots sounded on the back steps.

Marigold leaned on the board. Her chest ached with all the things left unspoken between them. She picked up the iron and finished her shirtwaist, then tidied up and put things away. Matters were always so serious between her and Seth. Tense. Complicated.

Why couldn't it be easy between them, like it was between her and Buck? Why didn't they laugh and go on picnics, play horseshoes together? Immediately she regretted those thoughts. It was unfair to compare the two. Seth was a man with the weight of the world on his shoulders, a man who took on responsibilities.

Buck might have a boyishness about him that was appealing, but would he look at her like Seth did? Would he lose sleep over a cat because it was important to her? Would she ever want him to kiss her the way she longed to kiss Seth?

Seth was all man. Serious perhaps, sensible, unflappable, self-controlled. But loyal and deserving of loyalty— Dewey had worked for his father, accompanied Seth on cattle drives and survived Comanches, and still worked with him. Trustworthy and dutiful—he'd cared for his mother since their father's death, saved their ranch in Missouri, took in his friends' children without a question. Generous and kind—apparently, he'd stayed up the better part of two nights waiting for Peony and had awakened her in the middle of the night so she wouldn't worry any longer. Why? Because it had been important to her. She would never forget the way he'd said those words. Like he'd crawl to the end of the earth or lasso the moon if it

was important to her. She placed her hand over her heart
to dull the ache that persisted when she thought of him.

She grabbed a shawl and went out the back door,
needing to clear her thoughts.

Seth spotted Marigold in the darkness as she walked
from the side of the house, heard her walking through
the grass.

"It's cooled off," he said from the corral fence where
he was leaning.

She started, then pulled the soft shawl around her
shoulders. "Considerably." She glanced in the empty
corral. "What are you looking at?"

"The stars."

They spread out across the sky like glittery jewels.
"Do you know the constellations?"

"Some." He glanced up. "Orion. That one's easy."

"Orion's even in the Bible. Did you know that?"

"I did not."

"In Job and, I think, in Amos."

He pointed to the stars. "Ursa Major…and Ursa
Minor."

"You do know your constellations."

"The easy ones." He studied the sky. "Imagine the
sailors navigating ships with only these stars to guide
them."

"I can't imagine." She took in the whole of the night
sky as she spoke. "'Silently, one by one, in the infinite
meadows of heaven, blossomed the lovely stars, the
forget-me-nots of the angels.'"

"Who wrote that?"

"Longfellow, in a book called *Evangeline, A Tale
of Acadie*."

She was a wonder. "Where do you store all of that?"

"I just remember things I've read."

"Probably why you're an excellent teacher."

From the distance came the sound of a lowing cow.

"Sounds like such a mournful cry," she said. Then, before he could ask her why she looked so sad herself, she continued. "I know a lot of people have suffered loss."

She looked at him. "You and your mother. Everyone we know. It seems the whole country has been in mourning since the start of the war."

She turned her attention back to the stars and continued.

"My story isn't all that different from anyone else's. I've told you, I lost both of my parents and my sister. But I was fortunate that my father made provisions and I had the house. What I didn't tell you is that after Daisy was gone I took care of my niece. She was all I had left. I had written and tried to reach her father, but he never responded, so I didn't even know if he got my letters. He followed the gold rushes. We rarely saw him. I didn't even know if he was alive or dead. Violet and I went on, just the two of us.

"I taught school, and she was one of my students, so we were together all the time. I even put her to bed in my room because she was afraid and often ended up in my bed anyway."

Seth didn't know if he wanted to hear how this story ended. She'd never mentioned these things to him before. The tremor in her voice and the way she spoke of her niece made it plain this was painful to talk about.

Perhaps she needed to say the words. Maybe telling her story was a way to deal with the pain and start to heal. He was honored she felt she could trust him. If she wanted to tell him, he wanted to hear it. He wanted to reach for her and wrap her up in the safety of his arms, but she stood away from him, her arms hugging herself inside the shawl. Her sister had taken ill and died. Had her niece suffered the same end?

"We had friends, and the ladies from church. Violet had friends at school. We attended church and social gatherings. In the evenings we read and sewed and I told her about her mother and her grandparents.

"And then one afternoon as school ended and we gathered our things and left the building, Wade Berman stood outside waiting."

Seth's mouth was dry. "Who is he?"

"Wade was Daisy's ne'er-do-well husband. He mostly showed up when he was out of money or in between whatever else he did."

Unless other provisions were made, which was rare, men had legal rights to their wives' property. "Did he get your sister's money?"

"No. As I've told you, my father was a banker and an investor. He made sure Wade would never get a dime of his money. But I gave him some of mine."

He frowned. "Why?"

"Because he was taking Violet. I wanted to be certain he could provide for her."

"He—he took her?"

"Yes. He's her father. He brought a deputy with him. I had no say."

It was obvious Marigold was hanging on to her composure by a thread. He wanted to reach out to her, but she wouldn't want that.

"That's why I can't stay and love those boys, Seth. They are not mine. I know how that ends up. I'm not losing anyone else. I've always had to accept other people's decisions and make the best of them. I felt like life was happening to me, and I wanted to choose my own path. That's why I came here."

He vividly recalled the pain he'd seen on her face and in her eyes when she was unable to disguise it, and now he understood why. "Did you think I wouldn't understand?"

"I don't know what I thought."

"You're not responsible for the boys, Marigold. You took them under your wing aboard the train. You stuck with them when I was hurt, and you've been here every day since. What you did for them—for all of us—well, I can't thank you enough. You've been more than generous with your time. I'll talk to them, so they don't make it harder for you when it's time. Feel free to leave whenever you like. You don't owe me anything."

"I owe you for saving Peony. Twice. Your arm wouldn't have been broken, or your ribs hurt, if you hadn't gone back to save her."

"I told you we're even. You took care of the boys. I pulled your cat from the rubble."

"And saved her from coyotes."

"She was smart enough to come back on her own."

She finally took her gaze from the sky and looked at him in the moonlight. "Thank you for understanding."

"Choose a life that makes you happy." He meant it. He cared for her, cared what happened to her, but he wanted her to be happy, not burdened with his responsibilities.

She turned and walked back to the house.

He knew what it was like to forfeit time, energy and self to duty. She deserved her own family someday. Her own children. Her own life.

Midweek, Seth made a trip to Dr. Mason's to have the cast removed and his arm examined. She declared him healed, but warned him not to do heavy lifting or put himself in a position to fall on it for a couple of months. She gave him a brace to wear while he worked. While in town, he went to Will Canfield's office and asked for a few minutes of his time.

His weightless right arm felt strange as he shook hands with the man.

"What's on your mind, Seth?"

"Now that I'm able to do chores, Miss Brewster is ready to move into town. It'll be less travel for her."

Will didn't disguise his surprise. "I thought all of you were getting along fine."

"We have been," he said with a nod. "But stayin' with us wasn't the original plan. She'd be more comfortable in town."

"All right. I'll talk with the council. We'll put out a few feelers and see what we come up with. I'm sure finding a place won't be a problem. We had plenty of offers before she'd even arrived, and now that everyone's met her, she'll be even more welcome."

"Thanks, Will." He turned the brim of his hat in his hands. "Russ is seriously considering the position as mayor. I hope this town knows it's letting itself in for one hard-headed city official."

"I think that's exactly what they're looking for. Before you go…" Will plucked a couple of printed flyers from a stack on his desk and handed them to Seth. "Will you deliver one to Miss Brewster as well?"

Seth nodded.

"It's information for setting up a time with Walter Kerr. He took my official portrait and now he's photographing prominent businessmen, families and the like. Of course, he'll want the schoolteacher, but I'd like to have him get a few portraits of your family. Perhaps a few of you with the horses."

"Sure."

Will reached for his waistcoat. "Tomasina and I are going over some house details with Buck this afternoon, and she'll skin me alive if I'm late."

"Havin' work done on your house?"

"No. We're having a new one built. A smaller one. The one I built with the intent of a governor's mansion is too big for our family. I'm expecting to win my seat in congress and when I do, we'll be living here six months out of the year, so we only need an adequate home."

"And the big house?"

"I have a few ideas, but nothing is settled yet. Unfortunately, I don't foresee anyone we know wanting such a grand place."

Or being able to afford it, Seth thought. "Thanks for your time."

"I'll let you know as soon as I know something about lodging for Miss Brewster."

Seth gave Marigold the paper about the photographer as they sat down to supper that evening. "Will asked you to make an appointment with this fellow for a portrait."

"All right."

Dewey came in, freshly washed, and took his seat. Evelyn and Marigold set the food on the table. Seth asked a blessing over their food and their health, and they ate.

"I was thinkin'," Seth began. "I told you I'd dig more trees for the park area across from school, and now there are all those fruit trees from the city council. I checked, and Daniel's keeping them watered and shaded at his place."

"What were you thinking?" Marigold asked.

"What if we made a day of it and asked for volunteers to dig out the hackberry trees? Get as many people as possible to help dig the holes at the spot on Lincoln Boulevard and plant them."

"That's a good idea. I'd be happy to help organize."

"Do you think we could be ready by this Saturday?"

"I think we could."

"Is your arm strong enough for all that digging?" Evelyn asked.

"Dr. Mason has already warned me not to overdo." He cut his roast beef into bites. "That's why I thought gathering volunteers would be good."

Marigold picked up the fork Harper had dropped and wiped it on her apron before handing it back to him. "What about your trees, Seth?"

"What about them?"

"You can't dig six holes by yourself."

"Dewey will help."

Marigold glanced at Dewey and he nodded. "We was fixin' to do it tomorrow."

Seth shrugged under the two women's gazes. "Dr. Mason gave me a brace to use to support my forearm. I'll put it on and wrap it before I pick up a shovel."

Evelyn shook her head. "You're every bit as stubborn as your father."

He ignored her comment. "Pass the potatoes, please."

"Every bit as handsome, too," she added as she handed him the bowl.

"Ma."

His mother ignored his subtle attempt to halt the flattery. "Isn't he handsome, Marigold? Boys, don't you think Seth is a handsome fella?"

Harper wrinkled his nose. "What's hansom?"

"Awww." Tate made a face.

Little John waved his arm and knocked over his cup of milk.

And Marigold? If Seth wasn't mistaken, she blushed becomingly, right before she jumped up for a towel.

"Dewey, will you take me into town after supper?"

"Happy to, miss."

She mopped up the milk. "Thank you. I'm going to go upstairs and get ready."

And she fled up the steps.

"I'd like to make a couple of stops if you don't mind," she told Dewey as they neared town.

"Don't mind a whit. I got all night."

"It's my understanding that Buck Hanley lives on Fourth Street, just west of Grant."

"I believe you're right."

"There first."

He stopped in front of the small house. "I'll circle a couple o' blocks, so we're headed back the right way when yur done."

It wasn't full dark, so she was able to make out the stone path and the white-painted door. Light shone behind the curtain on the front window. She drew herself up and knocked.

"Comin'!"

She flexed her fingers and straightened her shoulders.

The door opened, outlining Buck's tall form. His hair wasn't combed back in smooth waves, and his shirt wasn't neatly tucked in. "Marigold!"

Chapter Thirteen

Marigold stood before Buck in his doorway. "I hope this isn't an imposition. I wanted to speak with you. Alone. And I didn't want to wait."

"Uh...no. No, it's all right." He took a step to the side and tipped his head. "Do you want to come inside and sit down?"

"I should probably stay out here."

"Of course. Sorry." He stepped out, leaving the door open, creating a rectangle of light on the path that was now growing dark.

The sound of wagon wheels and horse's hooves grew louder as Dewey led the team closer. "That's Mr. Dewey turning around. He brought me."

Buck glanced at the wagon and back at her.

"When we had our conversation and you asked me about courting, I told you I'd need to think about it."

"I remember."

"I did think about it. A lot. I like you, Buck. I do. You're fun to talk to and you're interesting and smart. I enjoyed our dinner together, and I had a nice time playing horseshoes with you."

He reached a hand up and ran it down the back of

his head to his neck. "I'm pretty sure I know where this is leading."

"You didn't do anything wrong. Under different circumstances maybe…I don't know, maybe it would have worked out with us. You're a good catch. You'll make some girl a fine husband."

He planted his hand on his hip and she reached for his wrist.

"I'm just not that girl. Once I was sure about it, I didn't want to leave you waiting or wondering. I needed to be up front with you, because you deserve honesty and courtesy."

He gave a half laugh, half snort. "I wish you weren't bein' so ever-lovin' nice about this. You could have made it easy for me to not like you or to blame you or something, but you're sparin' me any hard feelings."

She took away her hand. "Isn't that good?"

"Yes. Thank you. Thank you for bein' brave and comin' out here to tell it to me square like this."

"It's the least I could do."

His gaze traveled over her face and her hair in the light from inside. "I hope whoever wins your heart appreciates what a gift he's getting."

"I'll bet I can count on you to ask him."

He chuckled. "You can."

"Good night, Buck."

"Good night, Marigold."

Back in the wagon, she asked Dewey, "Will you pull past Dr. Mason's office for me, please?" Lights were on, as she'd figured. Marlys had told her she was at the office late on Thursdays. "I'll be a while if you want to leave for an hour or so."

She pulled the chain that rang a bell inside, and Marlys unlocked the door to let her in. "Marigold, I wondered if you'd come this evening. I have one other person bathing right now, and a tub open for you. Shall I heat more water?"

"Please. I'm ready for my mineral bath." This seemed the perfect time to use the prize she'd won at the horseshoe competition. She needed someone to talk to, and Marlys had become a friend.

Marlys directed her into a bathing chamber that held a deep tub with one high end and gleaming faucets. A plush rug, white towels and a fluffy wrapper were luxurious surprises. "Change into the wrapper behind the screen while I fill the tub and prepare your bath. Almond oil?"

She nodded. As she stepped behind the screen, she wasted no time. "I turned down my first suitor this evening."

"Mr. Hanley?"

"Mr. Hanley."

"I have just the combination of minerals and oils for this particular ailment. I'll make you a tea as well."

On Friday, Marigold spoke with Leah about planting the trees the next day. Leah was amenable, but surprisingly she had a request for Marigold.

"Would you be willing to help with the layout of the park?" Leah asked. "Since we'll have that many trees, we should have a plan."

Being included in planning something for the town was an honor. She rested her fingertips on her chest for a moment in surprise. "Yes, of course."

"I'll ask Will and Tomasina to come over this evening. If you and Seth could join us, we could put our heads together."

How exciting to be included in developing the place

across from the school that she already enjoyed. "It's going to be a park then?"

"Why not? We don't have a town square or a place to gather for special days. Until now we've been closing Eden Street and gathering or meeting at the churchyard. But with all the trees that will eventually provide shade, we'd have an actual park."

Marigold smiled. "And there's a well right there to keep the young trees watered."

"I know something else that's going to please you."

Marigold looked at her friend expectantly.

"Will and Daniel are in negotiations for the sale of Will's house."

She cocked her head, waiting for the news that would please her.

"He's offering it at a considerably low cost, low enough that Daniel can afford to buy it."

Marigold studied Leah. "And you want a mansion?"

"No. Daniel would in turn donate the house to the town."

"I see."

Leah's expression lit up. "For a library."

A library! Marigold clasped Leah's forearms and hopped up and down, grinning from ear to ear. Her head spun with ideas. "Books. We'll need books."

"All in good time. Let's not get ahead of ourselves. Daniel would wring my neck if he knew I'd told you. Don't say anything. It's still in the planning stages and nothing is official yet."

"I won't say a word."

"About what?" Beatrix said as she entered the schoolhouse earlier than usual.

Marigold released Leah. "Beatrix, we're planning a

day-long event tomorrow to plant trees and create an actual park across the street."

"That sounds nice."

"Do you think Colton could get away from the livery?"

"I suppose he could. I'll ask him."

"I told Marlys about it last night, but I should spread the word around town."

"Why don't I start the children working on their spelling lesson while you do that?" Beatrix offered.

"I'll see you this evening." Leah took the empty pails from the day before and left.

Marigold left Beatrix with the students long enough to visit the newspaper office, Aunt Mae's, Booker & Son and all the nearby establishments to pass the word about needing volunteers.

At supper Seth agreed it was a good idea to plan the layout of the planting, so after they'd eaten and she and Evelyn had done the dishes, he brought two saddled horses around to the front of the house.

"We're riding?" Marigold asked, surprised.

"Do you want to?"

"Yes." She adjusted her skirt over her knee to pull herself into the saddle. "What does one do with all these skirts?"

"I can't answer that question." He called over his shoulder, "Ma?"

Evelyn came out onto the porch.

Marigold gave her an imploring look. "How do I ride with skirts and petticoats?"

"If you don't want your stockings to show a bit, you have to wear a split skirt. But when you don't have one, you simply make the best of it. Make sure you have the skirt secured well, so it doesn't blow in the wind.

I don't think Bright Star would get startled, but your skirts over your head might make for an embarrassing moment." She laughed.

Tate joined Evelyn on the porch. "I'll help Mrs. Halloway while you're gone!"

"You're a big help, son." Seth swung himself up and onto his saddle. He wore his revolver in a holster against his hip. "Thank you."

The boy looked pleased with himself.

"It's plenty light out, so you'll be able to watch the ground ahead as we're riding." Seth nudged his horse forward and she did the same.

"How will we see the ground on the way home?"

"We'll have moonlight tonight. I know the way. I've traveled it many times. But you should know that it's not safe to ride a horse in the pitch-dark when it's an unfamiliar trail. The horse could step in a hole or bruise its hoof on a stone."

As they rode, Marigold wanted to tell Seth about Will's house, but she'd promised Leah she'd say nothing. She did have something she hadn't told him, however.

"Did Dewey tell you I went to see Buck last night?"

"Didn't ask and he didn't say. Figured it's your business where you go."

She looked over at him. "I went to tell him I'd made a decision about him courting me."

He rode beside her in silence.

"I told him I didn't see a future for us."

"You turned him down?"

"Yes."

"So, Buck Hanley won't be courting you."

"No."

He reached up and adjusted his hat.

"I went for a mineral bath, too."

"How was it?"

"Rejuvenating. I might save my next one for the next time I throw hay."

He chuckled.

"You should try it."

"Maybe I should."

When they arrived at Daniel and Leah's house, Seth tied the horses to the post out front. Daniel answered the door with a friendly smile and ushered them into the parlor. Will and Tomasina had apparently walked the couple of blocks from their place and were already there. Tomasina sat on a divan, holding an infant. Her curly bright red hair was held back with silver combs, and she gave Marigold a smile. "I don't believe you've met Andrew yet. He arrived just before you did."

Marigold perched on the divan beside her. "He's a beautiful baby."

Tomasina's green eyes sparkled with happiness. "Would you like to hold him?"

"May I?"

"Yes, of course." She handed her the wrapped bundle.

"He barely weighs anything." Marigold admired his fine pale lashes, translucent skin and sweet pouting mouth. It had been quite a few years since Violet had been this tiny, but she remembered it well. She and Daisy had stared at her for hours, mesmerized by the blessing that was theirs to love and enjoy. She inhaled his scent and the memories unleashed a flood of emotions. Marigold's eyes stung and she blinked back unshed tears. In short order she handed the baby back to Tomasina.

Leah came from the kitchen, with Evie on her hip. Marigold was familiar with the seven-month-old baby, since she saw her often in the mornings. Evie pointed to the baby.

"That's Andrew, isn't it?" Leah said. "Can you say 'baby'?"

"Ba!" Evie said.

"She said it." Tomasina clapped for her.

"She calls me 'Ma' and her father 'Da,' so we haven't moved beyond one-syllable conversations yet." Leah kissed the baby's cheek.

"Da!" she said and waved her arm in the air toward Daniel.

He came to his wife's side and wrapped his arm around them both. The baby reached for him and, when he leaned forward, grabbed his nose. He grimaced and disengaged her chubby fingers.

Leah handed Evie to him. "I'll make us tea, and then we can get started."

"I'll let you," Tomasina said, sitting back with a sigh. She gave Marigold a sideways look. "I've herded cattle from San Antonio to Schuyler. I've roped a calf from the back of a galloping horse and run two miles to catch a horse that threw me. But I've never been as tired as I am since having this hungry, spitting, wetting little package of sweetness." She touched her baby's hand affectionately. "But as my daddy always said, 'I'll sleep when I'm dead.'"

"You've truly done all that?" Marigold asked, amazed.

"The first time I saw Tom, she was herding longhorns down the middle of town," Will told her. He launched into a story about his wife winning a sharpshooting contest.

"I should be getting lessons from *her*," Marigold said to Seth.

Leah brought tea, and Will took the baby so the ladies could enjoy theirs first. Leah brought out paper and pencils, and they set to work planning the layout of the park. Before long, Andrew cried.

"Take him up to the nursery," Leah told her, and Tomasina excused herself to feed him.

"Your home is beautiful," Marigold told Leah. "Last time I was here, there were a lot of people, and I didn't really have an opportunity to see it."

"Thank you. Daniel built it before I arrived. It's almost like he knew the perfect home for us."

Before long they had a plan they all agreed upon, leaving room in the center of the block for a bandstand. Leah served pie her housekeeper had baked that day, and it grew late. But instead of being tired, Marigold left the house with a feeling of expectation.

"I'm excited about tomorrow," she said as they stepped out into the night.

Seth untethered the horses. "Would you like a hand up?"

"I'm not going to get soft now. If Tomasina can rope cows, I can surely mount a horse." She grabbed the pommel and pulled herself up, adjusting her skirts rather ungracefully.

Seth had been right about the moonlight. It was surprisingly bright as they rode home. She was thankful she'd brought a jacket, because the night air was chilly.

When they reached White Rock, she threw a leg over the saddle and slid to the ground. Her legs were a little shaky, but she led Bright Star into the stable and close to the rack that held the saddles. After unbuckling the straps, she lifted the saddle onto the wood rail, removed the saddle blanket and wiped down the horse, all while

Seth tended to his gray. She led the animal to its stall and made sure Bright Star had feed and water.

"You did real fine," he said, and followed her out and across the yard to the porch. She had her foot on the top step when he asked, "Why did you turn down Buck Hanley?"

She turned, standing three steps above him.

He stepped up one.

"He's a fine man," she said. "His attention was flattering. He made me laugh. But I knew he wasn't right for me."

He took another step up. Now their faces were almost level and he stood close. "How?"

"Well, I've seen others, like the friends we were with tonight. Like Sam and Marlys. Like James and Hannah. Marlys is a doctor and Hannah has her dressmaking shop. They also have husbands and children. They have it all. I'm sure it's not easy, but they make it work. I want that."

"And you couldn't have had it all with Buck?"

"No." She turned, but he stopped her by taking her wrist and turning her back to face him.

They were so close, she could smell the starch in his collar. Starch and sunshine and man, that's what he smelled like. Her senses reeled.

He loosened his grip on her wrist and moved her hand until he could thread his long fingers through hers. He had calluses on his palms. Her heart started a crazy thumping beat. She remembered what his mustache felt like as it touched her upper lip. She remembered how gently he'd kissed her, and how easy it was to lose herself in his kiss. He placed his other hand behind her waist and barely encouraged her toward him.

His breath touched her lips. His eyes shone dark in

the starlight, and she let hers drift shut. In the eternity that passed before his lips touched hers, she wasn't sure if she said his name or only thought it. His kiss tasted like the cinnamon from the pie he'd eaten.

How was it she'd lived to be twenty-three years old and never known something as pure and gentle as his kisses existed? What did they mean?

He drew away and raised his hand to slide a knuckle over her lips. "We have a busy day ahead tomorrow."

She withdrew and backed away. This time he let her turn and go inside.

Plenty of helpers showed up the next day, and men, women and children all pitched in. As promised, Seth had worn the brace on his forearm and wrapped it. Marlys even checked it when she spotted him.

Seth led wagons to the spot along the creek and those with shovels set to work. Digging deep enough to keep sufficient root systems intact was arduous work, but with the cold water from the creek right there, workers drank and splashed their heads and faces. Others helped carry and lift the saplings into the wagon beds. When the wagons rolled along Lincoln Boulevard with their haul, the men were welcomed with smiling faces and good-natured teasing.

Will, Marigold and Leah displayed the layout they'd created of the planned park. With August's help, Marlys and Sam, Daniel and Reverend Taggart set out stakes where the trees should be planted, and Hannah poked a piece of paper labeled with the type of tree on each one.

"What's this big empty space?" Hannah called out.

"That's the future bandstand," Will answered.

"We have a band?" Jennie Simms, one of Marigold's students, asked, evoking laughter.

"Not yet," Freddie answered. "But we're getting prepared."

Seeing them made Marigold wonder about them. Freddie Simms was quite obviously single and looking to court someone, and three students in her class were named Simms. "Freddie, is Jennie your sister?"

"Nah, she and Dwight and Frank are my brother Billy's kids."

"You're their uncle," she said, understanding now.

Buck gave Marigold a grin. "You've had a lot of families to keep straight."

A dozen men and women had been digging holes where the stakes had been inserted, and as Seth and his crew arrived, they joined in to dig more. As the trees went into the holes, the children filled buckets from the well and saturated the roots and freshly turned earth. By late afternoon, with everyone dirty and aching, the townspeople surveyed their day's work.

Daniel Gardner whistled and got everyone's attention. "Aunt Mae and several others have been busy cooking all afternoon. They're asking everyone who wants to come back after chores and cleaning up to join us for a late picnic on the school grounds."

That met with cries of excitement.

"Pa, you can bring your banjo!" Ivy Ernst shouted. "Miss Brewster taught us to sing 'Old Dog Tray.'"

"Judd, I didn't know you was a picker," Freddie called. "I'll bring mine, too."

With good-natured jesting, the men bantered over who would do a worse job with the song. Once the shovels, wheelbarrows and pails were packed, the crowd dispersed. Marigold rode with Evelyn and the boys. Seth and Dewey had brought a second wagon.

A couple of hours later, dressed in her ecru brilliantine dress with a scalloped overskirt bound with slate-colored satin, Marigold tied a matching sash around her waist and secured her hair atop her head. While going through one of her trunks searching for the sash, she'd discovered a large round lace doily that had been her mother's. She wrapped it in tissue and set it aside. She'd been considering a gift for Beatrix, and the doily seemed appropriate.

"Am I overdressed?" she asked Evelyn as they met downstairs. "The other ladies always look so nice."

"You look lovely and the dress is beautiful. You shine no matter what you're wearing."

"I agree." She hadn't seen Seth standing in the doorway, and her face warmed under his gaze. "The boys are waiting in the wagon," he told her.

The festivities had started by the time they arrived on the school grounds. Someone had cleared a spot and surrounded it with stones where a fire would be lit once darkness fell. Already food was being carried to makeshift tables.

There must have been ten cakes, some plain, some fancy, and two of them were layer cakes topped with chunky applesauce, whipped cream and nuts. Some of the women had brought slaws, cornbread and jars of pickles and beets to add to the bounty from Aunt Mae's kitchen.

"Miss Frazier made all these desserts today," Aunt Mae announced.

Deborah stood to the side, her hands clasped in front of her, smiling as others commented on her creations.

Though she was a formidable baker, Marigold couldn't help but think that for a prospective bride, Deborah hadn't seemed to show any interest in the young men. She turned to Leah, who stood beside her, and asked, "Has Deborah been courted by anyone?"

Leah tilted her head as if in thought. "I haven't heard anything about her courting, and news about the brides travels fast. For example, I know you had dinner with Buck Hanley."

"He's a nice man. He asked to court me."

"And?"

"And after lengthy consideration I told him no." She was grateful it hadn't been awkward between her and Buck today at the planting.

Leah nodded. "You'll know the right person for you when you're ready."

"Is that how it was for you?"

"I didn't trust my feelings for a long time, because I'd made mistakes, but yes. I knew I was supposed to be with Daniel."

"Reverend, will you say a blessing over the trees and our meal, please?" Aunt Mae waved to get his attention.

"A prayer for fruitfulness and growth." Reverend Taggart grinned. "Seems God has already been working on that in Cowboy Creek, doesn't it?" He thanked God for the gathering of friends and family, prayed for their safety and provision, petitioned the Lord for good weather and rain for crops and trees and thanked Him for the bounty of food.

"Amen!" everyone shouted.

Marigold met more of her students' parents, which was nice in this informal setting. The parents of seven-year-old twins Abigail and Jane introduced themselves. She'd heard that Noah Burgess, one of the town founders, had been reclusive in the past and still only came to town on rare occasions. He wore a beard to mask burn scars on his jaw and neck, though the uneven pink skin was evident. Grace was friendly and sweet.

She met Freddie's brother, Billy, father of Dwight, Frank and Jennie. He was a widower, and every bit as friendly as his younger brother. "My youngins talk about you all the time. Miss Brewster said this, and Miss Brewster did that. I been lookin' forward to meeting this special schoolteacher."

"They're bright children, Mr. Simms. Polite and respectful as well."

"That's their ma's doin'," he told her. "She was soft-poken and kind, but she didn't take no sass."

"She sounds like a wonderful woman."

He nodded and dropped his gaze.

After everyone had eaten, Marigold helped wash and rinse dishes in Aunt Mae's enormous kitchen. With a dozen women and girls helping, the task didn't take long.

"I didn't think I'd see this all cleaned up tonight." Aunt Mae took off her apron.

"You cooked all day," Sadie Shriver told her. "No reason you should clean it all up, too."

The fire had been lit, and its brightness glowed across the lot as they returned to the gathering. Accordions, fiddles and even tom-toms with leather stretched and tacked over the top joined the banjos. Billy Simms started off with "Old Dog Tray," and the school-age children were delighted. All of them knew the lyrics and sang along. When the last notes died away, Jennie Simms announced, "Stephen Foster wrote that song."

Marigold beamed at her student.

"He died five years ago," Jakob Willis added.

"He wrote over two hundred songs." Michael Higgins's voice surprised Marigold. She spotted him seated on the ground in front of his father in the circle around the fire. His father had trimmed his beard for the occasion and sat perched on a crate. Michael glanced at Marigold and grinned. "Two hundred songs. Isn't that somethin'?"

Emotion rose in her throat and prevented her from replying, but she smiled through a blur of tears.

"Reverend, you start us off with a song now!"

Reverend Taggart, standing beside his daughter and holding Ava, started a hymn.

A stunning soprano voice stood out, and Marigold spotted the petite singer with ginger-gold hair standing beside a fair-haired man with a mustache and goatee. She knew all the verses and sang each one in a clear lilting tone.

People chose more songs, repeated their favorites, and the singing went on for an hour or more. The hour grew late; both children and adults were exhausted from their day.

"I hope to see all of you at the service tomorrow morning," the reverend said.

"If you sing 'Old Dog Tray,' I'll be there," a man shouted.

"Cookie Kuckelman, if you show up tomorrow, we'll sing 'Old Dog Tray'!" someone else shouted.

Everyone laughed and said their goodbyes.

Will approached Marigold. "Thanks for helping to arrange all this."

"It was Seth's idea. I only passed the word along."

"Everyone working together is what makes Cowboy Creek a great place to live and work. And raise families."

When she said good-night to Will, she heard a voice behind her. "Miss Brewster?"

She turned and recognized the petite woman who had sung so well.

"I'm Pippa Kendricks."

"Pleased to meet you, Mrs. Kendricks."

"Call me Pippa. Everyone does. I couldn't help but hear how you led the first song so assuredly."

Marigold thanked her. "I have a knack for remembering songs and poems."

"And a lovely voice. Did I understand correctly that you've taught music to the children?"

Leah's prediction came to light. "You're the person who arranges music and plays for the opera house, aren't you?"

"Indeed I am. It's one of the most exciting things that's happened to this little town since I've been here. My husband works for the railroad, and I travel with him often, but I always make time for plays. The stage is my passion."

"I heard you sing. You're quite good."

"Thank you. I was wondering though, if you would consider joining our little troupe for our next performance."

"I'm not a performer. No one would pay to hear me sing."

"We could certainly use your help playing for rehearsals. Sometimes Hannah is just so busy with her dressmaking, and I feel guilty for putting the pressure on her, but she's all we've had. Until now."

"How often do you rehearse?"

"Sometimes we go months without rehearsing, and then two or three times a week before a play."

"I suppose it will depend on what time of year it is and how busy my schedule is. Why don't you let me know when you have something scheduled, and I'll see if it will work for me?"

"Thank you so much. I'll do that."

After saying goodbye to Pippa, Marigold scanned the dwindling crowd for Seth. She found him shaking out blankets, and went to help him fold.

"You look pretty tonight," he said when she joined him.

That was the second time he'd complimented her tonight and she was once again caught off guard. "Thank you."

"In the fire your hair catches all the light and almost glows."

"My hair?"

"Yeah. I like it best in the sun, though. It kind of shimmers as if the light comes from inside."

She set a blanket on the stack on the open buckboard. "What are you doing?"

"Folding blankets."

"I mean talking about my hair. Why are you talking about my hair?"

"I was just giving you a compliment."

She flashed one hand, palm toward him. "Don't give me any more compliments. Don't be nice to me."

"What's wrong with you?"

She had no idea what was wrong with her. She'd enjoyed one of the best evenings of her life. She'd felt pride and hope and admiration for her students and the women who had traveled here with her. Being able to enjoy the evening, to enjoy her life, was nothing anyone took for granted. It was evident in the way people spoke and sang and interacted with each other that life was precious.

"I don't know." She shook her head. "Don't pay any attention to me."

These people had survived so much as individuals, but they'd come together to start afresh and make a better life for themselves. They'd found a place—and possibly many reasons—to unite, with similar goals and dreams, and their children were now reaping the benefit of this new opportunity. She had everything to be thankful for and glad about.

"Not paying attention to you is impossible," he told her.

She ignored his provoking statement. She wasn't going to let him confuse her more than he had been. "Let's get the boys. It's getting late."

There was a light shower early Sunday morning, and Marigold couldn't help remembering Reverend Taggart's prayer the night before. By the time church began, the skies had cleared. A slender older fellow played the organ that morning. Sam told her he'd been the organist when Hannah and her father had first arrived. "It was months before anyone knew she could play. She was sickly and stayed in her room at Aunt Mae's a lot."

"Hannah? She looks so healthy."

"Turned out she wasn't really sick. She was expecting and hiding it."

"Oh. But Ava is…?"

"She and James knew each other before coming here. James is Ava's father."

A steam whistle nearby notified of an arriving train. The townspeople had grown used to the sound and Reverend Taggart paused in his opening prayer.

After the songs and the reverend's preaching were

done, Marigold spoke to a few of her friends as she made her way toward the door.

She shook the reverend's hand.

"Blessings to you this week, Miss Brewster."

Little John caught up to her and took her hand. The sun shone brightly. She turned her face upward to the warm breeze. "Rain and sun on the new trees' first day. Isn't that just like God to provide what we need?"

A man obstructed her path, bringing her up short. It took her brain a moment to analyze his face. She came in contact with so many people she didn't know or had only recently met, but this forbidding face was all too familiar.

He didn't look the same as the last time she'd seen him. His face was thinner—his entire person gaunt, his skin pallid, save the rash on the lower portion of his cheek and neck. But she still recognized Wade Berman.

She became aware of Little John releasing her hand and backing away.

"Wade?" Her thoughts still hadn't come together. "What are you doing here?" She looked around but there was no one with him. "Where's Violet?"

"You and I need to have a conversation," her brother-in-law said.

She looked farther, glanced at the children leaving the churchyard with their parents. "Is she all right, Wade, has something happened?" Panic gripped her and she got dizzy on her feet. "Where is Violet?"

A strong arm came around her, and Seth steadied her. Her vision cleared. She didn't care that people turned to look at her—and at Wade.

"Violet is fine," he said.

"You're sure?"

"I'm certain. Who's your friend?"

"Seth Halloway," Seth said from beside her.

She took time to notice that Wade wore a nice shirt, brown jacket and tie. She hadn't seen him dressed so nicely since his and Daisy's wedding ceremony. Her money must have been adequate enough to dress him well.

"Wade Berman." He didn't offer his hand and neither did Seth.

Marigold's anger grew. "What is it you have to say that you couldn't write?"

Wade gave Seth a piercing glance.

"Whatever it is, say it in front of us both," she insisted.

He cleared his throat and adjusted his stance. "I'm not well."

"You don't look well."

He grimaced. "No. It's serious. And it's only going to get worse."

"You need more money."

"No. Money won't help. Well, money always helps, but it won't fix me."

"We have a brilliant doctor of eclectic medicine in this town," she offered. "I believe they call the science homeopathies."

Wade waved off her offer. "That's not why I came. There's nothing to be done." The side of his mouth twitched. "I'm dying."

She was sorry for him but her thoughts went immediately to her niece. "What about Violet? You've taken her, now what will become of her?"

"I'll need to leave her with someone. You're the best choice."

Relief, grief and gratefulness roared into her being

like a tidal wave and rushed back out, leaving her nearly limp. She clung to Seth. "You're leaving her with me?"

"In truth, the child has made my life a misery since the moment I came for her. No one I've left her with has been able to handle her. She's uncooperative. Cries all the time."

Marigold was so angry, she trembled. She wanted to run at him and strike him for taking Violet, for leaving her, for making her miserable. Seth tightened his embrace, holding her close against his side. Had he not, she might have done something she would regret.

Wade opened his jacket and handed her a parchment envelope. "That's everything you need. Written by an attorney, signed by me and witnessed before a judge. You won't have a legal problem."

Seth released her so she could reach out. Her fingers shook on the envelope, but she opened it, slid out the creased document and read it. Her gaze went back to Wade's. "When? When can I get her?"

"Follow me." He turned, found unsteady footing on the path and started toward the few remaining buggies and wagons. One carriage stood on the street, likely a rental from the livery. Upon the rear seat was a small form in a pastel lavender dress.

That train whistle earlier! He'd brought her here by train!

With Seth close behind, she ran toward that buggy. Toward the child with the curly red-gold hair.

Seeing Marigold, Violet sprang to her feet.

Marigold found a burst of energy and closed the distance, extending her arms.

Violet leaped forward into her embrace and Marigold caught her. She held the girl so tightly, she caught herself before she caused harm, and she loosened her embrace.

ut kept her in her arms, the child's legs locked around
er waist. She held Violet's head in one hand and looked
t her dear face, the eyes so like her sister's, and kissed
very spot on her cheeks and forehead, pressed her own
ace to the girl's, breathed in her scent and felt the warmth
f her little body against her breast.

Violet swiped the tears from her aunt's face, then
lung to her and sobbed.

Chapter Fourteen

Seth felt tears on his own cheeks, swiped them with his sleeve and swallowed down the sting in his throat. This must be what if felt like to be reunited with loved ones in heaven, he thought. Beauty. Love. God's very best gift.

But this reunion was present and tangible. Almost sacred.

None of the twenty or so people who had noticed Marigold's behavior and followed at a polite distance made a sound. The only sound was his own heart beating and the sobs of the child with hair just like her aunt's shining in the sunlight.

Finally, Violet moved back and looked up at her aunt. "Are we going home?"

"We're staying here. This will be our home."

The girl looked past Marigold's shoulder for the first time, directing her gaze away from Wade and darting to Seth. Her attention dropped lower, and he turned his head to look down at the boys, their three faces wearing quizzical expressions.

At last Marigold released her hold and let the girl stand on her own. She wiped Violet's face with her finers, smoothed her hair and grasped her hand as though he'd never let go. She led the child over to where her brother-in-law had been silently watching. "I want to keep her with me now."

"As I supposed."

"Tomorrow I'll take this document to an attorney and make sure everything is in order."

Wade seemed unaffected. "It will be."

"You stay until then. I'll compensate you for your trouble."

"I've already had a talk with Violet." He looked down at her, but didn't touch her or bend to her eye level. "You're back with your aunt now. This is where you're staying."

Violet said nothing.

With a stiff nod, Wade took off at a slow ambling gait toward the conveyance, where he reached in and brought out two bags, which, with obvious effort, he placed on the ground. Then he climbed into the buggy and led the horses toward Eden Street and the hotel.

Seth watched him go for a moment, and then studied Marigold's face. She was still disbelieving. She turned, glancing at the scattering of observers, then led Violet to where Seth and the boys stood, Evelyn at his side, making little sniffling sounds.

"This is my niece, Violet. I've been staying with this family," she told the child. "Mrs. Halloway, Seth…and this is Tate, Harper and Little John."

"She'll stay with us, of course," his mother said to Marigold. "We're happy to have you." She gave the girl a watery smile.

He felt as though he should say something, but could think of nothing befitting this shocking turn of events or the ordeal this little girl had endured. So he smiled what he hoped was a welcoming smile. "Hello, Violet."

Violet clung to Marigold without reply.

Seth took the initiative to get moving. "Let's head out then. I'll get her bags."

Marigold sat in the back, with Violet crushed up against her. The boys sat across from them, observant and silent, while Seth drove the team with his mother beside him.

Dewey came out to help with the horses. He reached to help down Marigold and the boys, and his eyebrows shot up. "Land sakes! You found another one."

Marigold made the introductions, then she took Violet's hand and they all walked inside. "I'll heat water and we will bathe you before dinner. I remember how much I longed for a bath after my train ri—"

"Peony!" Violet's cry stopped everyone in their tracks.

The cat had come to greet them in the kitchen and skidded to a stop and gazed at Violet. The girl dropped to her knees and extended a hand. Peony touched her whiskers to her fingers, gave a little lick and then climbed right onto her lap and rubbed her head against her arm.

"She got fatter," Violet said.

"She eats just the same." Marigold went to heat water.

A warning bell went off in Seth's head. That cat did look a little wider than it had previously.

He carried the battered satchels up to Marigold's room. The space smelled like her, like her delicate orange scent. What would she do now? Her contract said nothing about additional lodging for another person. He didn't mind having her niece here, of course. He would

ssure her, but hesitated to bring up the subject of her
eaving again. She'd had her mind set.

Peony came to inspect the luggage, touching her nose
o each edge, the latches and the handles. Seth hunkered
down beside her and spanned her midsection with both
hands. She balked for a moment, but soon rolled over,
and he felt her belly.

Hopefully Marigold's good mood would last until he
had to tell her this news.

While Evelyn prepared a cold meal, Marigold car-
ied warm water to the tub in the enormous pantry beside the kitchen. She helped Violet undress and washed
her hair. Her hair was truly just like Marigold's, so she
knew how to tame the curls and had supplies ready. She
worked up a lather with mild castile soap and massaged
it into the girl's head.

"It smells good," Violet said. "I haven't smelled this
for a long time."

"Who washed your hair for you while you were
away?"

"One of the ladies did it. One was nice, but some
weren't."

Did she want to know? "I'm so sorry. I'm sorry I
couldn't keep you with me."

"Don't be sad anymore, Aunt Mari."

"I won't, darling." She worked a beaten egg through
the strands of hair to prevent the ends from drying out,
rinsed it out and then rinsed again with a mixture of
vinegar and rosemary water.

She'd almost forgotten how slender and delicate Violet was in comparison to the sturdy boys she'd been
bathing. She suspected, in fact, that her niece was thin-

ner than she'd been previously. She could see her ribs
and prominent spine as she dried her.

The dress she'd taken from the satchel was wrinkled,
and didn't look as though it had been pressed. It was
one she remembered and surely it was too short now.

"I think you've grown a little taller. Bend over and
shake out your hair."

Violet leaned forward and Marigold ran her fingers
through the tresses, a familiar ritual neither had forgotten. When her niece straightened again, she wound curls
around her fingers and let them spring into place to dry.

Violet looked into her eyes as Marigold kneeled before her. She wrapped her arms around her neck and
Marigold was overcome with emotion. She pressed her
lips together to hold back a sob. She leaned back and
held the child's upper arms. "The Halloways are nice
people. They're kind and generous. They welcomed me
to their home when I got here. Seth took in the boys as
his own. It's safe here. We're together. Always."

Violet nodded.

She would do everything in her power to always
keep this child safe.

Seth noticed the seating arrangement but said nothing. He and his mother always sat at opposite ends of the
table. Dewey was to Seth's right, with Harper between
him and Marigold. Tate was to Seth's left, with Little
John beside him. His mother had obviously done some
strategic planning so as not to dislodge anyone or upset
their routine. She simply moved herself right, closer to
the corner, nearer to Little John, and made a place for
Violet on her left, between herself and Marigold.

He said the prayer as everyone bowed their heads.
"Thank You, Lord, for bringing Violet here safely. We

hank You, Father God, for her protection. Help us know how to comfort her and help her. Let her know we care about her and how much we want her here with us. Thank You for this food and for each other. In Jesus's name, amen."

He'd prayed a similar prayer when the boys had arrived. Tate obviously remembered, because he nodded at Seth, as though confirming the adequacy of his prayers.

Violet merely nibbled at her food, unlike the boys, who had been ravenous upon their arrival. She was so delicate, he feared she'd blow away in a strong wind. Her appetite would pick up once she was exposed to the fresh air, sunshine, riding lessons and chores. She drank her whole glass of milk. He asked if she'd like more, and she politely replied, "Yes, please."

Marigold poured more and Violet drank it down.

He and Marigold exchanged a glance.

The little girl's hair was still wet from her bath, but charming curls framed her face and fell over her shoulders. She looked strikingly like Marigold, even her hazel eye color and the shape of her face. Of course, he had no idea what Marigold's sister had looked like, so her similarity probably wasn't surprising. No one would ever question they were related.

He often saw both parents in the boys, depending on their expressions, but he saw nothing of Wade Berman in Marigold's niece. Thank goodness.

He turned to the two older boys. "Tate and Harper, you're excused from chores tonight. You can show Violet around the house and the yard. Play on the porch if you like. Don't go near the stables or the barn without me, you hear?"

"Yessir." Tate turned to the newcomer with a serious expression. "We ain't been here that long, neither."

"We're off to do chores." Dewey followed Seth outside.

The two women got up and stacked dishes. Marigold heated water for washing and scraped soap shavings. She gave Violet an encouraging smile. "I'll be right here, I promise. You go on ahead with the boys and look at the rest of the house."

Never the bashful one, Tate asked, "Did your parents die, too?"

Evelyn and Marigold looked at each other and then away. Suds dripped from Marigold's fingers as she listened. The children were just on the other side of the kitchen doorway now.

Violet must have nodded because there was no audible reply. Marigold bit her lip.

"What about Seth?" It was Violet's voice. "Isn't he your father?"

"No. He's our pa's goodest friend."

Marigold let her eyes roll up. She hadn't even broached grammar with these children yet. They'd been here only a few weeks, and she figured working it into their reading and spelling curriculum would happen soon enough.

"Marigold is your aunt?" Tate, asking more questions. "What is an aunt anyhow?"

"My mama was her sister."

"You look pretty jess like her!" That was Harper's higher-pitched voice.

"We got beds 'n' things upstairs." Tate was talking again. He and Violet were the same age. "C'mon, we'll show you our soldiers and books. Did you bring any toys?"

"My dolls."

The sound of shoes clambered on the stairs and their voices grew muted.

At a sound behind them, they turned to find Little John had come back to the table and climbed up on his stool. He looked back at them with wide eyes. "Pwease, a cookie?"

Evelyn got him a cookie from the crock and handed it to him. "More milk I suppose, too?"

"Tanks."

She kissed the top of his head. "You're welcome."

After the dishes were dried and put away, Evelyn swept and Marigold went upstairs to change sheets and put away Violet's things. She made up the bed and then sat on the edge. This bed was adequate for the two of them now, but Violet would need her own soon.

Her heart swelled with joy. Such a small problem when everything else was boiled away. Violet was safe. She was *here*. Tomorrow Marigold would take that paper to Russ and make sure nothing was amiss. She had lost a lot, but she hadn't lost everything. God had answered her fervent prayers for Violet's safety and comfort. She slid to her knees on the wood floor and clasped her hands in thanks to the good Lord. "Lord, Your mercies are new every morning."

She felt Little John's presence and opened her eyes to find him staring at her. "Come pray with me," she said, motioning him closer.

He got on his knees beside her and folded his hands. "Thank You, Jesus," she said.

"Tank You, Jesus," he said, mimicking her.

She ruffled his hair.

There was a tap on the door frame.

"Come in."

The other children filed in.

"It's time for nightshirts," she told them.

Tate took Little John's hand and led him out.

She took her time helping Violet into her nightdress and tying back her freshly washed and nearly dried hair with a ribbon. "I'm so sorry I couldn't help you. I prayed for you every day and every night." She set aside the brush. "Your father said you cried a lot."

"I hate him for taking me away."

"I know. We have to forgive him, though."

"Why?"

"Because holding onto those feelings and not forgiving only hurts us, not the other person."

"I don't want to."

"I don't want to, either. But we're going to try. Together, all right?"

"All right." She stood on tiptoe to see her hair in the washstand mirror. "What about our house back home?"

"I sold the house. It was worth quite a lot. I could buy us a house here if we wanted. I don't know yet what we're going to do." She unfolded a shawl from her drawer and wrapped it around Violet's shoulders. "But we're going to be together. And we're safe here. That's all that matters right now. Not where we live."

"Why did you come to stay here?"

She explained about how she'd taken the teaching position and how the job came with room and board at students' homes. Then she explained about how she'd met the boys aboard the train, and how Seth rescued them when it derailed. "He rescued Peony, too, and he got hurt saving her. I promised to stay and help with chores and the boys until he was better."

"He doesn't look hurt."

"He's fine now. He's trying to find me another place. Or he was. I don't know what we'll do now. But it will be fine. You trust me, don't you?"

Violet nodded solemnly.

Marigold cupped her dainty chin. She was so beautiful. She reminded her of Daisy when she was a girl. She reminded her of everything important and meaningful.

"Wherever we are together, you and I, it will be home. All right?"

"All right."

She walked over to the door. "We read in the boys' room before bed, so let's skedaddle."

They went to the boys' room and found Seth there already, holding up a book. He beckoned in Violet. "Do you know this story?"

Violet nodded.

"What happens at the end?" Tate asked.

"Don't answer that," Seth said with a chuckle. He placed his fingertip on Tate's nose. "You will have to wait and see." He found where they'd left off and read.

Peony surprised everyone by showing up and leaping onto Violet's lap, where she sat beside Marigold at the end of the bed. Violet stroked her fur, and the cat purred loudly.

"She missed you, too," Marigold whispered against her hair.

After the story and good-nights, she lay beside Violet, stroking her hair until she fell asleep. She could hardly believe she was right here. Close enough to hold and kiss.

"Thank You, Lord," she whispered. She would say it every day for as long as she lived, and the words could never express her gratitude.

Once her niece was soundly asleep, she left her with Peony and tiptoed out of the room. Seth was at the kitchen table with his ledger and a cup of coffee.

"I heated water for your tea."

"That was kind of you." She poured the teapot half-full of boiling water and let the leaves steep. "I'm sorry I was snappish earlier."

"It's all right." He rolled his pencil between his fingers. "You and Violet are both welcome to stay here. You don't have to find another place to stay if you don't want to. If you do still want to go, I'll help you."

She turned and studied him, his dark hair mussed, his skin darker from all day yesterday in the sun. "I still can't believe it's true." She pulled out a chair and sat. "It's the answer to my prayers."

"I know."

"I mean, I didn't pray for Wade to get sick. I didn't even wish it on him."

"I know," he said again.

"I prayed fervently for her safety and comfort. You know…?" She looked at him, her eyes wide and shining with more unshed tears. "I didn't even pray for her to be with me, because I didn't want it for me. I wanted her safe, and I thought for my own peace of mind I needed to let her go. I just prayed for her to not be afraid or hurt."

"And now she's safe."

She remembered her prayers. "I trusted that God was working in my life." She'd believed He loved her and cared about her. She knew with all her being He wanted what was best for her and for Violet. She'd asked Him to show her how to get past the loss and be a whole person. "I chose to be thankful for the good things I'd been given and my blessings."

"And you were blessed again."

That moment, sitting there in the quiet kitchen with Seth, knowing Violet was upstairs sleeping under the same roof, she almost felt as though she was dreaming. "Is this really happening?"

"It is."

She sipped her tea and thought. "I could buy us a house of our own."

He looked at his ledger. "You could."

"I don't know what I want. I promised Violet everything would all be all right now. After tomorrow I'll be certain about the documents. Russ will help me."

He tapped the pencil against the tabletop. "Are you sure you want to give Wade more money?"

"He's her father. He's sick. Dying apparently. I'll only give him enough to perhaps buy him medical treatment and make his last days more comfortable. You saw him. He did the right thing. I have to believe he was even led by God to find me and bring Violet here. Why else would he do it?"

"To get more money."

"Maybe. In any case, he brought her to me, and I'm thankful." She finished her tea and carried her cup to the basin. Before she headed back to her room she turned to Seth. "Thank you for everything, Seth. Thank you for your generous offer to let us stay."

"You're as much help to us as we are to you," he said, giving her his full attention. "It would be of mutual benefit, so I suggest you give my offer some thought."

He was happy for her. He really was. In fact, Seth was happy for both her and Violet. Imagining what was happening with her niece had to have been torture for

Marigold, and Violet had to have been miserable being taken away by a stranger, even if he was her father.

He didn't like his selfish thinking, but he felt left out. Why did she need him? She had her family now. He hadn't realized she had modest funds to take care of herself if need be, but there it was. And she had a secure position with the school board. Of course, they still had riding and shooting lessons to continue. Violet would need to learn how to handle horses as well. He had things to teach Violet that Marigold could appreciate—things she might even find valuable enough to entice her to stay.

He had plenty on his plate right now. He had three boys to concern himself with, so why was he adding more to the duty list?

Because he cared about Marigold. More than cared. He'd fallen in love with her. In truth, he might have loved her since the moment he'd laid eyes on her.

Maybe it was wishful thinking, but maybe he could get her to care about him, too.

"I'll take you into town this morning," Seth told Marigold the next day. "I'll go with you to meet Russ. If he's not in his office, we'll go to his house."

She was grateful for his assistance. "All right. But what about the children?"

"Ma, will you come with us and stay at the school-house with them until it's time for school to start?" Seth asked Evelyn.

"Leah will arrive first," Marigold told her. "If I'm not back before the students arrive, you can ask her to stay with you."

"Of course," Evelyn said. "I'll have to take Little John."

Marigold had one more stop this morning. "I'll want to go to the bank as well."

Seth nodded.

After the children had eaten and gathered their books and lunch pails, Seth led them out to the wagon. Marigold took one more look at Violet on what would be her first day in the new school. Her hair was braided and she wore a dress that was nearly too short.

"I'll need to have more clothing made for her," she told Evelyn as her niece went outside.

Evelyn agreed. "I'd love to see what Hannah would create for her—for you as well, with your lovely hair and eyes. That young woman does wonders with her designs. She's done so well, she's hired at least three people to work in her shop. She has two machines that sew by pedaling. They're made like the machines that stitch leather, but are for cloth. I've seen them."

"I've read about those."

"They use the machines for seams and the like, but bodices and all the fancy work are done by hand. Hannah herself made all my Sunday dresses."

"Violet and I will visit her shop soon."

When they got into town, Russ was already at his Eden Street office. They stepped into the interior, which smelled like new wood and coffee. A young man in a suit and white shirt stood and came from behind a desk to greet them.

"Simon." Seth shook hands and introduced Marigold.

"Your brother is having his second cup of coffee, and he's alone," Simon told them. "Go on in."

Russ looked up from a stack of papers. His waistcoat was draped over the back of his chair, and he had a pencil behind one ear. He got up and shrugged into his coat. "You two are out and about early."

"Marigold needs you to look over something," Seth said.

"Of course. Please have a seat."

Marigold handed him the envelope and perched on a glossy wooden chair with arms and a padded seat. She briefly explained what had happened and how Wade had shown up after church the previous day. "I must be certain this paper says my brother-in-law is relinquishing his legal rights to my niece."

Her heart raced as Russ read it over. He held the paper to the light streaming through the window behind him. "It looks to be in perfect order. What I can do is telegraph the persons who signed to verify." He glanced at her concerned expression. "I'll do it this morning."

"Thank you," she said, relieved.

"Often I hear back immediately, but of course, sometimes people can't be reached right away for a reply. Will you be at school?"

She nodded.

"If I get a reply, I'll send my assistant immediately." Russ placed the document on his desk. "Will you want to adopt this child?"

"I don't know. I haven't thought about that. I can talk to her. She's my niece, so that probably wouldn't really be necessary." She paused a moment. "Would it?"

"Not for legal purposes. She will be permanently in your care in any case."

"Thanks for your time," Seth said.

Marigold glanced at Seth, then back to the lawyer. "Do I owe you anything?"

Russ smiled and shook his head. "No. You're almost family."

After expressing her thanks, she walked from the building ahead of Seth and out onto the boardwalk.

The sound of iron on iron rang loud as they passed

the livery. Reaching Third Street, Seth cocked his head. "Let's take a quick detour right here."

Three horses were in the corral behind the saddle shop and livery. The large black one shook his head and walked to the fence. Seth stopped and reached to scratch behind his ear.

"Isn't that Russ's horse?" Marigold asked.

"Yes. He's the one Russ and I bred some years back. His sibling from the same sire carried me all through the war. He's good stock. Good lines and strong limbs. Can run distances and he's good on rough terrain."

"Do you still have his sibling?"

"Nope. Comanches took him down."

"Oh. One of the horses in Dewey's story. I'm sorry."

Seth patted the horse's neck. "Me, too. Did you want to head to the bank?"

"If you don't mind."

The bank was two more blocks south, so they continued on. Marigold withdrew funds and had a bank check made out to Wade Berman. Then, on the way to the schoolhouse, as they passed in front of the bakery, the smells drew them to the window.

A white-haired gentleman waved them in. "Good morning! Aren't you the new schoolteacher?"

"Yes, I'm Miss Brewster."

"I remember you won bread and rolls in the horseshoe competition, and I haven't seen you to fill your orders yet. Would you like something this morning? I have plenty of everything. How about enough for your class?"

"That's quite generous. You select them for me, please. Whatever you know children will like."

He filled a paper-lined crate with dozens of pastries and deep-fried dough rings. Seth reached to carry them.

"There's enough for your gentleman friend as well."

"Much appreciated, sir," Seth told him.

She thanked the baker and they continued toward school. "This is going to be no ordinary day at school," she said with a nod to the treats he carried. Then she sobered. "I wasn't even there to introduce Violet on her first day."

"I'm sure Ma has taken good care of her."

She conceded with a tilt of her head. "I'm sure she has."

As they grew near the schoolhouse, they heard the cheerful laughter and squeals of the children. The students were in the side yard, playing a game of statues, and apparently August was "it" because the others were running from him until he touched them, at which time they froze in place.

"Leave it to Ma to be creative. They're having fun."

Evelyn and Beatrix stood outside the circle, watching and cheering. Violet stood between them, also watching. Little John ran around and between the others, not paying attention to who was "it," but having a grand time.

"It's Miss Brewster!" one of the young people called.

"Aunt Mari!" Violet ran to meet her.

"Hello, darling. Didn't you want to play with the others?"

She shook her head. "I was waiting for you."

Marigold hugged her. "I had to take care of that paper your father gave me. You know that."

She nodded.

"What do you have there, Mr. Halloway?" Evelyn winked at her son.

"Form two neat lines and we'll show you," Marigold instructed the children.

They obediently lined up before Seth and Marigold.

"You may select one and eat it out here." She whisked the cover from the crate and Seth lowered it.

"Oh, my." Twins Jane and Abigail, as well as Violet, had been nearest and were first. They each chose a pastry. In orderly fashion, the children selected their special treats until Michael stood last in line. He'd come last, letting the younger children go ahead of him. He stared at the remaining golden fried dough rings and his eyes widened.

"Go ahead," Seth urged him.

"I ain't never had one b'fore."

"These that are left are small," Marigold observed. "You'd better take two."

Eagerly, he selected two and walked away smiling.

There were enough for each of the adults as well.

"Thank you for winning the horseshoe competition." Beatrix licked her fingers.

Seth took a bite and chewed. "I suspect the baker would have given these to us anyway. Or to Marigold, rather."

Marigold looked up at him. "Why do you say that?"

He leaned toward his mother and Beatrix as though sharing a secret. "I think he was smitten by her smile. Or maybe he saw the sun shining on her hair."

The ladies chuckled and Beatrix nodded. "I can see how that could happen."

"Yes, indeed." Evelyn looked completely serious. "Now, mind you, that won't happen in every shop. For instance, Amos Godwin has his wife, Opal, in the store with him. He won't be giving away any more boots than agreed upon."

Seth's burst of laughter volleyed across the schoolyard.

Marigold gave him a shove with her shoulder. "You're embarrassing me."

Violet finished her pastry and reached for Marigold's hand.

"Did you enjoy it?" she asked the girl.

"Yes."

Marigold called the children. "It's time to go into the building and have class now. Let's thank Mrs. Halloway and Mrs. Werner."

They called out their thanks. Tate and Harper gave Seth quick hugs and darted inside.

"Thank you for the treat, Mr. Halloway," Michael said.

"You're welcome, Michael. But I was only the delivery boy."

"I seen you ridin' your horse once. The gray with speckles and a black mane. It's the handsomest thing I ever seen."

"You like horses?"

"My pa ran the station here b'fore. I fed and watered the horses what he changed out for the drivers."

"You must've been a little rascal back then."

"Yeah, but I'm strong."

"I see that. You keep doing your lessons, and you'll have even more skills to help you through your life."

"Yessir." Michael walked toward the school.

Marigold remembered Will's talk about how the town got started and recalled he'd mentioned how there'd been a stage station before the railroad came through. She was still curious about Michael and his father.

She studied Seth as he watched the boy walk away. He was compassionate and kind always, to children, to animals. He was brave. And not because he'd survived a war and fought Indians, but because he wasn't afraid to care.

Violet still clung to her hand. Evelyn had gone for her shawl and now had Little John in tow. Their wagon stood where they'd left it on the street.

"Thank you, Seth. For everything." Then Marigold turned to his mother and gave her a brief hug. The first time she'd done that. "And thank you for your help. Seth can tell you what Russ said."

"You're welcome, dear."

She looked at mother and son, and wished she could be as brave as they were. But she wasn't.

For now she had to settle with what she did best. She led Violet inside the schoolhouse, where she'd teach her lessons.

Chapter Fifteen

Violet was afraid to let Marigold out of her sight. She'd been through a traumatic experience, so her behavior was understandable. Marigold was patient with her, as were the rest of the family. The boys didn't quite understand, but they were accepting and tolerant. With that in mind, as the school day began she placed Violet and Jane Burgess together at a desk at the front, nearest her desk. Jane was a quiet girl, but friendly and helpful, and she would be a good partner for Marigold's fearful niece.

Late in the day there was a knock on the schoolroom door; it opened and Russ entered. She looked up from where she sat at her desk, with Jakob and Arnold beside her while going over their work. "Excuse me just a moment." She got up and hurried to the doorway. "Continue your studies, children."

He handed her the envelope with a confident smile and said in a near whisper, "Everything checked out. All the signatures have been verified. Violet is legally in your custody."

Relief washed over her with the force of a strong

wind. Her legs grew weak, and she grasped his arm to keep from buckling to the floor.

He steadied her with his other hand. "Do you want to sit?"

Michael got to his feet and gestured to his desk. "Are you all right, Miss Brewster?"

Russ helped her reach the seat.

"I'm fine, Michael. Thank you."

"Will you get Miss Brewster a drink of water, please?" Russ asked the lad.

Michael hurried toward the covered pail.

A few heads turned to see what was going on.

"Everything is fine," she said to assure them.

Violet got out of her seat without permission and came straight back to her aunt's side. "Is everything all right, Aunt Mari?"

Marigold whispered in her ear. "Mr. Halloway made sure the paper from your father is true and good. We will never be apart again."

Violet kneeled before her and placed her head in Marigold's lap. Marigold smoothed her palm over her niece's braids. Russ met her eyes and smiled—it was a kind smile, like his brother's. She couldn't wait to tell Seth.

Michael brought her the tin cup filled with water and she drank.

After a few minutes of collecting herself, the drink revived her. She stood with renewed vigor. "I have one more favor to impose upon you," she said to Russ.

"I'll do what I can."

"Just a moment." She went to her desk, withdrew the bank check and carried it back to where he stood. "He's at The Cattleman. Will you please see that he gets this?"

Taking the bank check, Russ looked at it without reaction. He tucked it into a pocket inside his waistcoat. "Yes, I will."

"Thank you, Russ. If there's ever anything I can do for you, you only have to ask."

"I'll remember. Have a good day."

"Oh, it's a very good day."

He left, closing the door behind him, and she shooed Violet to her seat.

She couldn't continue with the lesson. This was a time for celebration. "Children, put away your papers. We're going to sing."

Seth and Dewey were planting fields and didn't return in time for supper that evening. Marigold's impatience wore thin. "Do they do this often?"

"This is a ranch, dear. There are seasons when the men work from dawn to dark. Seth has been taking it easy because of his arm and those ribs, but he has planting to catch up on now or we won't have hay for the horses come fall."

"So...if Violet and I moved to town, you'd be alone here with the boys?"

"Except in winter if we're snowed in. Then we'll be tripping over each other in this house day and night." She put beans on to soak for the next day. "I'm used to it. It's not a hardship, and the boys will be good company for me until they're old enough to help."

"My father was gone weeks and months at a time."

"I'm sure that was difficult."

"Yes." She took the cups and glasses from a cupboard and wiped the shelf clean. "And then eventually I lost everyone."

"I'm sorry, dear."

She gave Evelyn a weak smile. "You've lost people, too. I admire your strength."

"The Bible tells me the joy of the Lord is my strength. I live by that every day."

"You must miss your son Adam terribly."

Evelyn nodded. "I do. I pray for him every day. I have to trust that he is well and that he's on a path that will eventually lead him back to his family."

"Like the prodigal son?"

The older woman smiled. "Like that perhaps."

Marigold had returned the cups and glasses to their shelf and hung the washrag. "Would you like to read the children their story tonight?"

Evelyn nodded her assent.

Later, with the boys snuggled into their beds and Violet seated with Marigold at the foot of Tate's bed, Evelyn sat in the rocker and read the last chapter of *Hans Brinker, or The Silver Skates.*

"We're gonna have to tell Seth what happened," Harper declared as she closed the book.

"He's gonna be sorry he missed it," Tate agreed.

"Seff mithed it," Little John mimicked. He kicked out of the covers to jump down and run into Marigold's lap.

She held him and rubbed his back. "You can remember the story and tell him how it ended."

He bounced, his feet brushing against Violet.

She pushed his feet away and slid closer to her aunt. "Please take me to bed now, Aunt Mari."

Marigold hadn't missed her pushing away Little John. She kissed the boys' foreheads and told them good-night.

"Sleep well, Violet." Evelyn headed to her room.

Marigold led Violet to their room, and tucked her in. Peony jumped up beside her and bumped Violet's chin with her nose. She giggled and stroked the cat. "Your whiskers tickle."

Marigold petted Peony's fur as well.

"Do you love those boys, Aunt Mari?"

She didn't want her time with the boys or her feelings for them to be a threat to Violet, but she understood her insecurity. "I'm very fond of them."

She explained in more detail how she'd come to meet them on the train, how they'd been together when the accident happened, how she'd helped care for them and come to stay here while Seth recovered.

"When I was gone, did you want *them* to be your family?"

"You're my family. You've always been my family. You and your mother."

"She was beautiful."

"Yes. She was."

"You're beautiful, too."

"And so are you because you look like your mother."

"Jane and Abigail said I look just like you."

"Only because they never saw your mother. Let's show them her portrait, shall we? We can take the one on the bureau there."

Violet looked toward the photo. "I remember that dress in the picture. It was yellow."

"I kept that dress, along with several others. They're in one of my trunks. One day you can wear them."

"Can I look at them?"

"Yes, of course. We'll get them out tomorrow."

The little girl looked at her with sad eyes. "I miss her."

"I miss her, too." Marigold touched her niece's cheek. "I love you. You never need to be afraid again. I promise. I'm always going to be here for you."

Violet brushed the edge of the covers with her fingertips. "Did you give my father money?"

"Yes, so he can go to doctors and pay for a nice place to stay."

"He's going to die, isn't he?"

Her niece was a smart child. She would never lie to her. "He said he was, yes."

"Should I be sad?"

Marigold thought over her words. "It's sad when anyone dies, isn't it? God loves your father as much as He loves you and me."

"I'm glad he had to bring me here, though."

It occurred to Marigold then that Violet had lost just as many people as she had. She sent up a quick prayer. *Lord, don't let this child be afraid to love or care for people because of her losses. Don't let her be like me.*

"Our feelings can be mixed up, can't they?" she asked the girl. "We're sad about one thing, but glad about another. That's all right."

Violet turned on her side and her eyelids fluttered before opening wide again. Marigold needed to let the child sleep, but she had to know something.

"Did you go to school while you were gone?"

Violet nodded. "Some days. It wasn't a real school, though."

"Why not?"

"It was in the back room of a café and we only read to ourselves and made pictures. We could go to sleep on mats if we wanted to."

"Was there a teacher?"

"There were ladies who watched us. I don't think they were very smart."

"How many children were there?"

"Five."

"It doesn't sound like a proper school at all."

"I was the best reader. If it got late, and we were still there, I read to the others."

Marigold couldn't imagine what kind of place Wade had taken her to. If he was off mining—or whatever else he did—he could have left her with just about anyone. "I'm so proud you were kind to the others. And I'm glad God was watching over you." She thought a moment. "Did you receive any of the letters I sent you?"

"I got one," Violet said and her eyelids fluttered again.

It was time to say good night, so Marigold leaned down and kissed Violet's forehead.

While she sat with her in the silent room, she heard the damper on the stove downstairs. Seth must have come in and decided to heat coffee. Once Violet was sleeping soundly, she tiptoed from the room and went downstairs.

There was no one in the kitchen, but the coffeepot was warm.

She found Seth seated on the porch, his bare feet on another chair in front of him.

"You must be tired," she said as she stepped outside. "Did you eat?"

He nodded.

She perched on the rail, close enough to smell his soap and shaving powder. "You took time away from planting to go see Russ with me."

"Some."

"I appreciate it." She smoothed her skirts over her knees. "Russ came to see me at school late this afternoon."

"Was it good news?"

"It was. The witness and the judge confirmed their signatures. There will be no legal worries."

He lowered his feet, leaned forward and caught her hand. His fingers were strong and callused. "That's good news, thank God."

She looked down at his hands. "You work long hours."

"Spring and fall as long as there's daylight," he agreed. "I'm glad to be able to work again."

"What about summer?"

He lifted her hand to his mouth and her attention focused on the gesture. He brushed his lips across the backs of her fingers. "Summer I pray for rain."

A tingle ran up her arm, and she shivered.

"Are you chilly?"

"Not really."

His mustache brushed her knuckles.

"What are you doing?" she asked him.

"Smelling you."

She pulled her hand back but he didn't let it go. "I just wanted to tell you the news."

"I'm happy for you. Both of you. Violet is fortunate to have you."

"We're quite a pair, aren't we?"

"We're not exactly a pair," she reminded him.

"I meant that one day we were on our own, and the next we have children to take care of."

"You have more than I do."

He chuckled.

She realized she'd been waiting to tell him—to share her good news, as though the pleasure would be more fulfilling once he knew. "I just wanted to let you know since you took me to see your brother."

"I'm glad you did."

"I should probably let you relax."

But he still didn't release her hand. In fact, he held it more tightly. "No, stay with me. I have something to tell you, too."

He pulled the chair he'd been resting his feet on close beside him, and she seated herself. "What is it?"

He stroked his fingers over the back of her hand. "Remember when Violet said Peony was fatter than she remembered?"

Marigold thought a minute. "Yes."

"Well, she is. She's not fat really. She's going to have a litter."

She blinked at him.

"Of kittens."

"Oh." She rolled that over in her mind, confused and then realizing… "Oh!"

"She'll probably have them end of May, first of June somewhere."

"Do I need to do anything?"

"Maybe give her a comfortable place to hide in a closet or somewhere. They know what to do, but they find a private place to do it."

She thought it over and then shrugged. "The kids will love little kittens."

"They will," he agreed.

"What will they look like?"

"I can't even guess."

"She's so pretty. I hope they look like her."

He chuckled and reached around her to hug her, even though they were both seated.

Her thoughts grew intensely serious. "What if Will finds us a place to live soon? It's likely, you know."

"Peony can stay here. Ma and I will take care of her."

"That would be a solution." Even to her own ears, she didn't sound confident about that idea.

"Until we have to think about that, we still have a lot to do. We need to continue your shooting lessons. And Violet will need to learn to ride."

"But what about your planting?" she objected. "Will you have time for those things?"

"I've decided to hire a couple of hands for a few weeks just until the spring work is finished. And I'll saddle horses in the mornings and ride with you and the children to school. They'll get in more saddle time that way. Your horses can stay in Werner's corral until school is over. He lets a couple of the other children leave horses there during the day. There's water and feed, and he's built a shelter. I'll ride back here and work."

"I'll pay for their keep," she offered.

"The school board pays for it, and it's not much."

"I'm confident I can get us home on our own after school."

"I'm confident you can, too. But you'll carry a revolver, so we need to work on aim."

"Yes, sir."

"We'll start tomorrow."

"Thank you, Seth."

They rose to their feet at the same time and his nose touched the side of her face. Though the contact had been accidental, she didn't draw away. He brushed his lips against her cheek in a sensory caress and restrained exploration. "Your skin is so soft."

He trailed his lips to her jaw, then her ear, his breath sending a shiver across her shoulders. "And you smell so good."

She turned her head until their noses touched and

cupped his jaw in her palm. His skin was warm and recently shaven smooth. He smelled good, too, like soap and shaving powder. These feelings were new and frightening. It probably wasn't wise to let herself learn more about them—she'd likely be gone soon, but she was curious...and irresistibly drawn to him.

She initiated the touch of their lips, gently leaning into him and closing her eyes. Thinking objectively wasn't really an option when he kissed her like this. She could move away any time she wanted. She could decide this was the last kiss they'd ever share. She was choosing to kiss him in this moment, choosing to discover a fervent tenderness in this shared moment.

She backed up a bare half inch. "I don't know if this is fair."

"To who?"

"To you...to me. I don't know if it's wise."

"It's just a kiss," he said, but they both knew he was lying to himself.

"I had no idea," she whispered.

"Neither did I." He bracketed her upper arms with strong hands and drew her closer. "I want to kiss you every day." But before he could meet her lips again, the screen door creaked, and they moved apart. Her heart thumped erratically.

A small figure came out and closed the door behind, then padded across the porch floor. "I had a scawy dweam."

Marigold got up and swooped Little John into her arms. She sat on the padded rattan settee, and Seth joined them, scooting in close. Little John moved back so his head and shoulders were against Seth's chest, his legs and feet on Marigold's lap. Seth smoothed his hair and kissed his forehead, and Marigold rubbed his bare feet.

"You didn't cry this time," Seth said.

"No. I woked up in our room."

He didn't have the words to explain, but Marigold knew what he meant. Little John felt safe waking up in their room. "That's right," Marigold said. "You're safe."

She and Seth sat so close, their arms and hips were aligned. They shared Little John's weight between them and they shared affection for him—for each of the children in this house. The moment seemed so idyllic that its very perfection pointed out how Marigold was merely a visitor here. The child Seth held against his chest was his now.

But she had Violet. They would make their own family, wherever they ended up. A deep sadness filled her heart when she thought about the inevitable time that would come and she would leave here. She had the comfort of knowing the boys were loved and would be well-cared for. She would see them in her classroom and watch them develop and grow.

She would make the most of every moment until then.

Seth made good on his plan to have horses saddled when they were ready to leave the following morning. They tied their lunch pails to their gear with leather thongs. Seth explained to Violet how to mount the horse. He'd chosen a deep mahogany mare with a black mane and black stocking markings. "Her name's Liberty. She's gentle and will stand nice and still for you until you let her know it's time to go."

Violet looked to her aunt, who had already pulled herself up onto the saddle. "It's all right," she assured her. "Seth won't let anything happen to you. If he says Liberty's gentle and safe, she is."

Seth looked at her with an expression she hadn't seen before. He nodded and locked his fingers so Violet had a step. Once she'd pulled herself up, he smiled at her and looked at Marigold. "I'm not teaching you or Violet or Tate to mount using a step or stump, because there won't always be one. You need to have the strength in your arms and shoulders to pull yourselves up."

"You're a good teacher," she replied.

The boys giggled over her remark, and she wrinkled her nose at them.

"Liberty's going to follow the other horses," Seth told Violet. "But should you want her to move, you nudge her with your ankles and knees. Nudge again to go faster. Tighten the rein gently to stop her. Never yank hard. She responds to your commands. I'll ride right beside you."

They started out, and Violet looked around, her eyes wide, but not frightened.

"You're doing well," Seth told her. "Marigold, you lead the way to town. You're going to be leading them home by yourself."

By the time they reached the corral on Third Street, Marigold was proud of each of them. "We did it!"

Seth joined in the praise. "You did. And Violet rode all that way her first time on horseback."

Violet straightened her skirts. Tate untethered their dinner pails, and Seth led the horses, except his own, into the corral. "Everyone have a good day."

The boys gave him hugs and dashed toward school. He smiled at Marigold and touched the brim of his hat

n a gentlemanly gesture. "Have a good day, Miss Brew-
ter."

She ached to embrace him in the sunshine but settled
or a smile. "It's already a good day."

Chapter Sixteen

When Beatrix arrived that morning, Marigold gave her the tissue-wrapped gift she'd remembered to bring. The other woman unwrapped it to discover the delicately crocheted doily.

"It's beautiful," Beatrix exclaimed. "I don't have anything like it."

"My mother made it."

Beatrix's face showed her surprise. "Are you certain you want to give it to me? Perhaps you should keep it."

"No, no. She did a lot of needlework when she was sick. I have several. I want you to have it."

Beatrix gave her an enthusiastic hug. "That is so kind. Thank you."

"I can't tell you what a blessing you are to me and the children," Marigold replied. "It's a small token of my appreciation."

"But a thoughtful one. I will treasure it."

Leah arrived then with Evie. "I heard some very interesting news. Mr. Higgins has been given a job in town. And a place to live. Michael will be able to attend school full days."

"I'm sure either your husband or Will had something to do with that."

"I don't know, but I was glad to hear it."

Marigold asked if Leah was available to watch the boys for about an hour or so after school, so she and Violet could go to Hannah's dress shop. Leah was happy to entertain them at her house, so after school was finished and they'd dropped off the boys, she and Violet walked to the shop between Booker & Son and Godwin's boot shop on Eden Street.

The interior was narrow, but long, with dresses displayed on mannequins in the front and walls of fabric and bins of trim, lace and buttons farther back. Two ladies were shopping, and Hannah excused herself from speaking with one to greet them. "How nice to see you!"

"Hannah, this is my niece, Violet. She's come to live with me."

Hannah gave the girl a huge smile. "How wonderful. I know you're going to like it here. Have you met all your classmates?"

"Yes, ma'am."

"She's just as bright and pretty as you," Hannah said to Marigold. "How I envy that hair. Don't tell my father I said that. He'll come up with a sermon."

Marigold laughed. "Evelyn suggested you would have ideas for colors and fabrics. For us both."

Her face lit. "You dress so beautifully already, but yes, I am excited to create some fashions for the two of you."

"Violet's dresses from last year are already far too short."

"Bring them to me if they're good quality and still have plenty of wear. I'll be able to add trim or fabric to lengthen them. And for her new ones, I always suggest hemming extra material that can be let down as a girl grows. Obviously, I didn't stop growing for a long time. My poor mother despaired keeping me in skirts of adequate length, and she was quite good at inventing solutions that were beautiful as well as practical."

"I've admired your dresses and those the other women wear. I'm looking forward to this."

"Let's measure you both today. Step behind this curtain and we'll get measurements."

Once that was accomplished and recorded, the trio browsed fabrics. Hannah suggested a lovely coral. "We'll do a white inset bodice with this and a coordinating floral collar and trim, that way we'll keep this orange tone away from your face, yet in the sleeves and skirt it will be flattering to your hair and skin."

She draped the fabric around Marigold and then placed white around her shoulders and directed her to a mirror.

"Why, you're right," Marigold exclaimed. "I'd never have chosen this color."

"I can use the scraps as trim for something for Violet. Perhaps on a pastel plaid."

Hannah's ideas amazed her. "How do you know what will be so perfect and get these ideas?"

"I don't know. My mother taught me to sew, and my father taught me to believe in myself and what I could do with God's help. I've always had an affinity for color combinations and creating fashions." She pointed to a counter with neatly stacked woven baskets. "I have hundreds of patterns and order the latest catalogs as soon as they're printed."

"Evelyn said you've hired people to help you sew."

"I had to in order to keep up with orders. Women

are coming from nearby towns and even a few from as far as Wichita and Salina."

"I feel fortunate to have you take the time for us."

Hannah reached for her hand. "You're our teacher and my new friend. Of course I have time for you."

Marigold smiled at Violet. "We are so blessed." She patted Hannah's hand. "And now we're going to ride back to White Rock all on our own."

The ride was uneventful, except when a bee buzzed around Harper and he swatted at it so forcefully, he fell off the horse. Tate laughed uproariously while Marigold got down, brushed him off and got him back onto his saddle.

She was tired when they arrived at the stables, and there were no men around, but Evelyn came out. Tate helped, and the three of them removed the saddles and tack, brushed the horses and led them to their stalls with feed and fresh water.

"There will be a couple more for supper," Evelyn said. "Seth has a couple of hands this week. I baked bread and I have a roast cooking. We'll need to peel more potatoes. Working men eat a lot."

After settling Violet, Tate and Harper to their homework at the table, Marigold peeled potatoes, scraped carrots and set the pans on to boil.

Evelyn had been right about the hungry men. They devoured everything that had been prepared, and Evelyn went for jars of peaches to give them for dessert. Later, after they'd gone and the kitchen was cleaned, Seth suggested a shooting lesson. Though tired, she managed to hit a couple of cans.

"Where's the fields you planted?" Tate asked after they'd returned to the house.

"Several acres away to the east," he answered.

"Will you show us?"

"There's nothing to see yet. Just dirt in rows."

"Ain't never seen a new-planted hay field," Tate told him. "How can I be a rancher someday if I don't learn this stuff?"

Seth studied him, pleased the boy was taking an interest. But showing him a field? "Guess it won't take long."

"Let's all go," Tate suggested.

Marigold was seated on the porch step, watching Little John play with the marbles. She glanced up. "I'm willing. I'll let Evelyn know."

"All right." Seth headed for the barn and the rest followed.

Once he had the horses ready Seth gave Violet a leg up. She rode with Harper behind her, and Tate and Little John rode together. He led them along a path in the grass, beside fenced-in pastures and across a narrow creek bed to the newly planted fields. "We need rain now."

He and Marigold dismounted and walked through ankle-high grass, and he pointed across the landscape. "There are fields farther east, too. Come late summer, this will be waving heads of grain."

"That will be a sight to see."

He was looking at her when he said, "Yep."

Their kisses the night before came to mind, and she studied him shyly, but wasn't embarrassed enough to look away. Where would she be late summer? The thought of not being here disturbed her.

"We will see you at home!"

The distant voice penetrated her thoughts. Seth's head turned, and she followed his gaze. "What…?"

Already a distance away, Tate and Violet led Seth's gray and Bright Star behind their horses and they trotted in the opposite direction.

"Tate!" Seth shouted.

Marigold shielded her eyes from the setting sun. "What are they doing?"

"Tate, come back here!"

She took a few pointless steps. "They're gone."

He sat on the lumpy ground and watched as the shapes of the horses and riders got smaller and smaller.

"They just rode off and left us here," Marigold said, as if trying to get the notion to sink into her head. "Did they do that on purpose?"

He glanced up at her. "I'm thinking they did."

"But Violet is inexperienced. Will they be all right? Will they get lost? It will get dark soon."

"They'll be fine."

"You don't sound very worried. There are four children alone on horses out there."

"The horses know the way back, and they're dependable."

Marigold plopped down near him on the hard ground. She placed her elbows on her upraised knees and dropped her head into her hands. "I don't know why they did such a thing."

He moved closer and rubbed his hand in a circle on her back. "I don't, either, but we'll get to the bottom of it. They're definitely in some hot water for this stunt."

She straightened to look at him. "You won't hit them."

"No, I won't hit them. Marigold, they're kids. They pulled a fast one on us. It's not dangerous, but it's not acceptable."

She looked at the lowering sun. "Do you suppose they'll know they're in trouble and come back?"

"Nope." He got to his feet. "I've already been out here all day long. I have a nice comfortable bed to get to, so let's start walking." He reached a hand down and she took the help up. But before she could take a step he ordered, "Don't move."

She stood paralyzed. She moved only her eyes in an attempt to see and whispered, "A snake? Not a coyote? Where's your gun?"

"Shhh," he whispered back. "Just stand still. It's a skunk."

She turned her head slowly until she spotted the furry creature. "I am going to throttle those kids."

It rooted its nose in the grass and weeds, then sniffed the air. When it spotted them, it turned and waddled away at a swift pace. "It's gone," he said. "Let's get out of here."

He took her hand as they walked. The sky grew darker, but there was still enough light to see where they were going. A sound caught their attention, a high-pitched wail on the prairie wind. Marigold stopped short, Seth beside her, and listened. It came again. This time the hair stood up on the back of her neck. "It's one of them. It's Little John."

She gathered her skirts and they ran. She'd already ridden a fair distance today, and now walked a couple of miles. Her legs were tired, but she kept going, with Seth pulling her forward.

In the dusk, they spotted a horse coming toward them at a run. It was Tate.

"It's Violet!" he called, tears streaming down his face. "Somethin' scared the horses when we got to the crick, and she fell."

"Get up!" Seth gave Marigold a step up, and she landed ungracefully behind Tate. She took the reins, turned the horse and prompted it forward. Seth sprinted at an all-out run. Ahead, two more horses came into view and then she spotted Harper and Little John huddled around a figure on the ground. Little John wailed at the top of his lungs, spotted Seth barreling toward him and looked as though he didn't know whether to run to him or run away from him. His crying ended with a squeak.

"Where's the other horse?" Seth asked, running to Violet's side. She wasn't moving, and was a distance from the water, near a bank of smooth stones.

"It ran off," Tate told him. "Somethin' scared the horses. Harper jumped off, but she tried to hang on, and when the horse stood up, she fell back."

Marigold kneeled beside her niece, out of breath, her heart thumping. Violet's eyelids were closed, her face pale. No injuries were visible. She picked up an arm and felt along the bones, did the same to her leg, while Seth checked her limbs on the other side. Marigold ran her palms over her collarbone, her hips, but felt nothing protruding.

"Nothing seems broken," Seth said.

Through his tears Tate whimpered, "I'm sorry."

"We din't know she would be hurt," Harper added.

"I sowwy." That was from Little John.

"Her hair is wet," Marigold called out as she patted her head.

"Did you move her?" Seth asked the boys.

"We moved her here where it was dry," Tate said.

Seth glanced at the bank. "She might have hit her head on a stone."

Marigold helped turn her on her side. He felt the

back of her head and his hand came away with blood. "There's a bump. A pretty big one."

Marigold leaned over and separated her hair, searching for the source of bleeding. There was no blood on the ground. "I don't think it's a bad cut, but it must have been a hard fall." Her stomach lurched in fear.

"Bring my horse," Seth ordered.

Tate immediately brought the gray. "I'm sorry, Seth."

"We'll deal with what you did later. I'm going to get you home and get a wagon."

He tenderly slid his arms under Violet's limp body, held her against his chest and got to his feet. "Hold the horse still."

Marigold and Tate both did his bidding and he mounted with the girl in his arms. Tate got on his own horse and Marigold lifted Little John up behind him, then she helped Harper onto the remaining mount. She found quickly that Seth had been right about needing to know how to mount without a step as she climbed onto Bright Star's back behind Harper. The sight of Violet's red-gold hair draped from the crook of Seth's arm terrified her, but she kept her composure and followed with the boys.

It took only minutes to get Dewey's help to hitch a wagon and make a bed of blankets in the back. Evelyn ushered the boys inside. Marigold prayed beside Violet the whole time Seth led the team at a run toward town.

It took time to find Marlys because the office was dark. Marigold stayed there with Violet while Seth ran to the Werner home. Minutes later both Marlys and Sam arrived. He unlocked the door and lit lanterns in the office.

"Carry her to the first room down the hall," Marlys instructed. She examined the girl for broken bones first, then cleaned the wound on her scalp and asked Sam to go for ice. She lifted Violet's eyelids one at a time, looked in her ears and listened to her heart.

"I know that lump on her head is scary," she told Marigold. "But it's a good sign because the swelling is not *inside* her skull, as far as I know. She has no blood in her ears or nose. That's another good sign. But she seems to have a concussion."

"What does that mean exactly?"

"I'm unable to determine that exactly. As I said I don't think she has any bleeding in her head. But she has had a brain trauma of some degree, caused by hitting her head. She's breathing well. Her pupils are reactive. She's just not waking up. The best thing for her is rest."

"How long will this last?"

"I have no way of knowing. She could wake up tonight or tomorrow. It could take weeks."

"Or longer?" Marigold asked. "Could she stay like this?"

"It's been known to happen, but in my opinion, her condition is temporary."

Marigold trembled and groped for a chair, where she sat hard.

"What should we do?" Seth asked the lady doctor. "Take her home?"

Marlys looked at the girl. "I'd leave her here instead of moving her again. I can keep a close watch on her for any changes. You're welcome to stay with her."

Seth kneeled beside Marigold's chair. He took her hand. She looked into his eyes, her own revealing her pain and worry. She'd only just been given the gift of having her dear niece returned to her. And now this.

"I'm going to go get James and see if he knows where Libby Thompson lives," Seth told her. "She can come fill in for a day or so at school. You don't need to think about that, too." He opened her hand and pressed her palm against his cheek. "Look at me. She's going to be all right. You hear me?"

"Could you find the reverend, too?" Marigold asked in a hoarse whisper.

"Yes, of course. I'll be back as soon as I can."

She leaned forward and touched her forehead to his. He bracketed her head between his hands and then stood. "Don't you lose faith in your girl. She's tougher than she looks."

He stood and stepped back.

A tear rolled down her cheek, but she nodded and gave him a weak smile.

Seth found James at home. Hannah stood behind him with a shawl around her shoulders while Seth explained the situation. James knew where the Thompsons lived and was willing to ride and ask Libby to replace Marigold for a few days.

"Are you going for my father?" Hannah asked.

"I am."

"Tell Marigold I'm praying. James, on your way back, you'd better stop and tell Daniel and Leah what's happened."

James gave his wife a peck on the cheek and grabbed the vest he was never without. "I'll tell them."

The town had built a small parsonage to the west of the church, and Seth woke Virgil Taggart by pounding on his door. He opened it and peered out. "Seth Halloway?"

"Reverend, Marigold's niece has been hurt. We need you to come pray. She's at Dr. Mason's."

"Step in while I get dressed."

A few minutes later they ran into Marlys's office.

Sam had carried in chairs, and Reverend Taggart sat closest to Violet on the side opposite Marigold. He rested his hand on the top of her head and prayed.

Marigold gripped Seth's hand so hard, his fingers went numb, but her hold relaxed the longer the prayer continued. The reverend sought the grace and merciful healing power of Almighty God on behalf of this precious little one. He quoted Scripture in which Jesus had laid His hands upon people or had merely spoken and they'd been healed. "Lord, we are not anxious or fearful because Your Word says in the book of Philippians in chapter four that we should be careful for nothing, but in everything by prayer and supplication, with thanksgiving, make our requests known to You. We know You hear us, and we know how much You love Violet…and Marigold. Thank You, Father, for hearing our prayer and healing Violet's injuries, in Jesus's name."

Marigold squeezed Seth's fingers. "Amen."

Reverend Taggart stayed about an hour, and then stood to leave. "Don't doubt in your heart," he said to Marigold.

"Thank you so much for coming."

Shortly after, Sam went home to his son and Marlys retired to the back room, where they could call her if needed. Seth, though, stayed right beside Marigold.

"You could lie down beside her and rest," he told her.

She did, climbing on the small bed and curling up beside the sleeping child. She took Violet's hand in hers and kissed her fingers. "You rest and get better, my darling. We have a lot more to do together. We haven't even had a chance to get started."

Seth's eyelids got heavy, but he woke at the sound of Marigold's voice.

"Do you remember the lullaby your grandmother used to sing to you?" she asked the unresponsive child. "It's an old Welsh folk song."

He waited only seconds for Marigold to sing it.

"'Sleep my child and peace attend thee, all through the night. Guardian angels, God will send thee, all through the night. Soft the drowsy hours are creeping, hill and vale in slumber sleeping. I, my loving vigil keeping, all through the night.'" Her sweet voice trailed off. "I'll play it on the pianoforte for you when you come back to school."

His throat tightened with emotion. Violet had to wake up.

Chapter Seventeen

The following morning Violet was the same—frighteningly motionless. Marlys listened to her breathing and her heart, lifted her eyelids and looked at her eyes. "Rest is the best thing for her. If she doesn't wake up soon, you can take her home. I'll come out to the ranch to check on her."

Seth had fallen asleep in the chair a few times and then Marlys had come and offered him a bed in one of the other rooms. He'd slept a couple of hours.

James showed up to let them know Libby Thompson was taking over the classroom temporarily. "She sends her love, along with the Gardners and others who've heard the news."

"There's nothing you can do here," Marigold told Seth. "Dewey will bring the boys to school. Go home and work."

He held Marigold in a comforting embrace before leaving.

Aunt Mae sent breakfast for the two women. Marigold took a few bites. "What about her?" she asked. "She can't go forever without eating and drinking."

"We'll prop her head and shoulders and see if she

will swallow when we give her water. If she does, we'll make sure she drinks and give her bone broth."

Marigold moved back to the edge of the bed and held Violet's hand. "She was already so thin."

"We'll take care of her, you and I."

She was grateful for Marlys's wisdom and gentle encouragement. "Thank you for everything."

Violet swallowed when they gave her spoonfuls of water, so Marlys used a rubber tube with a clamp to regulate flow and slowly fed her a cup of bone broth. She washed her face and hands and smoothed her hair.

The doctor looked at Marigold. "I couldn't help but notice the way Seth touched you last night."

Marigold shook her head. "It didn't mean anything."

"It meant something," she insisted. "I saw him look at you."

"No. He has a ranch to run, and now the boys to take care of. I happened on him by accident. He's a man of duty. He couldn't refuse when his mother arranged for me to stay with them. He takes on responsibilities, and I've been one of those. He has been teaching me to ride and shoot, so I can take care of myself. When I asked him to, he directed Will Canfield to find me a new place to live."

"It's more than obligation."

"Perhaps. But I'm simply convenient."

"Marigold, I know what I'm talking about here. That man's in love."

"He told me my hair was pretty."

"Has he kissed you?"

"Yes." She blinked and looked at the lady doctor. "He gets this low timbre to his voice when no one is around to hear us talk."

Marlys gave her a soft smile.

"But I want to make my own choices," Marigold told her. "I've lost everyone who's ever meant anything to me—except Violet. She was taken away from me once, but that's not going to happen again. Love is fragile. You can lose it in a heartbeat. I want to be in control of my own life. I've seen you and your husband together. I've seen Hannah and James. I want that. I want it all. The love, the career, the right to choose."

"I think you're afraid."

"Of course I'm afraid. People who aren't afraid don't have anything to lose."

Marlys moved toward the door. "Some things are worth the risk."

Beatrix stopped in on her way to school, and Deborah brought pastries she'd baked that morning. "All of us at the boardinghouse are praying for your niece."

Evelyn arrived in the afternoon. She set a bag inside the door. "I came to sit with you and the poor little dear. I'll take the boys home from school later."

"Thank you."

"What can I do?"

Marigold explained what Marlys had told her about Violet's condition.

"Those little boys cried their eyes out most of the night, but they got up and went to school. They haven't seen Seth since it happened, because he came in and went straight out to the fields."

"They're not afraid of him?"

"I don't think so, but they haven't been with us that long, and this is serious. They're children, but they're smart and they know they did something that ended badly."

Marigold relived the evening, thought back over

being stranded miles from the house, walking over the field, Tate riding toward them… Violet lying still on the earth. She hugged herself and shuddered.

"Tate said they came up with the idea together. They planned to get you two away from the house and then leave you alone to walk home."

Marigold frowned in confusion. "Why?"

"As I understand it, they were trying their hand at matchmaking."

She couldn't wrap her mind around that disclosure. "What?"

"His words were something about leaving you alone so you could make friends and stay at White Rock always."

Marigold let her body go limp on the chair where she sat. "A plan to get me to stay."

Evelyn drew a quick breath. "And Violet was in on the plan."

"She what?"

"She wanted to stay at the ranch, too."

Marigold could only shake her head. "And I thought she was jealous of Little John."

"That's normal for kids."

"Oh, Evelyn, I don't care what they did. I just want her to wake up and be all right."

"I know, dear. Why don't you go freshen up and change clothing? I brought you clean things. I hope you don't mind that I got clothes from your room."

"Of course not. That's thoughtful." She stood. "I still have a complimentary mineral bath coming. I'll see if Marlys has time to prepare it." She leaned down to give the older woman a brief hug.

Marlys was delighted to prepare a bathing room. The space looked different during the day, with sun streaming through wide multifaceted windows set near the ceiling and creating sparkling prisms on the floor and water. The oils and minerals smelled exotic, and the steam and temperature relaxed her, as intended. She thought about everything Marlys had said to her about Seth. How he looked at her. How he took her hand, touched her face so tenderly. Had she deliberately overlooked those behaviors because she didn't want to see them? Because she was afraid? She'd been right when she'd told the doctor that people who weren't afraid didn't have anything to lose.

With Seth, the ranch came first. And the rest of his responsibilities fell in line behind that. She didn't want to be another obligation, because if she was, she'd most certainly fall at the bottom of his list of priorities.

She felt refreshed and so much better once she was dressed and had her hair fixed. She almost expected to see Violet sitting up when she returned. But the girl was still lying on the bed as though sleeping.

Leah came to sit for a time, and prayed with them before she left. Hannah visited, too, and brought a lovely wrapper she'd sewn for Violet that morning. Marigold wept when she saw the beautiful soft pale blue cloth with delicate stitching and butterflies appliquéd on the yoke. "You made this today?"

"With a prayer in every stitch. I'll help you put it on her if you like."

"She would love that."

Together they changed Violet's clothing, and then Marigold dampened her hair with toilet water and arranged it in finger curls. The child looked as though she might open her eyes at any moment. Marigold watched them for a flutter or movement. She whispered in her ear. Hannah took Violet's clothing to launder and made her way out.

"Shall I bring the boys to see you and Violet before we head to the ranch?"

She glanced at Evelyn. "Do you think it would help them?"

"It might."

"Yes, of course. Bring them."

The school was only across the street a short way so it wasn't long before Evelyn led in the three boys. They glanced at Marigold, but their attention was soon riveted on Violet. The trio stood at the side of her bed.

"Looks like she's sleepin'," Tate said.

"She is."

"When's she gonna wake up?" Harper asked.

"Donna wake up," Little John said.

Marigold choked out a reply. "Soon, I hope."

Tate got tears in his eyes. "We're awful sorry, Marigold."

"I know you are." She came around the end of the bed to kneel and draw them into a hug. "You didn't mean for this to happen. Accidents happen sometimes."

"You're not mad at us?"

"I'm not mad. I'm not happy that you did something dangerous by taking those horses all by yourselves. You knew that was wrong. But I'm not mad. And what happened to Violet is not your fault. Go ahead and talk to her."

"Can she hear us?"

"I don't know. But if she can, she wants to know you're here."

They took turns speaking to Violet. Little John climbed on the side of the bed and patted her hand. "Wake up and tum home."

Marigold hugged them and Evelyn led the boys out.

At suppertime, Aunt Mae again sent meals. Marlys warmed another cup of broth, and they fed it to Violet. Seth would likely work another long day, but Marigold expected she'd see him once darkness fell.

She fell asleep sitting up and dreamed she was walking up a steep hill, intent on making it to the top, growing more and more tired. People she knew from various places, like acquaintances back home, Buck Hanley, Russ's assistant, Simon, kept interrupting her progress with questions and papers to sign. She'd never make it to her destination if they didn't leave her alone.

"Aunt Mari?" Violet's voice, as sweet and soft as she remembered, mingled with the chaos of distractions, and she concentrated on hearing her, frustrated by the interference.

"Aunt Mari?"

Marigold opened her eyes.

Violet's eyes were open, and her wide hazel eyes showed her confusion.

"Violet?" She stood quickly and stepped to the doorway. "Marlys!"

Marigold darted to her bedside and reached for Violet's hand. "You're awake."

"Where are we?"

"We're at Dr. Mason's office. In Cowboy Creek. You took a fall when you and the boys were riding."

"My head hurts."

Marlys entered and went to the other side of the bed. "I'm sure it does. You have a big bump on the back of your head. Follow my finger."

Violet's eyes followed Marlys's finger as she moved it back and forth in front of her face.

The doctor picked up Violet's hand and slid hers underneath. "Squeeze my hand."

Violet obeyed.

She went to the foot of the bed and folded back sheet. to place her palm on the sole of her foot. "Can you push against my hand?"

She looked up and smiled at Marigold. "She seems just fine."

Marigold fell over her niece's form and hugged her gently, holding back a tide of relieved tears that threatened to spill over. She kissed her cheek and straightened "Praise the Lord."

"Are you mad at me? Are the boys in trouble?"

"No one's angry with anyone. We were worried sick All that matters right now is that you're all right."

"When you talked about getting a house for us, i' sounded fine at first...but I like Seth and Evelyn. And I like the boys. I wanted to stay and ride horses and play with them."

"You might have just told me."

"I'm sorry." She noticed the wrapper she wore. "What's this?"

"Mrs. Johnson made it for you."

Violet touched the cloth of the sleeve. "It's so pretty." Her expressive gaze lifted to Marlys. "When can I go home? I mean leave here?"

"I'd like to watch you at least until tomorrow," the doctor said.

"I am pretty tired."

"Rest all you like. We're right here."

Marigold lay down and curled on her side next to her niece. Marlys covered her with a blanket. She dozed but woke to thank God and look at her niece. This child had been through so much. First she'd lost her mother

en her father, a virtual stranger, had taken her from
e only home she'd ever known and subjected her to
eople and conditions Marigold didn't even understand.
he'd clung to Marigold, but she'd also adjusted to life
t the ranch and a new school. She'd made friends with
ane Burgess, and apparently she'd wanted to stay with
e Halloways.

Violet had lost just as many people as she had, yet
he was taking chances on caring for new people. Mari-
old recalled all the prayers she'd prayed for her niece,
ne in particular. *Lord, don't let this child be afraid to
ove or care for people because of her losses. Don't let
er be like me.*

In that moment Marigold realized she had wasted
me being afraid. Hopefully not too much time.

If Violet could learn to be brave and love again, she
ertainly could.

Marlys had said it well: *Some things are worth the
isk.*

Finding happiness was worth the risk.

Loving again was worth the risk.

Because what was the alternative?

She sat up.

The movement woke Violet.

At the same time there was a tap on the door and it
pened. Seth stepped inside. His gaze went from Mari-
old to Violet. "You're awake." He came close on the
ide where Marigold sat. "She's awake."

"Marlys said she seems to be just fine. She has a
eadache and Marlys wants her to stay until tomorrow."

He pulled Marigold into an embrace, and she relished
e comfort. Releasing her, he leaned over Violet. "You,
ttle girl, gave us quite a scare."

"I'm sorry."

"Don't worry about that. I know some little boys who are going to be very happy to hear you're awake."

"They were here this afternoon," Marigold told her. "They talked to you. Evelyn was here for hours."

The girl's eyes widened. "They were here?"

Marlys showed up with a fresh pitcher of water. "Are you thirsty?"

Marigold turned to Violet. "Seth and I are going to be right outside for a few minutes." She took his hand and led him from the room. She glanced around and guided him into one of the empty bathing chambers.

"Everything's all right?" Concern laced his voice.

"She's fine. Everything is good. Except me."

"What's wrong?"

She took a deep breath and paced to a table with a mirror above it. "Oh, my goodness, I look a fright."

"You look beautiful."

She came back to where he stood. "I've been a coward. Let me say this." She covered his lips with her fingertips. He took her hand. "I put up a wall around my heart. I told you—I told everyone—that I needed to make my own choices…and I do. But that was just an excuse. I didn't want to love the boys because they aren't mine. I had lost Violet and felt helpless. I couldn't bear to become attached to them and then lose them."

"Lose them how?"

"You might have married someone, and I'd be out of their lives."

"Who would I marry?"

"Any number of interested females. Molly Delaney for one."

He shook his head. "No."

"I felt as though I was an obligation to you. You always do the right thing, and having me in your home as the right thing. Your mother made the arrangements nd you couldn't say no."

"If anyone is an obligation, it's me. I got you and the oys—and Peony—out of that train car, and I was hurt, o you felt like you owed me something."

"I did feel that way at first."

Silence beat a suspenseful rhythm between them.

"And now?" he asked.

"I didn't want to care about you, either, so I wanted o leave White Rock before that happened."

"You're wise in so many ways," he told her, "but this n't one of them."

"I didn't want to love you because from where I was tanding, caring is weakness. I couldn't admit to myself r anyone else that I might want more. I wanted guarntees, and sometimes there are none."

"If it makes you feel any better, I was lying to myelf, too."

"You were?"

"I didn't think I had time or energy for a wife. I relized though that I didn't want to be alone. And I realzed pretty soon after you got here that I was in love with ou. I even had the idea recently that I could entice you o fall for me."

His words made her heart race. "It was working."

They stared at each other while she forced herself o breathe normally.

"Say the words to me, Seth."

He looked at her. Moistened his lips with the tip of is tongue. "I'm in love with you, Marigold. Completely, izzily, desperately, impossibly in love with you."

She hurtled forward, wrapping her arms around his eck and meeting his kiss with all the fervency she'd ept hidden these weeks. She poured the feelings that had been inexpressible into the kiss, understanding that moment that she was choosing him.

She bracketed his face with her hands. "I love yo too. I don't feel obligated to you. I feel honored that yo fell in love with me. I want to hear you say it every day

He held her wrists. "Miss Brewster, will you marr me? I'll have Russ change the paperwork, so your nam is on the boys' adoption papers. There's nothing I wa more than to be a family with you…than to be yo husband."

She couldn't smile any wider. "I'll marry you. But l me warn you, curly red-haired babies run in my family

"I suppose we will need a little zinnia in our bo quet."

She laughed.

He kissed her again, and she smiled against his lip "What will the children say?"

They didn't make the announcement until after sup per the following day. Violet had come home and no rested on the daybed Seth had used on the porch. Th boys held court around her, bringing her drinks, sing ing her silly songs and making her laugh—a soun more beautiful to Marigold than the truest note Pipp Kendricks could sing.

Evelyn sat in a chair mending a shirt and smiling the children's antics.

"We have something to tell you," Marigold an nounced.

"What is it?" Tate asked.

"Ith it?" Little John said, mimicking.

"I'm making us a horseshoe pit," Seth announced

"You are?"

"Where at?"

"Oh, boy!"

"You are?" Marigold asked.

He grinned. "I just thought I'd let everyone know."

She chuckled. "That is not the announcement."

Evelyn laid down her sewing.

Seth took Marigold's hand and drew her to stand beside him, where he put his arm around her waist.

Evelyn covered her mouth with her fingers.

Violet's eyes opened wide and she sat up.

The boys looked at each other.

"Marigold and I are going to be married," Seth announced.

It only took a heartbeat until all four children exclaimed their pleasure and excitement together. Evelyn dabbed her eyes with the shirt she'd been mending. The boys crowded around their legs and hugged them.

"Uncle Russ is working on the paperwork," Seth told them, "changing it so that Marigold's name is with mine. We're adopting you boys together."

"You'll be our ma?" Tate asked her.

"You can call me whatever you feel comfortable with. I'll be proud, whatever you choose." She noticed her niece's fallen expression. "Violet? Is something wrong?"

"You'll all be a family then."

"And you're part of our family." Marigold went to sit beside her.

"But I won't be adopted like Tate and Harper and Little John."

Seth moved to hunker down at the side of the bed. "Honey, if you'd be happy with Marigold and I adopting you, we'd be happy doing it."

"You would?"

"Of course. My brother can start the paperwork an
we'll take care of it all at once."

Violet leaned over and put an arm around both c
their necks, drawing their faces near hers. "And the
we'll all be family."

Not to be left out, the boys climbed on the bed an
joined the hug.

Seth rested his forehead against Marigold's and the
smiled into each other's eyes. "How many of those red
headed babies do you want?" he asked.

* * * * *

Don't miss a single installment of
RETURN TO COWBOY CREEK

THE RANCHER INHERITS A FAMILY
by Cheryl St.John

HIS SUBSTITUTE MAIL-ORDER BRIDE
by Sherri Shackelford

ROMANCING THE RUNAWAY BRIDE
by Karen Kirst

Find more great reads at www.LoveInspired.com

Dear Reader,

Getting reacquainted with all the wonderful characters from the previous Cowboy Creek series and once again working with fellow authors Sherri Shackelford and Karen Kirst was great fun. If you haven't read the entire series, I hope you'll look for previous books and enjoy them as well.

Seth and Marigold were interesting characters to develop. Marigold is a resilient, determined young lady who is hungry for love, but afraid to risk it. Seth is a hardworking, responsible rancher who doesn't have time in his life for an injury, a schoolteacher with a pet cat, or three challenging kids who need a lot of love and attention.

When they're thrust together, this couple has a lot to learn about themselves—and about love. We've all experienced losses, and we've all dealt with them in diverse ways. Seth and Marigold have something to teach us, and what we learn from them is that love is worth the risk.

I enjoy keeping in touch with readers.

You can contact me at: Saintjohn@aol.com.

Visit me on the web: http://www.cherylstjohn.net/.

Like my Facebook author page: https://www.facebook.com/CherylStJ.

See inspiration photos for all the Cowboy Creek books here: http://pinterest.com/cheryl_stjohn/.

Happy spring!

Cheryl St. John

We hope you enjoyed this story from
Love Inspired® Historical.

Love Inspired® Historical is coming to
an end but be sure to discover more
inspirational stories to warm your heart
from **Love Inspired®** and
Love Inspired® Suspense!

Love Inspired stories show that
faith, forgiveness and hope have the power
to lift spirits and change lives—always.

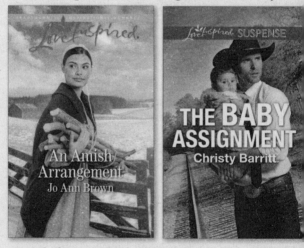

Look for six new romances every month
from **Love Inspired®** and
Love Inspired® Suspense!

www.Harlequin.com

LIHSTO

Get 2 Free Books,
Plus 2 Free Gifts—
just for trying the Reader Service!

SPECIAL EXCERPT FROM

Love Inspired HISTORICAL

When widowed Anna Linford comes to Cowboy Creek
as a last-minute mail-order bride replacement, she
expects to be rejected. After all, her would-be groom,
Russ Halloway, is the same man who turned down her
sister! But when they learn she's pregnant, a marriage
of convenience could lead to new understanding, and
unexpected love.

Read on for a sneak preview of
HIS SUBSTITUTE MAIL-ORDER BRIDE,
the heartwarming continuation of the series
RETURN TO COWBOY CREEK.

don't want another husband."

Russ grew sober. "You must have loved your husband
very much. I didn't mean to sully his memory by
suggesting you replace him."

"It's not that." Anna's head throbbed. Telling the
truth about her marriage was far too humiliating. "You
wouldn't understand."

"Try me sometime, Anna. You might be surprised."

One of them was going to be surprised, that was for
certain. Philadelphia was miles away, but not far enough.
The truth was bound to catch up with her.

"If you ever change your mind about remarrying,"
Russ said, "promise you'll tell me. I'll steer you away
from the scoundrels."

"I won't change my mind." Unaccountably weary, s[...] perched on the edge of a chair. "I'll be able to repay y[...] for the ticket soon."

"We've gone over this," he said. "You don't have [...] repay me."

Why did he have to be so kind and accommodating[...] She hadn't wanted to like him. When she'd take[...] the letter from Susannah, she'd expected to find t[...] selfish man she'd invented in her head. The man who [...] callously tossed her sister aside. His insistent kindne[...] only exacerbated her guilt, and she no longer trusted h[...] own instincts. She'd married the wrong man, and th[...] mistake had cost her dearly. She couldn't afford any mo[...] mistakes.

"I don't want to be in your debt," she said.

"All right. Pay your fare. But there's no hurry. Neith[...] of us is going anywhere anytime soon."

She tipped back her head and studied the wrought iro[...] chandelier. She hated disappointing him, but staying [...] Cowboy Creek was out of the question. Russ wasn't t[...] man she remembered, and she wasn't the naive girl she [...] been all those years ago.

Don't miss
HIS SUBSTITUTE MAIL-ORDER BRIDE
by Sherri Shackelford, available May 2018 wherever
Love Inspired® Historical books and ebooks are sold.

www.LoveInspired.com